Issue Nine

Edited by
Dean Wesley Smith

A WMG Publishing Inc. Magazine

Pulphouse
FICTION MAGAZINE

TABLE OF CONTENTS

SHORT STORIES

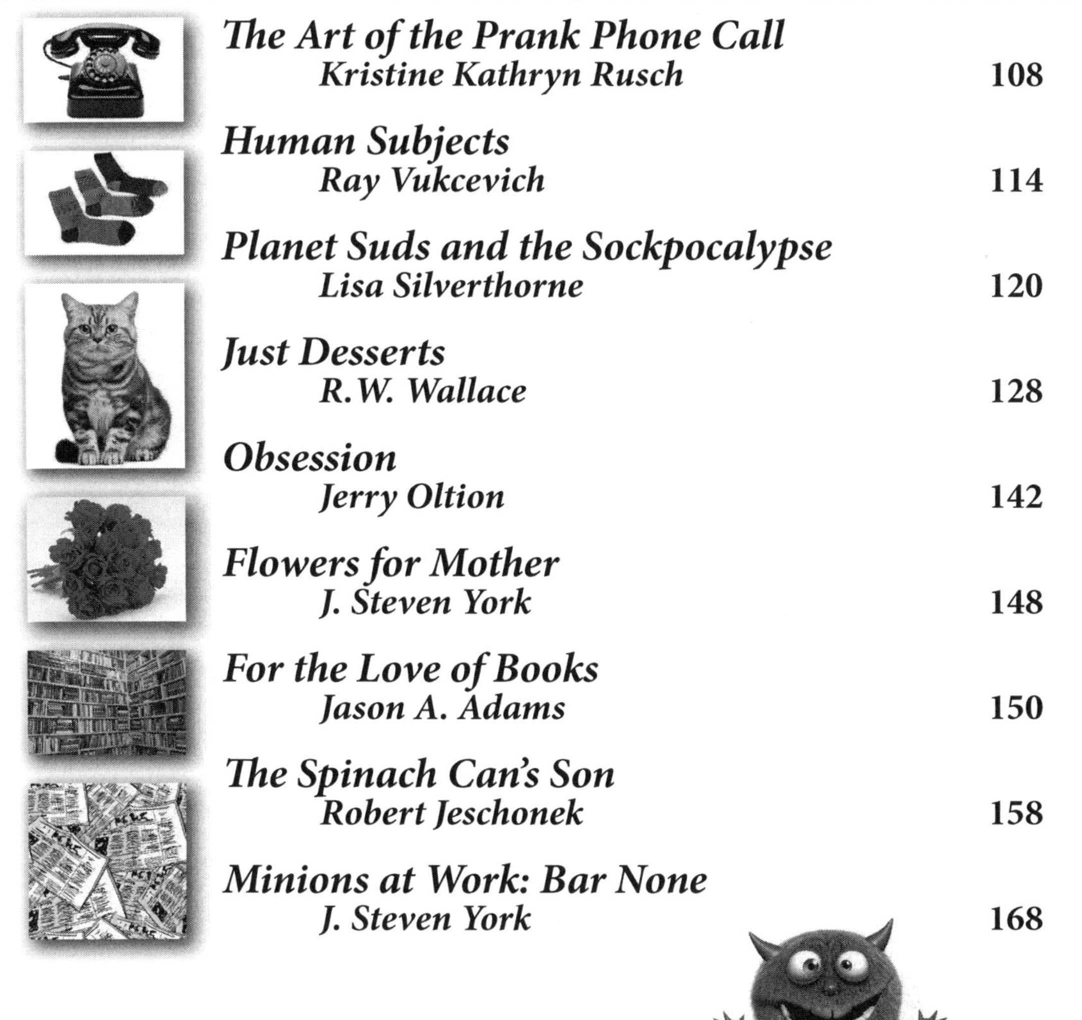

Pulphouse Fiction Magazine
A WMG Publishing, Inc. Magazine

Publisher
Allyson Longueira
Associate Publisher
Gwyneth Gibby
Executive Editor
Kristine Kathryn Rusch

Editor
Dean Wesley Smith
Managing Editor
Josh Frase
Designer
Dayle Dermatis

PULPHOUSE FICTION MAGAZINE ISSUE #9

Published by WMG Publishing Inc.

ISBN-13: 978-1-56146-240-7
ISBN-10: 1-56146-240-3

From the Editor's Desk

Dean Wesley Smith

FANTASTIC SUPPORT

As this magazine starts into its third year, I want to thank all the wonderful readers who supported our subscription drive in 2019 through Kickstarter. It was a wonderful success and will allow us to continue to bring you the best in short fiction for the next few years.

Thank you, one and all.

Pulphouse Fiction Magazine has always focused on quality and different fiction, both in its first incarnation in the early 1990s and in this new version.

And we focus across genres, something that many fans love. We are not a science fiction magazine, a fantasy magazine, a mystery magazine, a Western magazine. We are a fiction magazine.

High quality fiction.

Secondly, if I know of (or find) a story that has already been in print elsewhere and that fits *Pulphouse*, I have no problem bringing it to readers of this magazine. It will be new to the readers here. Every issue is a mix of original stories and reprints. And there is no way to tell which is which.

Why do I do that? Because my focus as editor is filling every issue with the best quality *Pulphouse* fiction I can find.

I get asked a great deal what makes a story a *Pulphouse* story?

As I said in a workshop offered only to *Pulphouse* supporters through the Kickstarter subscription campaign, it is a story that has three major elements.

First, every story must have extreme control of the ability to pull a reader into the story. The writer must bring the reader almost instantly into the setting and the world of the story.

Second, every story must have character voice. In other words, the character must come alive to the reader in one fashion or another.

Third, the story must be different, but in a different way. And this third element is what makes writing *Pulphouse* stories so, so difficult.

A prime example I use to explain this is "Spud Wrangler" by Kent Patterson from *Pulphouse: Issue Zero*. Kent pulled the reader solidly into the details of that opening scene, made us realize we were in a different form of Western story. Yet he had all the standard tropes and details of a Western.

And some incredible character voice.

Then Kent made his story different, but in a different way. The characters were not cowboys, but Idaho spud wranglers. And they had to stop a stampede of Idaho bakers. And he made it work and believable, while never leaving the Western story feel.

Plus it was a great story in and of itself, with heart and emotion. But even more importantly, it was different in a different way.

And that's how you write a *Pulphouse*-style short story. Seems easy, doesn't it? Many a writer has discovered it is not.

And all of the above is what makes this magazine so special. Every story is different, every story quality. Just reading this magazine is an adventure.

I hope you enjoy this start to our third full year. And thanks again for the support.

—Dean Wesley Smith
Las Vegas, Nevada

Stephanie Writt has this amazing ability to just pull you into a story with her characters' voices, and this story is no exception.

In this fourth story in Pulphouse, *Stephanie gives us just exactly what the title of the story says she is going to do. And in the process, a perfect* Pulphouse *story and a great way to start into this issue.*

Valley Girl Vampire to Save the World

Stephanie Writt

I BURNED MY high school prom to the ground.

But I had to! 'Cause, they like, all turned into vampires, and stuff. They were, like, everywhere.

So I torched them. Well, my date Jimmy did.

Don't look at me like that. I was so traumatized. I mean, look at me! I'm a wreck. I probably look like some pathetic Goth weirdo with my raccoon eyes. I came by these through *actual* crying. Not some eternity time starring at myself in the mirror until my soul shriveled up, or whatever. Real crying cause I was like, freaking out.

There was blood. Everywhere.

Jimmy was so smart and brave. He took his dad's rifle and shot the gas pipe on the side of the gym. Jimmy said it went to the heater room or something. I was like, totally screaming at him. 'Cause when he started shooting, he wasn't even aiming at the hundreds of vampires pouring out of the freakin' gym doorway.

I felt like such a dumbass, excuse my language, when the building blew up. Just, *pekew*. Stuff falling everywhere.

Jimmy grabbed me and we jumped back into his truck. He didn't put the rifle back in the gun rack. Just tossed it in my lap and told me to reload.

Then he threw the box of ammo at me.

I mean, he had just saved my life and all, but he didn't need to be a dick about it. All those metal pieces flying everywhere. Some of them hurt. For reals.

Might have left bruises even.

They might have.

So it's kind of hard to load a gun when the driver is driving like a maniac out of some chase movie. The brave, save-the-day Jimmy that was so freaking hot at the gym totally vanished. The Jimmy that like, sputtered and spit on me when he talked and kept yelling at me? Not sexy.

Plus, he hurt my feelings.

Also, my legs with his stupid box of bullets, and my feelings with his spitty fit words. His chances of getting laid were dropping by the second.

So apparently, vampires didn't invade just our prom.

We drove through the neighborhood by the school and people attacked other people everywhere. It looked like everyone was totally making out with everyone else. But really, they were sucking each other's blood. Weird, but sexy in that everyone's-dead-or-might-be-killed sort of way. A little *Lost Boys* with a splash of *Twilight*. I mean, not enough *Twilight*. Crazy swerving Jimmy was no Edward. And Jacob? Not even. I wish.

I like the abbie types. Yum.

Anyways, so these two freaky, scary guys leap in front of the truck and Jimmy just plows right into them. He doesn't even slow down. I bumped my head on the roof of the cab when he drove over them and I totally got a knot on my head. I thought I might have a concussion.

So, I tell Jimmy he needs to keep me awake because if I fall asleep I might die. 'Cause that's what happens in a concussion. And the jerk starts yelling at me again. Says I'm self-centered.

Me! Self-centered?

If he truly loved me he would have cared enough about me to make sure I didn't fall asleep and *die*! Like, for reals.

I was the one that was hurt. On my legs from the bullets, then my head from him being a crappy driver. He just kept hurting me again and again.

I didn't know if I could take any more.

I mean, I didn't want to end up like some of those girls in abusive relationships. Where they get so used to the beatings they like it and can't live without it. Like drugs.

And I'm no druggie. That's gross.

So, I was about to have a talk with Jimmy about maybe we should break up if he was just going to keep treating me like that, when we hit a brick wall.

For *reals*.

Not just like, metaphorically in our relationship, which was totally true at that time, too. So maybe that had some effect on what Jimmy did. But yeah. He drove into a brick wall.

I don't know why. I mean after we stopped it was hard to keep track of anything because he was breathing all heavy and steaming up the windows. And I thought I was losing the love of my life, so I was a little emotional.

It's hard to see through tears.

So I didn't die. Not right away. I mean, I don't know if blood or tears filled my eyes, but my vision got all fuzzy like when I put on a geek's glasses and they were all thick and stuff. You know, just to make them feel better about themselves. That a hot girl paid attention to them. Like an outreach program. I consider it community service.

So I couldn't really see anything, but I hurt a lot. I mean *a lot*.

I know you know I'm serious when I say this word, because I would not use it lightly, like ever. So excuse my language, but…

I hurt a *fuck ton*!

I know. I'm serious. I might have been dead.

But then this warm feeling thing sort of went all around me, like a swirl or whatever. Then I got really hungry.

Like hungrier than the week I only ate Red Bull and laxatives to get into that size two dress and beat out stuck-up Jessica Martin. Oh, I hate her. Thinks she's so much better than everyone. Well, I got Jimmy to ask me to prom and she got stuck with Dennis the fencer.

I mean Dennis is pretty in that manly sort of way. But he's too skinny. I like a man with a package.

So I'm totally hungry and the pain had gone away. Just gone. Like it had never been there. But I'm hungry. I told you how much. And I smell the most amazing delicious thing like, *ever*.

It turned out to be Jimmy.

Can you believe it? I couldn't at the time.

I mean he was always yummy, but never Yummy.

I figured he owed me for the bump on the head and the bullets anyways. He always liked it when I bit his neck. So I found his favorite place and we necked.

Well, I necked him.

He screamed a bit and punched at me. The blows only distracted me from the most incredible taste in my mouth ever. Like *ever*, ever.

So much Yum!

I felt so, so, so much better after I drank Jimmy. It was too bad he had to die. His wounds looked pretty bad.

But, you know, he *had* driven us into a brick wall.

So after Jimmy died, I needed comfort and support in my time of need.

We had crashed in one of the "questionable" neighborhoods around the school. Like a nudist except *bathing* is optional. That's when I met this vampire guy named Marvin. Asian guy, but he *totally* talked American. If his hair had been a little longer we could have totally hooked up.

Total gentleman though. He held the doors open for me on the houses we entered looking for people. The best was feeding off one person at the same time. Totally kinky.

So then there's like, this weird call, and both Marvin and I hear it or feel it. It's hard to describe if you're not one of us.

So we follow this call that's like, a vampire ringtone or something. It rang through our veins. And you will *never* guess where it led us.

OMG, not the cemetery, silly. That's too easy. Très cliché. (That's French. I know. I'm *so* smart.)

No, it led us to a Costco.

The one down by the Winco and that theatre with the fattening popcorn, but the seats that recline way far. It totally led us there.

So we ran there like, super-fast. Even in my four-inch spike heels. Though you know I've always had natural balance.

There's a ton of us at the Costco. All crowded around those tables near the line of registers, all piled high with gobs of that horrific clothing. And under that unforgiving glare they call light, we all look pretty gross.

I mean, they could have led us to like, a day spa or someplace with *water*.

So vamps everywhere, and right up in the center of the crowd pops this totally stacked guy. H-O-T Hot!

An ab-tastic chest into slim-waisted jeans. Tousled hair just right to kinda shade his eyes. Sexy hair. And, good lord, he was clean.

He jumped up on one of the clothes tables. He obviously understood style 'cause he kicked the clothes off the table out of his way. Just left them in piles on the concrete floor.

I love a man who understands the importance of fashion.

So hotty vamp starts this *total* vampire pep rally. I'm totally paying attention to him as he waves his muscular arms around as he talks. I just wanted to bite into them. Who wouldn't have paid attention to arms like that? I mean, really.

He started talking about the path of the vampire and bonding and stuff. Very team spirit. So I started to bounce around. Hello, *cheerleader*! And in my low-cut prom dress I attracted a little bit of attention. Maybe a little more than a little. Never a bad thing.

There were a lot of hot guys there. Some from my school that must have survived the gym blowing up. I was glad they didn't hold a grudge. The guys smiled when they saw me so I, like, knew it was cool. The girls scowled at me like always, so no big change there.

A bunch of other guys from other schools around town waved at me too. I bounced and waved back. Even did a little cheer kick.

Which was damn impressive in my mermaid-cut dress. You know, all tight on the hips.

They totally liked it, of course, so I cheered some more for them. And some other guys started watching, and yeah, so like, the *whole crowd* liked what I did. Which made the head vampire dude on the table a little PO'd.

Which sucked, because I wanted him to notice, but in a *good* way.

So, because I am brilliant, I had a couple of the guys on the floor lift me up onto the table with hotty vamp. To help him. You know, to do cheers up there and like, keep everyone's attention.

I think he was kind of peeved at first. But a little extra bounce in his direction and he totally changed his mind. Of course. I knew I totally had him when he put his arm around me while he talked.

Hugged me to him.

I mean, I couldn't really bounce or cheer after that, but he smelled so good. Like, warm-beating-heart-and-fear sweat. Not his, of course.

So, we weren't officially dating or whatever, but he claimed me as his in front of all those people. So we were totally a couple.

So when Howard, that's hotty vamp's name, Howard Johns, *swoon*!

So Howard Johns broke up the meeting and sent people on their assignments. Like, getting a bunch of different important people and bringing them to Costco.

Big whup.

Then Jessica Martin, hate her, ran over to me and started talking all weird at me.

Howard got mobbed by a bunch of guys asking questions and I got bored. We hadn't even kissed yet. I was really concerned about where our relationship was going. Like, if I was just a trophy or whatever, at least dust me off and make out with me once in a while.

So as I'm totally contemplating my future as Mrs. Johns, Jessica yanked me away from the group. Maybe some time away from Howard would make the heart grow fonder. So I let her.

But then, what she did next reminded me why I totally *don't* talk to her.

Because she's a lying, thieving, man stealing, hoe-bag!

Excuse my language.

But she totally is.

So, she told me this *totally* made-up story about how Howard was really evil, and he wanted to take over the world, so he created vampires by switching the blood tests to blood injections at our last physical for team sports and cheerleading, and stuff about his being a lab assistant, which like, totally fried her story right there 'cause lab assistants are never hot, and it took five days to germinator and blah blah blah.

I saw through her plan.

Jessica wanted Howard for herself so she totally made up the story to make him the bad guy so she could snag his hotness for herself.

No way was I gonna let Jessica Martin steal away my new life partner.

I played it cool and made her think I was all worried and stuff. She asked if I was going to go get my hostage guy, and I told her no, 'cause that would be lame and totally what the 'bad guy' wanted us to do.

I'm a thinker.

So she said she would go pretend to get her hostage guy, and then run away and I should come with her. I told her we should go our separate ways so it would be harder for Howard to find us. You know, if we split up.

She thought it was brilliant.

I mean, duh! Had she never watched any chase scene in any movie ever?

So she left and I went to war.

First, supplies.

With slim pickins (hello, Costco!), I couldn't be picky style or fashion. So I totally went for less is more.

I grabbed the smallest two-piece bathing suit I could find and tried to ignore the atrocious design. Honkin' bottles of facial cleanser and shampoo, plus a three-pack of brushes fell into my skirt I held like a basket, and retreated to the ladies room.

I must pause here a second because this next part...well, it's a bit difficult for me to talk about. Traumatic is the only word I can say about it.

I think I have PSTDs from it.

I had no idea, *none*, how much physical trauma I had experienced up until that moment. So I wasn't prepared...I mean, I don't think anyone could have been prepared for what I saw when I looked into that mirror in that Costco bathroom.

I looked...oh God, I just have to say it.

I was ugly.

Hideous!

I won't, can't, go into the details. I don't want you to experience what I did just in the telling. Too cruel. Just too cruel.

I like, *almost* wished that the vampire thing about not showing up in mirrors had been true. *Almost.*

To say the least, those next few hours were some of the most difficult and trying of my life.

You have no idea how difficult it is to clean my long flowing hair in one of those push-timed sinks, where the spout is three inches from the sink bottom. I had to keep pushing and pushing, over and over and...

Nightmare. Just a nightmare.

Eventually, I was able to restore a certain level of my natural beauty, and re-emerged from the bathroom.

To say I looked stunning may have been exaggerating a bit. But up against the few girls there, some of whom put my horrific reflection to shame, I looked damn good.

But when I came out, lookie what traitorous bitch, excuse my language, stood next to my man.

Little Miss Jessica Lying Skank Martin.

She had him all up on her against one of those giant rack thingies. She was like, cooing at him and he had his arms around her. Just like he had with me.

Cereal boxes everywhere—they were making it on the Cheerios!

I now know what it means to see red. 'Cause all I saw was her red lips kissing on him and I just wanted to rip them off her face.

So I grabbed her face to pull it off him, and I like, totally ripped off her head.

I was so pissed 'cause I got blood all over me and I had just gotten cleaned up.

Apparently, when you rip a head off a vampire, they die. For real reals.

Howard, the jerk, got all mad at me. I told him it was an accident, but he totally got pissed off anyways.

Then he hit me.

I was so afraid that I was totally becoming one of those girls that chooses men that beat them. And they go from bad relationship to bad relationship and can't ever get out.

I would not be that girl. Could not be that girl. I was way too strong and independent woman for that. So I ran.

I didn't know where to go at first.

Then I started thinking about that jerk face Howard (ex-hotty vamp) and all he said. I thought if he *was* the bad guy, like a for reals bad guy, which he must have been to hit me after I killed Jessica, even though I said I was sorry. If Howard was a true bad guy then all that Jessica had said was true.

Howard planned on taking over the world!

Well, I wasn't gonna let some pumped-up pretty boy on a power trip hit me, then take over the world and get away with it.

I could rip off his head too, but he looked really strong. Like, he might rip mine off first.

I needed a plan. Which meant I needed knowledge about vampires. And there was only one place I knew I could get all the info I needed on vampires to help defeat jerk face Howard.

Blockbuster Video.

The guys behind the counter ended up being more helpful than the movies.

They had seen them all already so they just gave me the important bits. The info kinda came out in jumbles 'cause they kept talking over themselves and then arguing with each other.

I understood. Hot girl in a bikini made men do crazy things. I always like to work that to my advantage. And in this case, I was working that advantage *to save the whole world.*

Which is why I am here.

You see, the guys explained to me that vampires have sires, which are the people who made them. If a vampire kills their sire and drinks all their blood they become super-duper powerful.

You two made me, sixteen wonderful years ago. And I know you love me, because you are my parents, and would give your life to me. So I need to take your lives to gain enough power to save the world from vampire jerk face Howard.

Don't worry. I won't just leave your bodies on the floor in a heap.

I love you.

I'll set you both up on the couch holding hands.

I mean, I would never bury you. You would get all dirty. Well, and me too. And I don't have time to get coffins.

So now you understand.

Don't thank me.

I do this for world peace.

Don't cry for me. It's just who I am and what I have to do.

I'm a giver.

Annie Reed writes powerful stories about strong women. And in this wonderful story, she takes that to yet another place that makes the story great fun.

Annie's stories appear regularly in many varied professional markets and I am proud to say she is also a regular contributor to Fiction River, *as well as having a story in every issue of this magazine so far.*

Her story "The Color of Guilt" was selected for The Year's Best Crime and Mystery Stories *2016. She is also one of the founding members of the innovative* Uncollected Anthology.

The Warrior Women of Apartment 3C

Annie Reed

PRE-WEDDING JITTERS drive the best of people temporarily insane. My roommate, Wendell, wasn't the most tightly wrapped person to begin with. When he showed me the sword he bought for his wedding ceremony, I thanked my lucky stars my room had a solid door and a working lock. Just in case.

"You bought a sword," I said, somewhat unnecessarily since the thing was right there on my couch in all its tarnished, ornate glory.

"Yeah, off eBay," he said. "Isn't it cool?"

Wendell was deep in battle mode. Again. In Wendell's case, that meant blowing video game bad guys to smithereens from the comfort of his battered recliner. A beer sat on the floor at his feet next to a bag of half-eaten microwave popcorn. Wendell had moved his recliner to the exact middle of the living room, just far enough away from the television that I'd have to high jump over the controller cord if I wanted to cross in front of him to get to the kitchen. Considering I didn't jump—or skip or hop, for that matter—this pretty much guaranteed I wouldn't be interrupting his game.

I was never very good at video games. Wendell said that was because I was a girl. As if. I just didn't care enough to spend hours and hours learning how to destroy things that didn't really exist anyway.

Wendell, on the other hand, lived for video games. Even so, ever since he and his girlfriend, Clara, had set their official wedding date, he'd been outdoing himself. I guess he needed to stockpile time with his inner game geek before he moved out of my apartment and into Clara's. From what I'd seen, dear old Clara didn't look like the type to put up with hours and hours of gaming every night. That was the nice thing about being roommates. I didn't care how long Wendell zoned out in his computerized never-never land. I had a television in my bedroom, so it wasn't like he was hogging our only one.

I leaned over the couch and peered at the sword. It was a pretty hefty thing, thick blade with some sort of design etched on the tarnished cutting edges and a deeper design carved into a dirty white hilt. It looked old. Really old.

What was he planning? Wendell, and especially Clara, weren't the type to dress up in medieval costumes for their wedding. As far as I knew, their wedding attire would be boringly traditional all the way, complete with black tux, lacy white wedding dress, and bridesmaid outfits a drag queen wouldn't be caught dead wearing.

"Don't take this the wrong way," I said. "But how could you afford this?" Wendell wasn't living with me just because I was such a stellar roommate.

"Got it cheap. It's just a replica. Cost me more for shipping than it did to buy it."

Cheap, huh? That sounded like something that would attract Wendell. But why would someone want to unload a sword so bad they'd eat everything except the shipping charges? The sword didn't exactly look like a replica. Did replicas tarnish? And what was that reddish-brown stuff in the deeper crevices of the hilt? Could that actually be dried blood?

"So," I said, drawing the word out. "How are you going to...incorporate...this thing into the ceremony?" It was probably wishful thinking to hope that Wendell planned to use the sword on Clara right before she said, "I do," but a girl can dream.

Buttons on the game controller clacked, and fake metal sounds came out of the television as Wendell engaged yet another digital character in a fight to the death.

"It's this cool thing I read about," he said. "It's like a separate vow for a warrior."

A warrior. To do what? Love, honor, and cut Clara's head off?

I told myself to behave. Clara wasn't my most favorite person in the world, which had absolutely nothing to do with the fact that my cat had to live in my room 24/7 in my own apartment thanks to Clara's allergies. But Wendell loved her, and that meant I had to put up with her. At least until after the wedding.

I left the sword on the couch, squeezed between the coffee table and the back of Wendell's recliner, and went to retrieve a soda from the fridge. I thought about making some popcorn for myself. Just the residual smell of hot butter substitute from the microwave set my stomach growling. That's how the manufacturers of the stuff suck you in—with smell. I didn't like the actual popcorn all that much. I tried to summon up the smell of burnt popcorn to make the craving go away.

"Hey, Rose?" Wendell yelled at me from the living room. "Can I ask a favor?"

I shut my eyes and popped the top on the soda can. "Sure," I said, wondering exactly how bad this would be. Clean the bathroom? Make him a sandwich? Order take out—my treat?

"Uhm...Clara's coming over later."

Great.

"Can you keep the sword in your room while she's here?" he said. "She pokes around in my stuff after...you know...."

"After you've poked around in her stuff?" I really didn't want that mental image rumbling around in my brain, but some lines are too good to resist.

"After I'm asleep." He actually sounded ticked off, and not because Clara searched through his things. Note to self: don't tease Wendell about his love life. "I don't want her to find it," he said. "I want it to be a surprise."

He was going to surprise her with a sword at their wedding. Only Wendell would think that was a good idea with someone as controlling as Clara.

"Sure," I said, and took a long, long drink.

Anything to help out a friend.

* * *

A SNEEZE WOKE ME UP.

This was disturbing beyond just the loss of what had been a pretty good dream.

First of all, it wasn't my sneeze. Second, it didn't sound like my cat's either. Third, I recognized the perfume. I should have locked my door after all.

"What are you doing in my room?" I asked Clara.

She jumped.

"I thought you were asleep," she said.

No kidding.

My nightlight gave off just enough light for her to snoop around my room. Her hair was a mess, and she held the front of a bathrobe—Wendell's, I saw—tight against her throat. Probably got right up out of bed and didn't bother to put anything else on besides the robe. I didn't need that mental image either.

I rubbed my face, trying to really wake up. My cat hopped down off the bed and wound around Clara's ankles. Clara sneezed again. Good kitty.

"Well, I'm not asleep now," I said. "I'd really like to know why you're in my room."

Clara's mouth set in a stubborn line. "I want to see it. I know you have it in here."

It? "What in the world are you talking about?"

"It. I know you have to have it. He doesn't have it anywhere in his room."

"I don't have any idea what you're—"

"Whatever he bought for the wedding."

She meant the sword. So much for Wendell's big secret. Although I might be able to help him salvage some part of the surprise since she didn't sound like she knew it was something out of King Arthur's Court. All I had to do was keep her from noticing where I'd stashed the box with the sword.

She scanned my room with the practiced eye of a professional snoop.

"You've been in here before," I said.

Another sneeze. "Have not," she said, and sniffed.

Then she proved me right. Not only had she been in my room, but she knew where everything was supposed to be and what was out of place. She bent over and hefted a plastic storage bin away from the side of my bookcase. I'd leaned the box with the sword against the bookcase, covered the top of the box with a sweatshirt, and put the plastic bin in front to hide the rest. I probably should have put the box under my bed, except that's where I stashed a lot of my stuff, and that didn't leave enough room for the sword.

"Hey!" Not only had she barged in my room, now she was rearranging it.

I started to get up but my feet got tangled in the sheets. By the time I got myself un-mummified, my sweatshirt was on the floor and Clara had hot-footed it out of my room, the box with the sword in her arms.

I should have left well enough alone. This really was Wendell's problem, but I was pretty ticked off by this time. Who did Clara think she was? I didn't care if the sword was supposed to be part of her wedding or not. She'd crossed the line.

She had the box open when I got in the living room. She hadn't turned on a light, but she didn't really need to. Wendell had left the television on with his game on pause, and that gave Clara just enough light to see what was inside the box.

"Oh, my God!" she said.

"You weren't supposed to see that," I said, still annoyed. And a little sad now too for Wendell and his ruined surprise.

"How did he…do you know what this is?"

Her hands hovered over the open box. She looked like she wanted to touch the sword but wasn't sure she dared.

"Uhm…it's a sword, right?"

"It's not just a sword. Look at the hilt."

She pointed with a shaky index finger at the spot where I'd seen dried blood.

"So?" I asked.

"It's white. Dyrnwyn. White Hilt. That's what he called it. This sword belonged to Riderch I of Alt Clut."

She might as well have been speaking gibberish for all I understood her.

"Wendell got it off eBay," I said. "It's just a replica."

"No." She shook her head vehemently. "This is no replica. This belongs in a museum."

"How would you know?"

She stopped looking at the sword long enough to give me a withering glance. "It's my job to know. Well, not exactly my job, but it will be someday. I'm a history major, which you'd know if you cared to learn anything about me."

True. I'd never asked Wendell what she did for a living, but as far as I knew, she didn't know all that much about me either.

"If it belongs in a museum, how could Wendell afford to buy it on eBay?" I said.

"I don't know. It's worth a fortune."

That's when her expression turned avaricious.

"Oh, no," I said. "This is Wendell's. You can't sell it."

"We're going to be married. We could both use the money, and I know just who I should offer it to first."

Typical Clara. Appropriate everything. Like my room. Like Wendell's surprise.

"What we're going to do is take that back to my room and not mention any of this to Wendell," I said.

"So he can use one of the Thirteen Treasures to do something dumb at my wedding ceremony? I don't think so."

She reached for the sword, her inhibition at touching it smothered by greed. I reached for her, my annoyance outweighing my better judgment. My cat streaked by, indulging in that favorite late-night tradition of cats everywhere: tearing through an apartment he hadn't seen in months at top speed for no apparent reason.

My cat stepped on the game controller, and the sound of metal striking metal and really cheesy music blared from the television, all at the same time Clara grabbed the sword by the hilt and I grabbed her.

The sword caught on fire. From the tip of the sword to the hilt, orange flames danced along the blade, and the smell of hot metal filled the air.

Clara shrieked, my cat hissed, and I tried to remember exactly where I kept the fire extinguisher before she dropped the thing on the carpet and the whole apartment went up in flames.

"Dyrnwyn!"

That yell came from the television.

Before I could even process that the hero of Wendell's video game was there on the television screen looking at us, or more particularly, at the flaming sword, words just as incomprehensible as those Clara had said just a few minutes ago poured from the speakers. With a crash of sound as loud as a thunderclap right overhead, the world went black.

* * *

I HAD THE MOTHER of all headaches when I woke up.

It took me a couple of minutes before I felt like opening my eyes, which was probably a good thing. Viewing the impossible too quickly isn't good for anyone's psyche.

I expected choking smoke and hot, crackling flames. What I felt instead was something smooth and hard beneath me. I must have fallen on the floor, only whatever this was didn't feel like carpet. I still had a handful of robe. Clara. Here's hoping she didn't break her neck, or I'd have some serious explaining to do to a heartbroken Wendell.

I tried to move and groaned a little when my head throbbed in response. Next to me I heard an answering groan, and somewhere in the distance, something roared. A deep, bone-rattling sound.

"Hurry. On your feet."

A male voice. Not Wendell's.

I opened my eyes fast, then tried to open them for real because nothing around me *was* real.

I was surrounded by dirty gray stone walls. Torches attached to the stone by iron brackets provided a flickering, dull light, just enough to barely let me see what looked like a big wooly rug hung in a doorway at the end of the room. Patches of something slimy and glowing faintly green clung to the stone. The place looked wet and dank and should have stunk like a sewer, but I smelled nothing. The stone was too smooth, the patches of glowing green gunk too uniform to be natural. The torches gave off no heat, but I wasn't cold either. I'd gone to bed in just a T-shirt and underwear. I should be freezing.

Next to me, Clara screamed. I turned to look at her, blinked hard, and felt like screaming myself.

Clara wasn't Clara anymore.

All her main features were still there. Same narrow nose, same close-set eyes, same stubborn chin. But her skin was unnaturally smooth, like it was made of soft plastic. The little birthmark on her chin was gone. In fact, all the imperfections of her face were gone. Her eyebrows looked painted on, and her hair resembled a solid piece of fake suede with lines that were supposed to be hairs etched into the material. She had no pores in her skin. When she opened her mouth and screamed again, her teeth were a solid line of white.

"What happened to you?" I asked. My voice sounded shaky and strange. Flat. Almost like I was hearing myself talk over a telephone.

"To…to me?" She pointed a finger at me. "What happened to you?" She poked at my arm. I didn't feel it. "You're not real!"

She was right. I wasn't. The skin on my arms was as smooth as her face. I'm not exactly furry, but thanks to my parents' genes, I wasn't hairless either. Except now I was. Smooth and hairless, pore- and scar-free. The scratch my cat gave me on the back of my right hand yesterday morning was gone.

I got to my feet in a hurry, which didn't do my head any good, but I was too scared to worry about a headache. What had happened to us?

The wooly rug moved. Clara screamed again. The rug turned out to be a man dressed in a fur tunic, or what passed for a man and a fur tunic wherever we were, and he had Wendell's sword in his hand.

"Time to leave," he said. His voice had that odd electronic transmission sound to it, too.

"You have our sword," I said. Stupid thing to say, but my brain wasn't capable of polite conversation right about then.

"*My* sword," he said. "You brought it back to me. For that I will protect you with my life."

Great. We were someplace we needed protecting.

"Where exactly did we bring it?" I asked.

"Here," he said.

Now that was a non-answer answer if I ever heard one. "Could you be a little more specific? Because, I have to tell you, this place doesn't look like anyplace I've ever seen."

He had the same kind of flat, plastic-smooth face that Clara did, only he had a bumpy discoloration on his cheeks and chin that passed as a beard.

"You're Riderch," Clara said, the hesitation and awe in her voice making her sound like a little girl. "If that's your sword, that makes you Riderch."

"At your service," the man said. He nodded his head in a formal way toward Clara. "Now—both of you—we must leave before the horde discovers us."

"The horde of what?" I asked.

"Goblins," he said.

Goblins.

Right. Because in this world hordes were goblins, not angry commuters stuck in bumper to bumper traffic on the I-5.

That's when it clicked.

I remembered where I'd seen this room before. Where I'd seen torches in iron sconces on a dirty gray stone wall. Where I'd seen a wooly rug of a man, not with a sword in his hand, but a crossbow. Where I'd seen fight after fight involving goblins and monsters and truly disgusting things that went bump in the night.

Wendell's video game.

We were stuck in Wendell's damn video game. Me and his annoying, controlling, last person I'd want to be stuck anywhere with fiancé.

Oh, man. If I got out of this alive, Wendell was going to pay. Big time!

* * *

I SPENT THE next five minutes trying to convince myself I hadn't gone completely insane. Because sane people aren't transported by a magic sword inside a video game where their bodies are transformed into cartoon caricatures so a digitized wooly rug of a man, who used to be a real man about a million centuries ago, could lead them down a fake stone passageway to escape from an army of bloodthirsty goblins.

Oh, yeah. I was sane, all right.

The digitized version of Clara, still clutching the video game rendition of Wendell's robe tightly around herself, had apparently decided to embrace insanity for all it was worth. As we trudged along behind Riderch through a ridiculously long stone corridor, she peppered our resident hero with question after question about his life and the sword Wendell bought on eBay.

Every now and then Riderch stopped to battle a slimy, squirming thing or what looked like an animated skeleton that jumped out at us from alcoves and niches in the stone walls. We cowered behind him while he slashed and hacked and jabbed his way through a computer programmer's idea of flesh and bone. For the most part, the gore wasn't all that gory. Wendell's game must have been rated T for Teen. I had to resist yelling, "Score!" every time Riderch dispatched another make-believe monster into the ether. That wouldn't have been the sane thing to do, not to mention the noise might bring the rest of the goblin world charging down the corridor straight at us.

Between battles, Riderch told us that after he died—ironically not in battle—he'd woken up in a strange place. "Not this world," he said. "It was incomplete somehow. Flat and barren of people."

An earlier version of this game?

"What did you do there?" I asked.

"I wandered," he said. "I discovered things that led me to other places and other things." He shook his head. "It was not a fit world for a warrior. After I discovered all that existed to discover, I found myself here."

Ricerch's first world didn't remind me of any specific game, but then again, I wasn't a video game freak.

Much of what Clara asked him meant nothing to me. They discussed battles he'd fought when he was still alive. Names and dates and political intrigue from a long ago era. I let my mind wander as he talked about Nudd and Mordaf and the burning of Arvon. While the details might excite Clara—nothing like a little primary research to take her mind off the impossible—I was much more interested in how we were going to get out of here and go home. I missed my apartment. I missed my cat. I even missed Wendell and the aroma of freshly microwaved popcorn. Nothing smelled like anything here. I guessed scent wasn't something video game programmers had to worry about.

"Have you ever tried to leave?" I asked during a lull in his lurid tale of a sword fight in which he'd first discovered his sword's unique ability to catch fire.

"Leave?" He snorted at me. "One does not leave the afterlife."

"I'm not dead," I said.

"You are here." He gestured with his hand at the dank corridor. "You would not be here unless you were dead."

Clara's flat eyes grew wide and her birthmark-free chin quivered. "I can't be dead. I'm getting married in three weeks." She started to sniffle but no tears fell down her cheeks. "I have to pick up my dress tomorrow."

Riderch looked at her, neither pity nor annoyance in his expression. Come to think of it, he only had the one bland expression, even when he fought.

"I won't ever see Wendell again!" Clara covered her face with her hands as the realization sunk in. Pretty soon her shoulders started to shake as she sobbed.

I had to admit it—standing in that impossible place, I felt bad for Clara. We didn't get along, to put it mildly, but she really did love Wendell. And in his own way, Wendell loved her. I was pretty fond of Wendell myself. Maybe I needed to make more of an effort to like her.

"We're not dead." I put a hand on her shoulder. "We can go back. We just have to figure out how."

"You don't even know where we are," she said around hiccupping sobs.

I had a pretty good idea, but I wasn't insane enough to share it, even with Clara.

"We'll figure something out," I said.

Riderch got us moving again. No one talked this time. Clara shuffled along with her dry eyes and morose expression. Riderch kept his hand on the hilt of his sword, the blade stuck through the leather-like belt at his waist. Every now and then I heard scraping sounds from the corridor behind us, but every time I turned to look, I saw nothing but more darkly empty space. Still, if intuition counted for anything, we were about to be attacked any minute. We really had to get out of here.

I was pretty sure the corridor was the same as a level in Wendell's game. How did he move up a level? All I knew was he crowed about his victory every time he made it to a new and more difficult level. I closed my eyes and tried to imagine the television screen in my living room. The clanging of metal on metal. Wendell's fingers punching buttons on the controller, moving the character on screen around as it delivered kicks and blows, swung its sword and shot arrows from its crossbow.

That was it. To get out of this never-ending corridor, we were going to have to fight, and fight something more than the things Riderch had slain so far. Like the goblins chasing us.

"Stop," I said.

Riderch pointed at the corridor in front of us. "We must keep going forward."

"Not if we want to get out of here."

"They'll catch us," Clara said. "If I'm not dead already, I really don't want to die here."

"Then we fight." I grabbed a torch and yanked it out of its iron sconce. "We can do it."

For a man with no expression, Riderch managed to let me know without saying a word that he thought I was an idiot.

"Look," I said. "It's three against—" I didn't know how many goblins constituted a horde, but there had to be a way to beat them. Levels always let the players win. Eventually. "Okay, I don't know how many, but there are three of us. And I don't know about you guys, but I'm getting really sick of this place."

Riderch and I engaged in a short staring match.

"You've never run from a fight, right?" I said, playing on all that Big Bad Warrior King history he'd been telling Clara. "Just because you're dead is no reason to start now."

He stared down his nose at me. "I have never run from my opponents."

Right. He'd been doing a pretty good job of it so far.

"So let's quit running away." I grabbed another torch and held it out to Clara. "Gotta start somewhere if you want to get back to Wendell."

She looked from me to the torch, then glanced back the way we'd come. For some reason, even though torches lit our way, back behind us the corridor faded into gloomy black. A programming glitch, most likely. Or else most players didn't turn around and chase the bad guys down.

Clara knotted the belt at her waist, cinching it up tight to keep the robe closed. "For Wendell," she said as she took the torch from me.

If she kept this up, I might want to marry her myself.

She brandished the torch in front of her, a steely look in her digitized eyes. "And my thousand-dollar wedding dress," she said.

Or not.

* * *

I LOST TRACK of how many things we fought.

First it was the horde of goblins. A horde turned out to be twenty, all of which were afraid of fire. Lucky for Clara and me. We kept them at bay with the torches while Riderch dispatched them with his sword.

Once the goblins were all dead, a hidden panel in the stone wall slid aside. When we walked through, we found ourselves in a series of caves. Where we found, of course, a cave troll. Or three.

Cave trolls don't die easy. For one thing, they weren't afraid of fire, so the torches were no use. Slingshots, of all things, did the trick. Clara and I found slingshots and plenty of small rocks in the cave. We ran around and between and under the trolls while we pelted them with rocks. While we kept their attention on us, Riderch skewered them with bolt after bolt from his crossbow. Pretty soon the trolls were dead and we moved up another level.

After that came huge panther-like creatures with enormous fangs and the ability to leap tall buildings in a single bound. If there had been any buildings to leap. On the next level we were faced with flying reptiles with huge teeth and poisonous barbs on their tails.

And so it went. In each level we fought increasingly harder opponents. We found whatever weapons we needed, even if some of the weapons, like the slingshots, seemed laughably inadequate. By the time we got to the final level, I'd picked up a wicked curved dagger, an invisibility potion, the slingshot, and a crossbow of my own, complete with what seemed to be a never-ending supply of bolts. At least I hadn't run out. So far.

Clara had stocked herself just as well. Weapons practically bristled from the belt at her waist.

If Wendell could only see us now.

What if he could? What if we weren't controlling our own actions, but instead a series of button clicks decided whether we won or died? That was just a little too weird to think about.

I knew we'd reached the top level when I saw what had to be the last thing left to fight—a humongous glowing centipede-type creature with pincers like a crab, a stinging tail like a scorpion, and a mouth full of jagged teeth that would have done a great white shark proud. To top it off, this thing was the size of a ten-story building. The digitized ground shook beneath our feet whenever it moved one of its dozens of legs.

"We can't fight that," Clara said.

She shrank behind Riderch while I frantically scanned our surroundings. We happened to be in an enormous flat area paved with the same dirty gray stones from the corridor umpteen levels ago. The ground faded into a dull, misty background in the distance. I couldn't see walls or houses or hills in that mist, or even the indistinct bony branches of leafless trees. Not only that; I couldn't see anything in this barren area we could use for weapons to fight what Wendell would no doubt call the Boss Monster. We'd have to use whatever we already had on us.

In which case, we were screwed.

"I will kill it," Riderch said.

"With what?" I asked. He'd be swatted aside with one flick of one of the thing's legs if he tried to use his sword. Bolts from his crossbow would be about as effective as trying to kill a grizzly bear with toothpicks.

He ignored me. He stepped forward, looking as kingly and noble as his expressionless self could, and drew his sword.

And damned if the blade didn't catch on fire, just like it had when Clara picked the sword up in my apartment.

In all the battles on all the levels before, the sword had been only a sword. No fire, no glowing energy, just a video game version of a finely honed blade. Yet here, when we definitely needed a little extra help, it looked like we had it.

Too bad the flaming sword didn't make a difference.

The centipede from hell took one look at Riderch and the burning blade, picked him up in a pincered leg, and tossed him and the sword aside like they didn't matter. Then it turned its attention on the two of us.

Clara screamed. Gone was the warrior woman who'd battled her way through monsters too numerous to count while dressed in nothing but Wendell's robe. The weapons hanging from her belt might as well have been charms on a bracelet for all she was going to use them.

I slapped her hard across the face. "Wendell," I said. "Remember him? How you're getting married and want to live to see the love of your life again?"

The monster centipede made a chittering, scritching, scraping cry. Its sheer size magnified the sound to almost unbearable levels. This must be what little baby dinosaurs felt right before a T-Rex ate them.

"I can't help you," Clara said through chattering teeth. "I can't—"

"Yes, you can." I grabbed her hand. "Together, right?"

I didn't give her time to answer. I ran to where Riderch lay sprawled on the gray stone, hauling Clara along with me. We had to dodge centipede feet on the way, which was like dodging redwoods falling from the sky, but we made it.

I couldn't tell if Riderch was still with us or not. If he'd been real, blood would have been splattered across the stones, but here he was simply still, his eyes shut, his sword still held loosely in his hand.

I grabbed the invisibility potion from my belt. We only had one shot at this, Clara and I. I could have tried this on my own, but I hoped if I actually beat this thing, I'd find myself back in my own apartment. I didn't want to have to explain to Wendell why I left his fiancé behind.

I handed the potion, which happened to be in a stoppered bottle, to Clara. "I'm going to grab the sword," I said. "Right before I do, I want you to pour this potion over both of us. Got it?"

She nodded.

"On three," I said.

On one, she pulled the stopper from the bottle. Two, and I bent over to reach for the sword.

"Three!"

The invisibility potion felt like someone had covered me with a fuzzy blanket. Not warm but scratchy and hard to see through. I still managed to draw Riderch's sword from his hand.

Nothing.

I held the sword aloft and shouted, "*Cowabunga!*" because it was the first thing that came to mind.

The sword caught on fire.

Not only that, a brilliant white-hot light shot out from the pointy end of the sword and sliced through the air about a foot to the left of the centipede.

If I hadn't been under the blanket of invisibility, the light might have blinded me. As it was, the energy beam made the sword almost impossible to hold. I struggled to point the sword at the centipede's head.

The monster screamed at us. No mistaking the rage in that sound. Clara, still holding my hand in a death grip, dropped the potion bottle. She scrambled after it, pulling me along with her. I lost my balance, lost my battle trying to hold the sword steady, and swung the thing in an arc as I tried to stay on my feet.

Somehow, in all that, I managed to cut the monster's head off with the beam of energy.

We didn't get a victory celebration. We didn't even get the satisfaction of watching the centipede's head splat on the gray cobblestone. One minute we were fighting for our lives, and the next minute the world around us went black. No fade to gray, just black.

Game over.

* * *

CLARA PACKED UP the sword and sent it back to the person who sold it to Wendell. Even though she swore up and down our adventure as digitized video game characters was just an hallucination brought on by a severe allergic reaction to my cat, she still used barbecue tongs and oven mitts to get the sword back in its box. Allergic reaction, my eye.

Wendell wouldn't talk to me for a week. Clara had decided all on her own to return the sword—not that I wanted it around my apartment any more than she did—but Wendell got mad at me, not her, because I let her see the sword in the first place. I would have been more upset at the silent treatment except I was too busy cuddling my confused cat and making microwave popcorn just to enjoy the smell.

One night two weeks before the wedding, as I was walking through the living room inhaling a bag of popcorn, Wendell told me he decided not to be mad at me anymore.

"It wasn't really your fault," he said. "Clara always manages to get the better of me, too."

I decided to let that go. He'd never believe me if I told him I beat the Boss in a medieval sword and sorcery game while Clara wanted to run and hide.

"Besides," he said. "I found something better for the ceremony." He grinned. "Way better."

I stopped inhaling. I knew that grin. "What did you buy?"

"It was a super great deal."

Oh, no.

"You're going to love this." He waved a computer printout at me. "I paid for express delivery. It should be here tomorrow."

The printout was from eBay. *One silver chalice, antique, motivated seller.*

I put down the popcorn, shoved my wallet and keys in the pocket of my jeans, and shrugged on my jacket.

"Where are you going?" Wendell asked.

"Video game store," I said.

His jaw dropped open. "You? Why?"

"Research."

I needed a game guide for an adventure game set in Camelot. Preferably one featuring Arthur and the Knights of the Round Table, and the quest for the Holy Grail.

Just in case.

In this issue, Robert J. McCarter gives us a stunningly original and wonderful story of a kid growing up to love the stars. And maybe a little bit of understanding into dreams.

This is his fourth story in these pages, all of them different, and I am glad to say there will be more coming. He's published seven novels and his short fiction has appeared or is forthcoming in The Saturday Evening Post, Fiction River, Andromeda Spaceways Inflight Magazine, *and numerous anthologies.*

Breathing in the Stars

Robert J. McCarter

TIMMY'S FIRST MEMORY is of the Milky Way. A thick band of stars splashed across the night sky. They were stopped at a rest stop just outside of Flagstaff, Arizona. The cold woke him up while his father carried him to the restroom. His eyes fluttered open and filled with stars.

He sucked in the cold air, trying to breathe in the beauty, and pointed at the stars as he bounced against his father's chest.

"Stars, Timmy," his father said with a chuckle. "Those are stars."

"Stars..." Timmy repeated with reverence.

He cried when he couldn't see them anymore, but never forgot that feeling.

* * *

THE FIRST—AND LAST—thing Timmy wanted to be as a boy was an astronaut...or cosmonaut, or rocket man, or...the word didn't maters to him at all, he just wanted to be out there. Free of gravity, nothing to hold him down, floating and spinning among the stars.

When he was eight, he watched the 2056 mission to Mars, as they reached the red planet, with rapt attention. He entered every virtual simulation, watched every available stream.

He didn't want to ride his bike unless he was pretending to be Flash Gordon. He didn't want to study unless it was the kind of thing astronauts studied—which his mother told him, with all seriousness, was history and English. Astronauts had to have command of both, she said, so he studied. And they needed to have command of math and physics. They needed to be physically fit and strong. They needed to be the best of the best of the best.

But Timmy had asthma. Bad asthma. When he was nine, the day the doctor told him, "I'm sorry, son, but there is no cure," was the worst day of his young life.

If he couldn't be an astronaut, he couldn't go to the stars. A sub-orbital flight wasn't going to cut it. A night at one of the space hotels, which cost more than both his parents made in five years, was never going to happen, and was not nearly enough anyway.

He needed to be out there. He needed to be in the darkness, in the void, surrounded only by the stars. As little between him and the distant lights as possible. His young mind reeled, knowing some of the stars were already dead before their light even reached him.

He didn't want to be an astronaut or a cosmonaut anymore. He wanted to be a starman. He needed to be a starman.

But he was never going to leave the gravity well. He would ever have his feet affixed to the ground anchored by the inhaler the doctor had prescribed.

***

AT TEN, TIMMY spent more time in virtual than in the real world. The tech was good, it felt almost real, but he knew it wasn't.

He would find himself playing in a sim, on a mission for some galactic good guys that would save the universe from the galactic bad guys, but inevitably he would abandon his post, either as a sole operator or as part of a crew.

He would ignore the comm, or his commanding officer, or the alien or android on duty, and make his way to the airlock. He would put on his EVA gear, he would enter the airlock, wait impatiently as the air cycled out, and then open the hatch. He would jet out, he wouldn't look back, but be out *there*, among the stars, doing his best to find the feeling, that same feeling from when he was just a tiny boy being held by his father looking up at the Milky Way for the first time.

But in never worked. He never felt it. He couldn't suck in the cold mountain air from his stuffy bedroom. He didn't feel the light of the stars filling him. The virtual reality goggles squeezed his head, spoiling the illusion. It wasn't enough. It wasn't real.

***

AT FIFTEEN, HE discovered mescaline, offered to him by a sixteen-year-old temptress named Riya, with brown skin and hair as dark as the void of space that ran down to her waist.

She took him out into the desert, east of LA, driving her father's beat-to-shit Tesla. She drove until the glow on the horizon faded, and pulled over onto a dirt road. Tim snuck a hit from his inhaler, just in case.

"Here we are?" she said with a playful smile on her lips. "Ready?"

He nodded, and she popped a tiny piece of the peyote mushroom in his mouth and kissed him and told him to chew. To swallow. To not be embarrassed if he needed to puke.

Tim chewed, the intense bitterness filing his mouth. He swallowed. He kissed her back, his hands reaching under her T-shirt and finding her bra. She pulled him closer. She kissed him harder.

They fumbled through their young passion and after, they spilled out of the car into the night, stumbling among the cactus, the hot desert air filling his nose, the taste of her still on his lips, and he looked up.

The mescaline was with him then and he lusted more for the stars than the girl by his side. He opened his mouth, he gasped, he sucked the stars in, letting them fill him up. He felt them. He heard them. They spoke of time unmeasurable and peace unfathomable. They made him feel small and feel big at the same time. Finally, he had the stars back.

Tears flowed down his cheeks as the stars filled him up. They whirled in the sky above him. They seemed to pulse, to breath, to be alive.

"I need you," he whispered to the stars.

Riya gasped and said, "I need you too. You are so beautiful, Tim, so fucking beautiful. I could just eat you."

"Take me!" Tim said to the stars.

Riya pulled him down to the ground, pulled at his clothes and kissed him while he stared at the stars.

"I love you," he said the stars. They could hear him. They were talking to him.

"I love you too," she said to Tim.

Tim thought it was the stars talking back to him.

***

RIYA AND THE mescaline and the stars became one thing to Tim. Escape and ecstasy. Freedom. All he wanted to do was drive out to the desert on moonless nights, pop some mushrooms, make love to Riya, and wait for the stars to talk to him.

It was better than when he had been a boy. He could feel the stars. He could hear the stars. He loved the stars.

Tim found that dealing with his parents or his friends or his studies were a weak echo compared to peyote and the stars.

"Are you listening to me?" Riya asked during lunch in their noisy high school cafeteria. They had been together for almost a year. Graduation was coming soon. Riya wanted to talk about the future; Tim wanted to breathe in the stars and not the greasy smell of cheap food.

"What?" Tim asked, his eyes taking in Riya's deep frown, knowing he had missed something.

"I was asking about prom. We are going to prom, right?"

He nodded, not really thinking. "What about Saturday night? The moon won't be up until late."

"Is that all you care about? Your damn stars. I thought you loved me?"

"I…I do. I just…" He couldn't explain it. He did love her and not just because of the stars, not just because of the escape and the ecstasy. He loved her smile and her laugh, and her sweet, musky smell. He loved how sure she was of herself, knowing that she would be doctor one day.

Riya left in a huff, broke up with him a week later, and Tim found himself grounded again. Starman no more. He didn't have a car. He didn't know where to get the mushrooms. He missed Riya, but he would die without the stars.

***

PEYOTE WASN'T THAT hard to find. Tim didn't need Riya. A week later, he snuck out of the apartment one night, taking care not to wake his mother, and made his way to a park not far away. He flopped down on the ground and stared up at the washed-out, gray sky.

The peyote bud was a slightly different color and bigger than what Riya had given him, but he didn't care. He popped it in, and the now-familiar bitterness assaulted his tongue, so harsh, but he sighed and waited.

When the mescaline hit, he felt each blade of grass beneath him, he heard the swing creaking slowly in the wind, the hiss of tires on the freeway, honking, and a siren in the distance. He smelled the grass and his own sweat.

He smiled and then it twisted on him and he saw himself from high above, just a teenage boy alone in ripped jeans with overlong brown hair, his face covered in pimples. He was a dot. A speck. Nothing. He didn't matter. He would accomplish nothing. He would be nothing. There was nothing about him that mattered.

He sucked in air, but his airway constricted and he couldn't breathe, his inhale a slow hiss. The noise of the highway drilled into his head, an evil sound. The grass poked at him and the squeak of the swing was like fingernails on a chalkboard.

Tim patted at his pockets, but he had forgotten his inhaler. He hated it, the anchor that kept him grounded on this world.

He tried to sit up, but the word spun around him, and he fell back down to the grass. The hiss of the highway started sound like jeering, he heard voices, distant voices, and knew they were talking about him, laughing at him, knowing he was nothing.

That laughter was the last thing he heard before he passed out.

***

"ARE YOU OKAY?" Riya asked, her dark eyes moist. He hadn't seen her since the breakup. They were in his cramped, messy room; he had just gotten back home from the hospital and was grounded forever.

Someone found him in the park, had called 911, had saved his life.

Tim nodded, having a hard time meeting those eyes, finding himself grateful to have her near, to breathe in her sweet scent, but feeling so ashamed.

She slipped her hand into his and he smiled. "I do love you know," he said. "It's just—"

"Good," she said, cutting him off. "Because I'm pregnant. My parents…they are so traditional. They are freaking."

He was silent for a long time. Thinking of that first night in the desert with Riya, with the stars. Thinking of his own parents and their divorce. Trying to figure out what he needed. He need the stars and Riya too.

He swallowed hard. "Then we'll get married," he said with a nod.

"Really?" Tears started falling from her beautiful eyes.

"Of course. I was stupid. Of course, I love you more than the stars." He wasn't sure if he was lying, he just knew he needed both.

He put his hand on her stomach and looked into her mahogany-brown eyes. A child. Their child. The thought terrified him and excited him.

"But no more mushrooms," she said, wiping at her cheeks, her eyes hardening.

"Once a month?" he asked. "Just…just sometimes?"

She hesitated, staring at him for the longest time. She put her hand on top of his and pressed it to her belly, bit her lip, and nodded.

***

ON THEIR WEDDING night, in the bridal suite, Riya held something behind her back and said, "I have a surprise for you."

Tim smiled, hoping it was a peyote bud and trip to the desert, but she was pregnant, showing now, and would never do that. When she pulled a pamphlet from behind her back, he did his best not to show his disappointment.

"Over in Pasadena, the California Institute of Technology has a program in astrophysics."

Tim shook his head. "We can't afford that. We just graduated. I don't even have a job yet."

She jumped onto the bed next to him, still in her frilly wedding dress. "My parents. The will help us get set up, get ready for the baby, but…" A cloud passed over her face. "Only if we are both in school."

Tim took the pamphlet, fingering the shiny surface. "Astrophysics…"

She nodded. "Yes. The stars, Tim, the stars."

He felt a wash of emotion. He was grateful and knew he was not good enough for Riya. "The stars," he echoed.

He wouldn't be out among them, but he would get to know them, understand them, listen to what they were saying.

Tim wiped the tears from his eyes, grabbed his wife, and kissed her hard.

***

ASTROPHYSICS WASN'T THE same as those nights in the desert with Riya, the stars pulsing and alive, haloed in rainbow colors. It wasn't the same without the mescaline bitter on his tongue. He missed it and he knew he always would. Life had gotten busy and it had been almost a year since Riya and he had imbibed.

"Come on, Sara girl," he said to his daughter, six years old and getting too big to carry. "Can you walk? It's time to go to the bathroom."

She grumbled and shook her head, her dark hair brushing against his cheek.

"We're at the rest stop," Tim said, taking a deep breath of the cool, sweet mountain air. "Your mama's ready to take you in. You have to go now. We have hours more to drive and no good places to stop."

"I don't wanna."

"Well, that's nice," he replied, catching Riya's smile. "But it doesn't matter, you have to go now. Then we'll be at our home soon, where daddy gets start his new job watching the stars."

"I hate stars."

"Yeah, well look at this." He jabbed her ribs and her brown eyes flew open and she looked up at the dark night sky, the stars arrayed all around them, framed by pine trees.

"Daddy!"

He smiled and nodded. "It's the Milky Way, Pumpkin. Part of our galaxy."

"I...I love the stars," she gasped.

Tim chuckled. "Me too, but know what I love more?"

She shook her head.

"You and mommy."

He tickled her and put her on the ground and she ran to her mother. Tim took a moment, staring up into the dark, breathing deeply, breathing in the stars.

Ezekiel James Boston lives in Las Vegas and has no fear of writing stories on topics that others run screaming from. And that, combined with his incredible skill as a writer, makes him a perfect Pulphouse *author.*

In Ezekiel's third story in these pages, he gives us an original piece of superhero fiction like no other superhero world you have ever read. And, on top of that, the story has real heart and a wonderful character.

Retired from Henching

Ezekiel James Boston

MIKE SMITH'S STOMACH lurched and tightened. His fingers clamped onto the steering wheel. The entire bus rocked as all ten plus tons of it was lifted from the road.

Not meant to be lifted from the side, the walls, the ceiling, the roof creaked and whined. The small waste bins that Mike always set throughout the bus clattered as they fell.

For the most part, he had his passengers trained to actually put their trash where it was supposed to go—instead of just leaving it in the seat or on the floor. The bins, their contents, and other loose debris rattled as it settled into the corner of the left wall and floor; currently the lowest point of the bus.

Expecting a flyer to come down through the front folding doors, Mike looked up to only see the full moon in the clear Jonesboro winter night sky. The clock ticked over to 11 p.m.

He typed in the code to release the money hopper from the farebox. You were only supposed to do that if a robber demanded it. Doing so turned on all hidden recorders and alerted the authorities. Still, being reprimanded for punching in the code prematurely aside, Mike only cared about increasing the response time. Hopefully dispatch would notice him leaning against the driver window and the road six feet beneath them at a forty-two—no, forty-three—degree angle. If so, the Power League should be here in no time.

The light-on-mayonnaise, heavy-on-mustard ham and cheese sandwich Mike had for lunch wanted to come out.

He kept it in.

The engine continued to rev. His speedometer claimed he was going eighty. Mike lifted off the accelerator.

According to the census, the average American citizen was eight times more likely to die from being struck by lightning than to die from being caught in the crossfire of battling ultrahumans. If the public noticed that the best insurance only paid out thirty-three percent on damage caused by ultrahumans, they'd suspect it was a lie.

It was. Mike knew. He had been a henchman to four of the world's worst villains and, in America alone, there were more annual deaths by ultras than worldwide by lightning.

Since no one was coming in the front, he checked his rearview to eye the back-side door.

Most of the ad sliders along the inner roofline had come loose. Only a couple still dangled there, but that was the only movement.

He checked both side mirrors. No one was in sight above the vehicle holding it up with telekinesis or some kind of anti-gravity gun; and no one—no anything—was beneath the bus holding it up.

No matter how many times his vehicles were lifted from the ground, it was always startling. Not knowing how made this one more unsettling than the others. He had moved to a small Arkansas town to specifically avoid any trouble with ultras.

From beneath the buss, a baritone voice demanded, "Where is she?"

Mike's butthole clenched. That voice belonged to Amelia's husband: Randolph Turner, better known as Black Specter. One of America's most powerful ultras. Mike checked all his mirrors again, but didn't see him.

Randolph said, "Tell me!" The bus rotated to a full ninety degrees. "Or I'll crumple this up with you in it."

Mike said, "I don't know, Randolph. Haven't seen her since you told me to quit and get out of Dallas. And I did." Mike felt like an idiot babbling. "I left the city, state, hell, I even moved out to BFE to keep out of any sort of trouble." He added that last part on the off chance that Randolph went back to being a hero.

Randolph asked, "You haven't seen her?"

"No." Mike remembered the stealth suits Amelia was trying to perfect before he left. He opened the side window and stuck his head out into the cold night to look beneath the bus. The chill seeping into the bus made short work of his County Transit polo.

Sure enough, there was a vague six-foot-eight, barrel-chested outline beneath the bus holding it up with one arm.

After seeing Randolph do something similar to a boat in the past, Mike had figured out—and shared with Amelia—how the then-hero's super strength worked. The guy had raw strength, but everything he touched and lifted got engulfed in a field of energy that distributed the weight along the entire object. That was how he could have his hand on the window and the window not simply shatter from the ten tons of pressure.

Mike squinted. "Hell, I can barely see you."

Randolph tilted his head. "Why are you wearing a turban?"

Mike corrected, "It's a dastar."

"Whatever." Randolph took a hold of the bus with both hands and put it back on its wheels. "Why are you wearing it?" He cracked his knuckles and his voice took on a dangerous tone. "You give up on Christ?"

"No!" Mike cleared his throat. "No, I still believe there's a plan for me." He didn't believe in Christ, but Randolph did and the big guy wasn't against forcing others to believe, too. After having been launched into the air by Randolph the first time, Mike changed his stance on religion. He was still agnostic, but had started going to the church Randolph suggested after catching him to see if anything rang true or if the holy spirit got a hold of him.

It hadn't, but Randolph had, and being thrown high enough in the air where it gets damned freezing and air becomes too thin to breathe was a life-changing event.

Randolph's outline walked to the front of the bus to be at the window. This close, Mike could make out the mask on Randolph's face obscuring his features. His shaded eyes were narrowed and accusatory. "But you don't believe."

"Not yet." Mike doubted he ever would, but as long as Randolph was around, he was open to the possibility. He sat back in his chair and pulled his coat on. It'd be a good ten to fifteen minutes after closing the window before the bus would be nice and toasty again.

Randolph looked up and down the deserted two-lane road of US Route 49 with high grass on both sides.

Mike did too.

No headlights either way. It was just them, the windchill, and a distant owl hooting into the night. Jonesboro pretty much rolled up its sidewalks at 7 p.m. Mike had just dropped off that last of the Walmart employees and had been heading back to the depot when Randolph hijacked him.

Randolph removed his mask and looked again.

He still had the strong jawline and piercing blue eyes, but his jet-black Elvis Presley hairline had receded a good two inches. Randolph's physique would probably never change, but the ten years had left their mark. Mike made sure to keep eye contact when Randolph faced him.

Randolph asked, "Still going to church?"

Mike nodded. "Yup. Every Sunday." It was true. He had done so in case this moment ever happened.

When they were on friendlier terms, Randolph had shared that he had a power that let him know when people were lying, and Randolph appreciated that Mike never lied to him. Mike wanted to tell Randolph that he didn't lie to anyone, but the big guy had acted as though that made him special in Mike's eyes. And, while Mike didn't lie, he knew when to keep his mouth shut.

Randolph asked, "Tithe?"

Mike nodded again. "Fifteen percent."

"Good man." Randolph's hard expression eased. "Good man." He nodded absently to himself as he looked down the road.

Mike didn't want to press the conversation, but he held the bill validator up where Randolph could see.

"You pulled it?" Randolph shook his head slightly. As a former hero, he knew the process and what it meant. "I didn't demand it."

"I know." Mike shrugged. "But my bus was off the ground. I figured the sooner I pulled it, the sooner the league would show up."

Randolph shook his head. "They're not going to show."

"They're not? Why?" Mike didn't like the dismissive way Randolph said that. That tone used to make him smile a dirty I'm-on-your-side smile. Now there was only anxiety. The thought of a country without heroes, like down in the Primazone, sent chills through him.

Mike asked, "Why? What'd you guys do?" His accusational tone rung in his ears. He hoped it wouldn't piss Randolph off.

Randolph pointed to the farebox stand. "Go ahead and put it back."

Mike did.

When he looked back, Randolph was holding up a device that looked like a miniature Rubik's Cube.

"Amelia made it." Randolph smiled at it. "It blocks all frequencies within fifty feet. I had it on before picking up the bus." Randolph gave Mike a smug I-caught-you-caring-about-heroes grin. "What'd you think we did?"

"Nothing." Mike stopped his head from shaking a no-you-didn't denial. "It just sounded like—"

"Here's the deal," Randolph butted in. "I'll keep my ears tuned for your voice. You see her, you call me. If that'd be too obvious, just say her name. Got it?"

Randolph put his mask back on. "Good. Start driving again."

Mike did.

Randolph lifted the bus from the side and flew them down to about where Mike would've been if he hadn't been stopped. Randolph gave him his little two-finger salute before he flew up, up, and away.

Mike tried to think of what he could say about the alarm. He had put the money box back, but the alarm could only be reset by a shift supervisor or higher.

Randolph sped back to Mike's window.

Mike jumped in his seat, but kept the wheel steady.

Running next to the bus, Randolph asked, "Still got that cross I gave you?"

Mike reached into his coat and dug the cross made from two small nails banded to form a crossbar across a longer nail from under his polo. He pulled it up and showed Randolph.

"Good man." Randolph nodded and flew up and away again.

The bus's radio crackled to life. "Smith. Dispatch here. Any passengers on your route?" It was code. They had gotten his alarm and were checking in. Mike grabbed his radio hand unit.

To give the all-clear, Mike said, "No. I'm alone here. Just heading back to the depot."

He hoped they didn't ask what happened.

He hoped they wouldn't even mention it.

He hoped and waited.

***

WHEN THE FIRST waft of bacon came, Mike presumed it was from the Williamsons next door. They were writers and kept hours odder than him. But then the smell grew so strong that it made him cut blow-drying his hair short. Hearing grease popping made him wrap the length up in a towel to also cover his forehead. He wrapped a second around his waist, and stepped out of his bathroom.

Across the bedroom—well, bed area—of his shotgun apartment, his old boss, Amelia Schmidt—Mike made a mental correction, *Amelia Schmidt-Turner*—walked two plates of bacon and scrambled eggs from the two-burner range to the narrow wooden table set Mike had gotten because he had started dating. Seeing her turn from the kitchen, with plates of freshly cooked food—no servants anywhere—made him doubt it was really her.

Amelia's always long raven hair aside, she wore blue jeans and a thick gray Dallas Cowboys sweatshirt. As she walked, he noticed that she wore running shoes and that her legs and hips were notably wider. He also noticed, as she turned to face him, that she had a bit of a tummy and full arms. Where her face had been lean and gaunt, she had cheeks and a smile. For once, she looked healthy and happy. When he used to dream about seeing her again, this was exactly how he had imagined her.

Wait. This was *exactly* as he imagined. Fulfilling Randolph's request, Mike frowned and growled, "Amelia."

"Fine." She rolled her eyes and snapped her fingers. The luscious full-figured appearance vanished. Amelia, almost exactly as Mike remembered her, appeared. She still wore the Cowboys sweatshirt and jeans, but they hung on her slim, runway-model frame. Her running shoes were gone, replaced with heels, and her raven hair was cut short into a pixie cut.

She put her hands on her hips and asked, "Better?"

"No." The answer jumped out of Mike's mouth. He grinned and shrugged. "But at least it's real." Expecting the table to be empty, his eyes flicked to it.

The plates of food were still there.

"Wait." Mike started edging forward. He asked, "That's real?"

She flared her hands out and they landed back on her hips. "After ten years, you're amazed at *that*?"

"Yeah." Mike hurried past her and sat in his normal seat. He started on the hot bacon first. Randolph would be here any second and would, as usual, eat everything in the blink of an eye. Mike chased the delicious strip with a fork-shovel of eggs.

Amelia said, "He's not coming."

"Mmh?" Mike looked up to see her holding one of the small Rubik's Cubes of hers. He leaned back in his chair and chewed more casually.

"And look at you." She sat across the table from him—there was no other option—and pointed her finger at him. She had an impressed smile. "Sitting like that."

Mike covered his mouth, stopped chewing, and asked, "What?" Before Randolph, she'd seen him in only a towel hundreds of times before.

"You." She picked up her fork and jutted it toward the window behind him. "Like this."

"Oh." Mike nodded and swallowed. "Yeah, when I first moved in here, I kept to the usual habits. But after the first couple of years, I thought, if Brass or some other vigilante hunts me down here, I don't want to see the red dot on the curtains a split second before I'm shot." He picked up a piece of bacon. "It's real nice not living like I'm walking on eggshells.

She groaned. "Oh, I'm jealous."

Amazed at how this still felt normal, Mike asked, "Is Randolph that bad?"

"No." She took a small bite. "It's the children. They're just like him."

"Kids?" Mike stopped eating. "You guys have kids?" That smack of reality made him set his fork down. He tightened up. "Wait. Why are you here?"

"Don't worry." She tittered. "They're not yours."

That didn't relax him in the least. She hadn't used her emotion control on him.

Insisting, Mike asked, "No, Amelia. I'm seriously asking, *why are you here*?"

"Fine." She set the fork down. "I need you to hench for me again."

Mike's eyes started to twitch and blink. His guts felt like two massive hands had grabbed a hard hold of them and squeezed.

"Just for a bit." She looked him over. Her expression turned more and more annoyed at his reaction to the request. "It'll be just like old times."

His shoulders started to rise up as the sudden urge to use the restroom came upon him. Nausea hit his guts.

She waved a hand at him.

The chair squeaked a little as Mike leaned back, instantly relaxed. His limp hand knocked the fork from the table and it clattered on the linoleum. Though he hated her using any of her powers on him, he was too relaxed right now to care.

The weeklong suspension from work, the threat of Randolph arriving, her asking him to hench again; all of the stress in his life evaporated. He knew she didn't have to wave a hand to use a power on him, but he had asked once and she had obliged ever since. And he appreciated it.

"I can't." His smile felt sloppy. She'd slipped him a hint of euphoria.

"You can." She leaned forward. "Listen, I'm sorry for what I said when you quit. I was hurt. And, after all this time, I realized that my brilliance isn't as keen without your subtle influence." Her eyes took on that brainstorming twinkle. "Just being around you gives me ideas on how to get out of my mess of a marriage and plan a brighter future for my children."

"Well, I don't want to be a part of it." Mike always had the ability to make others around him a scooch better than they were on their own and he thoroughly enjoyed seeing his affect in their eyes. Still. He couldn't.

"I mean, I can't be a part of it." The hyper-relaxed sensation started to fade. Mike sat upright again. While the idea of returning to his old life felt promising, knowing what Randolph would do diminished his appetite.

He nibbled on the bacon. "Randolph would kill me. Straight up murder." Mike pointed up. "I mean, literally, he'd throw me straight up into space."

She gave an incredulous look. "You're exaggerating."

"No, I'm not." He set the bacon down. Mike reached to retrieve his fork and realized it'd been a while since he last mopped. Amelia was always the fastidious type so she doubtlessly noticed, but hadn't said a word about it and didn't look uncomfortable.

Amelia said, "Randolph wouldn't do that."

Mike set his fork on the table.

Spearing eggs with her fork, Amelia was absently shaking her head against the mere suggestion that her husband would do such a thing.

Her head kept the slow shake. "While Randolph does occasionally kill, he wouldn't do that. Well, not to you."

"Yes, he would." Mike insisted. "He told me he would, and has Randolph ever not made good on a threat?"

"Did you see him today?" She stopped shaking her head. A small frown started to form. "Did he threaten you?"

About to say no, Mike thought about Randolph's *Or I'll crumple this up with you in it.* Technically he had, but that probably wasn't the threat she was talking about.

"Yes, and yes, but!" Mike made sure to add the *but* to keep her attention. Otherwise she'd go off with what she thought was enough information. "The threat we're talking about happened the day I quit your employ ten years ago. Randolph said I could leave Dallas on my own or he wouldn't hold back next time he *threw me up to Jesus*."

"Next time?" She pounded the table. The plates and fork rattled.

Mike jumped in his chair. He then lifted his plate and fork.

"He threw you up to Jesus?" She pounded the table again. "That asshole!"

Waiting for a third pound, something she used to always do, Mike kept his plate off the table.

Amelia gave the table a small bop. "He promised me that he wouldn't do that again unless he really had to."

Mike set his plate and fork down. "And he probably hasn't." He didn't want to defend Randolph, but she needed more of the story. "He threw me up about a week after you finally allowed him into your workshop."

"You had that threat over your head for two years?" Her lips twisted up in thought. "I knew I noticed a change in you."

"Yeah." Mike nodded at the memory of looking down at the world as he rocketed upward. He remembered wondering on the way up if he was going to hit the plane. He remembered clawing at his throat for wisps of freezing air and blacking out. And waking up hurtling back down toward earth. Of course, Randolph had caught him. But that part of the memory wasn't as important.

Mike and Amelia's history together dictated that he was supposed to share what he had remembered. He didn't. The nature of their relationship changed when she fell for the then-hero. Mike wanted to, but he sure as hell wasn't going to try anything that could be remotely misinterpreted by Randolph and his ultra-jealous nature.

He decided to sit there in silence with her.

"Something needs to be done about that." She gave the table another bop. This one looked contrived.

Mike figured she had planned out how this vein of conversation would go to get him to hench for her again, but without him sharing his experience, she couldn't get his buy-in.

Mike said, "It's history. Don't sweat it."

As usual, when making a plan that involved him, she started to avoid eye contact. She never could look him in the eyes while her plans would put him in peril. And, no matter what he said, he was going to be a part of it.

Appetite gone, Mike pushed his plate away. But only slightly. There wasn't much room on the tabletop.

He yawned. "Well, thanks for cooking, but it's been a long day."

"Fine." Amelia pushed her plate a little too. It tinked into his. "I get the hint. I'll leave." She got up. "Hope you don't mind if I come by every once in awhile, unannounced of course, for a meal and visit."

Mike stayed seated. "I prefer you didn't."

She gave a careless smile. "I'm going to."

Mike's chest expanded as he drew a deep breath and—instead of uselessly trying to talk her out of it—heaved a defeated sigh.

"Before I go, though…" She pulled up her left sleeve, revealing one of her bracers that controlled a great many of her gadgets and automatons. It was much sleeker than before.

She punched in a code and said, "Take off that towel."

"What?" While he used to love that command when they had slept together, it came across as quite emasculating. Worse, suicidal, if Randolph found out. Mike had to refuse her. He had grown stronger through the years. He had to say no.

Her gaze drifted to the towel on his head. "I want to see it."

"Oh." That was only slightly better than wanting him to remove the one around his waist. She was the reason he had to keep the top of his head hidden. His gaze dropped to the table. Taking the towel off his head felt like undoing years of therapy. But she commanded it. And—whether he was under her employ or not—he had taken an oath to do her bidding. He swore to do anything but lie for her. And he took off the towel.

Amelia's eyes widened when the bottom half of the thick, huge Calibri font *1* made of black nanites on his head came into view.

Mike set his will to controlling the nanites. To keep them in the shape of the 1 instead of letting them cover his body in his old henchman uniform. Controlling them wasn't easy. The effort made him grimace, but he enjoyed the small sign of defiance.

Seeming not to notice, Amelia sneered at his hairline blocking the top of the one. Her expression turned to disgust as she noticed his wet hair went down past the seat of the chair.

She pulled up her right sleeve and typed commands. "One, we will eat next week. You will make your scrumptious quiche lorraine and, by then, you will have shaved your head bald before I lay my eyes upon you." She glanced carelessly at him. "Understood?"

Straining, Mike kept control of the nanites and nodded. It was so pleasing to show her that he could resist her will in some way.

"Good." Amelia tapped the bottom of the 1 on his forehead with her right hand.

The nanites stopped their struggle. It felt like they were gone.

She said, "Until next week." And vanished with a push of a button on her left bracer.

Hoping to never have to hide his head again, Mike rushed into the bathroom to check out his forehead. The bottom of the 1 was still there, just above his eyebrows, and the same size. The nanites rippled like they would when Amelia updated their programming.

Mike said, "Maybe." He tried to will them to slide up and be hidden by his hairline.

The thickness of the 1 thinned as the nanites did as mentally commanded, but a trace amount, enough to keep the 1 obvious, stayed.

Mike sighed and went back to blow-drying his hair. He liked it long and didn't want to be bald again. He looked into his reflection's eyes and tried to come up with his own plan. "One week."

***

UPON WAKING, MIKE lazed, moving the nanites that he could remove from his body around his room. He still had huge sums of money from his small portions of past heists in offshore accounts. He spent the day weighing options on where to relocate. He could move anywhere.

From interviews Randolph gave when he was a hero, Mike knew the ultrahuman could identify someone by their heartbeat up to two hundred and fifty miles away. The best plan was to go into the heart of Russia. They had no love for American ultrahumans and Russia's own ultrahumans, the *Kontrol' Material,* had battled Randolph and the Power League to a standstill on a couple different occasions. Without the Power League, Randolph would be outclassed.

Mike's Russian was a bit rusty, but…

Every plan he came up with to hide from Randolph was as solid as could be, but—as long as he had the nanites on him—there was no way he could hide from Amelia. And she was dead set on using his presence to spark ideas. Which would be okay as long as Randolph didn't find out; which, Mike was certain, he would. He just had to stay hidden.

When night came, Mike made himself a thermos of black coffee, packed a change of clothes in a backpack, and left everything else in his apartment. He got into his late model Honda Civic and hit the road, heading to the plot of land he had just outside of Cardwell, Missouri.

He had always worried about his past catching up to him and never grew attached to his possessions. However, he always thought that it'd be a grown-up sidekick to a hero murdered in the past to come for him. He would have never thought it would be his old boss and her jealous and crazy-powerful husband.

In thinking about it, the only thing Mike might've wanted to take was his employee of the year award from the transit authority, but that life was now behind him.

He abandoned his empty thermos and car—with the keys on the dashboard—on the side of MO-164. Shivering, he let the nanites cover his body in his old all-black henchman suit.

They warmed his skin instantly.

Further, they coated the inside of his mouth and esophagus. A super-invasive upgrade. But they warmed the winter night air, making it feel like he was breathing during a warm spring day.

Mike jogged out into the perfume of tussock sedge dotted throughout the copses of rusty black haw bushes that tottered between being tall shrubs and small trees until he hit real trees—tall white oaks—at the demarcation of his land.

A quarter of a mile farther in, he came to the large clearing that he had made. The moonlight showed that the efforts he had made years ago to make the soil infertile in the shape of Texas had mostly kept. Wild grass had started to edge in on the sides some, but the clearing was mostly dirt.

Mike went to the white oak north of the panhandle and looked up in the branches. The shovel he had placed there was still present.

He climbed. Like before, the nanite suit worked with him like a powered exoskeleton to make every move easier. He was up and down with the shovel in a jiffy. He then went to where Dallas would be in the clearing and struck the shovel into the ground.

Mike turned and dumped the dirt. But when he turned back, a hole the size of his buried footlocker had been dug twenty feet deep—deep enough to avoid accidental unearthing—and his footlocker was at his feet with the lock twisted off.

"So." Randolph's voice came from above him. "You didn't call me when she met with you." He removed his mask as he floated down to the earth. "And don't say you haven't seen her because I can smell her breath on you."

Holy shit. Everyone had always been so caught up with Randolph's unbelievable sight and hearing, that no one—not even Mike—had thought that all of Randolph's senses were heightened.

Mike said, "I said her name just like you said to, but she also had one of those cube things."

Randolph frowned. "She said it only works on electronic frequencies."

To keep what he wanted to say from spilling out, Mike pressed his lips together.

Randolph cocked an eyebrow at him. "Go ahead. Say it."

"Maybe she lied." Mike kneeled next to the footlocker. His nanite-covered knee sank into the earth. He could feel the texture of the ground through it, but not the temperature.

Randolph chuckled. "She doesn't lie to me."

"Really? When was the last time you checked?"

Randolph stopped chuckling.

Mike opened the footlocker. His old fake passports were in there on top of a bed of strapped bills. He had exactly a million dollars' worth of twenties, tens, and fives. He picked up the passports and tossed them to the side as though they weren't one of the main reasons he had come here.

He picked up the old laptop that Amelia had modified for him and opened it. Even after all these years, it came to life with Amelia's own Linux-based operating system. The battery still had sixty-one-percent energy.

Randolph said, "When we got married, she said she would never lie to me."

Mike nodded at what Randolph said and added, "And she probably meant it at the time." Acting as though he was after information on the laptop, Mike closed the footlocker, set the computer on top, and sat cross-legged.

He could feel Randolph's eyes upon him. He ignored it and clicked into old spreadsheets showing how much he had put into Bitcoin and codes to the cryptolockers.

Sounding suspicious, Randolph said, "Why are you wearing your old henchman uniform?"

Mike spared him a glance. "Because it's cold." And went back to checking on his wealth. His spreadsheet of Shadowcoin and codes to cryptolockers was more impressive, but a vulnerability had been introduced into the currency making it possible for some organizations to track money movement. He made a mental note to sell the funds.

Randolph asked, "Is Amelia here with you?"

Mike answered, "No, but—"

Ultraviolet black light bathed the area in purple.

Randolph swung at Mike and yelled, "You son of a—"

The punch landed on Mike's jaw. Instead of being turned into a pulp of flesh, blood, and bone, Mike fell backward. Strong ultraviolet would sap at Randolph's immense power, but whatever this was, it instantly rendered him powerless.

Mike held his jaw and got to his feet.

Randolph was looking at the massive light source above. He broke toward the trees.

Mike chased and tackled Randolph around Wichita Falls; twenty feet short of the white oaks' shade to the north.

Randolph struggled to get Mike off of him. Used to always just being stronger, Randolph didn't have any real techniques to make it happen.

Mike, on the other hand, practiced Brazilian Jujitsu and had the strength of the nanites on his side. He mounted Randolph, got him in a rear naked choke, and rolled over onto his back to keep Randolph exposed to the light.

Randolph reached back. His fingers were trying to find Mike's eyes.

"Do that—" Mike tightened his arms to restrict Randolph's breathing "—and I'll put you out."

Randolph stopped struggling.

Mike loosened his grip a bit so Randolph could breathe, but retained control.

The nanites coated Mike's eyes and dimmed the bright purple.

Coming down on a rope, Amelia cackled. She could've just punched in the codes and teleported, but sometimes she loved to enter the area by other means so that she could showboat. And this was one of those times.

She said, "Great job, One! I knew I could count on you." Wearing her old skin-tight nanite uniform and long trench coat made from extra nanites, she sashayed over to them. A nanite cross, just like the ones Randolph gave to his converts, dangled from her right hand. It emitted ultraviolet light. She put the nanite chain over Randolph's head and draped it from his neck.

Amelia said, "Randolph, honey. I want a divorce."

Randolph pulled at Mike's arm for more air.

Mike loosened a little more.

Randolph said, "Our vows were until death do us part."

Amelia grinned wickedly. "I was hoping you'd bring that up." She tucked the cross into his suit and stood. She then reached into her coat and produced a gun from the small of her back.

She said, "You'll only have power when I allow it. *If*, I allow it. Divorce me and you could go back to being a hero or a villain of your own design. But we won't be a team in any sense."

Randolph said, "The only way we won't be a team is if you use that."

Amelia shook her head at him. "You're not listening. I'm giving you a choice, hubby. Either give me a divorce, or I send you to patrol the halls of Heaven." She pressed the gun against Randolph's chest. Right over his heart.

Mike kept from freaking out.

Normally, at this close range, the bullet would go through Randolph and into him. However, the gun was made from Amelia's nanites and so were the bullets. He'd been caught in Amelia's crossfire before and knew the bullet nanites would just be added to his mass of nanites instead of hurting him.

Mike looked at Amelia.

She winked at him in that way she had when he'd become her number-one henchman. When Mike saw the wink before, he thought it was love. Now he knew it was a limited form of love—eternal servitude—on Amelia's terms. If she won tonight, there was no way she was going to let Mike stay retired.

Retaining just enough nanites to keep his body coated, Mike eased his excess nanites into the back neckline of Randolph's suit.

Randolph wriggled.

Mike clamped onto Randolph and held him still as his excess nanites gave Randolph an undersuit. Mike also wrapped the cross in nanites to extinguish the light from it.

Randolph said, "You wouldn't. You love me. And we're not divorcing."

She moved the gun around his chest and said, "Choose."

Randolph bellowed, "I'd rather die!"

A gunshot went off. Then another and another.

Cold as the Arctic, Amelia said, "All. Three. Hearts."

Mike didn't even know Randolph had three hearts. Explains why he was so hard to kill in the past.

Amelia stepped back and stretched, carefree, under the ultraviolet lights. "Being a widow will have to do."

Mike tossed Randolph to the side and covered the man's head with the nanites.

What was left of Amelia flew away in a nanite-coated bloody pulp as the bright ultraviolet lights overhead were shattered.

Randolph was hovering above the ground. His right hand was covered in Amelia's blood and still balled up in a fist. There was a murderous gleam in his tearing eyes.

Mike commanded his nanites to recede from the cross.

Instantly powerless, Randolph fell to the earth. He stood and balled his fist again. "I'm going to kill you for that."

Mike had the nanites stiffen.

As though in a full body cast, Randolph went still, but he cussed until Mike had the nanites cut off his air flow.

Mike said, "You once threw me up to Jesus. Well, guess what?" He pushed Randolph into the hole and started shoveling dirt in.

The nanites made the work easy.

Patting the shovel on the filled-in earth, Mike then collected the extra nanites from around the clearing, and hoisted his footlocker from the dirt. He was now truly retired from henching.

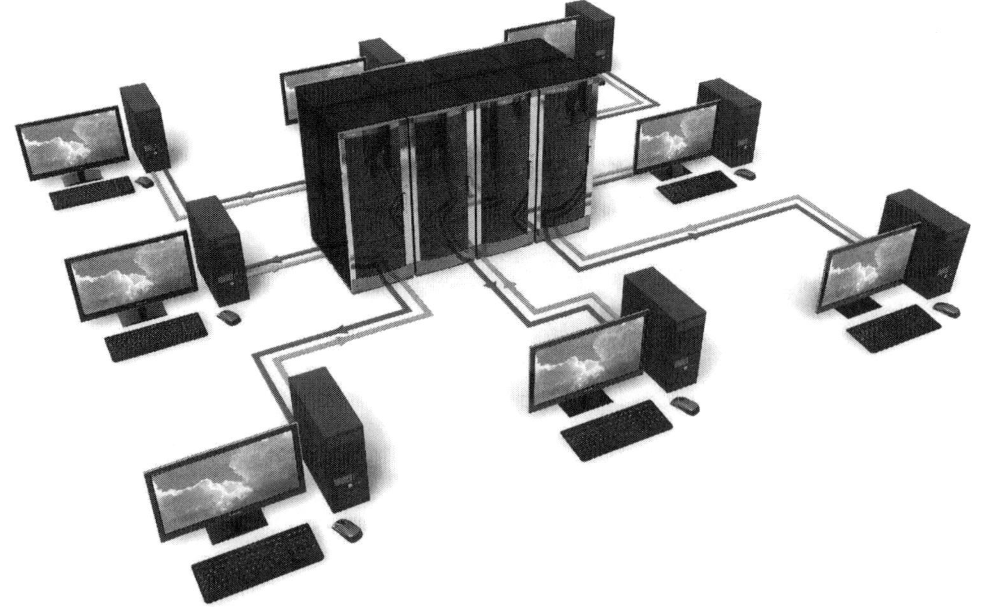

David Bruns, in his first original story in this magazine, follows Ezekiel James Boston with another fascinating and innovative take on superheroes.

I told him when I asked for this story for Pulphouse *that he should write more in this incredible world. I sure hope he does. The stories would be great fun, just as this one is.*

The Networked Path of the Cyber Zamurai

David Bruns

SUPERHEROES ARE BORN, not made.

That was the saying back in the '90s. Might've been true then, but not now. Today's superheroes are all made. First, the biotech companies do their gene-splicing thing, then the tech guys come up with some kind of cool weaponry, and finally the marketing groupies take over. Color palettes, hairstyles, regional food preferences based on area of operation, and of course, the costume. Then there's usually a big celebration as the new superhero is welcomed by the local community....

A light flashed in my peripheral vision.

"HeroNet, what's your emergency?" I said into the microphone on my headset. The software on my heads-up display showed me the caller was located on the north side of Brookdale.

A woman's voice, wracked with sobs, came on the line: "Please, my baby is still in there! They say the fire is too bad to risk sending anyone in!"

I had the local cameras up by now and had redirected a drone to the coordinates. My breath caught in my throat. The apartment building was raging like a Roman candle. Two fire trucks were on scene, spraying water, but their pitiful streams were the equivalent of a Boy Scout peeing on a campfire—

"Are you still there? Send a superhero! Please!"

I scanned the list of Trademarks—that's what we call the big guys—but they were either on another case or out of service for the day. (Union rules: you don't bother a superhero on their day off.)

"Hello?" she screamed in my ear.

"I've got someone on the way, ma'am," I said in my most professional-woman-in-charge customer service voice. Okay, a tiny lie. I hadn't actually sent anyone yet, but I did have a plan. I snatched up my mobile and thumbed to Rico's personal number.

He answered on the second ring. "Bartelli's Pizza, you buy, I fly—"

"Rico," I broke in. "I need you on a case. Burning building, baby trapped inside." I rattled off the address. "Go, man. Now!"

My boyfriend, Rico, is a good example of what happens when the superhero pipeline doesn't complete one of their creations. He'd been given the ability to fly through some genetic witchery, but the tech company that was supposed to develop him into a full-fledged superhero went out of business, which meant no costume, no cool tech, and definitely no coming-out party. When a company goes bankrupt, you call sell the assets, but it's still illegal to sell a human being, even one that's been modified. All the other agencies already had a guy who could fly, so Rico spent his adolescence in a sort of legal limbo until he gave up on his dream of becoming the Latin Rocket Man. He delivers pizzas now, goes by the handle Fly-Boy.

And sometimes, like now, he picks up a job as a free agent.

My boyfriend showed up on the drone's vid-feed as a streak of red, flying straight into the flames. He'd explained to me how he created his own vortex when he flew so the fire never touched him, but it still looked cool as hell to me. The seconds ticked by and no Rico. Finally, he burst through the roof of the building, carrying a small bundle. With an impressive swoop, he deposited the baby with the paramedics. I zoomed in the drone feed so I could see his smile as he accepted a hug from the tearful mother. Rico had great hair and an even better smile. It's too bad he never got to be the superhero I knew he could be....

"Finley!" My reverie came to an unpleasant end when Luther Meansby's face filled my heads-up display. My shift supervisor is not an attractive man at a distance, but to have his jowly mug fill up every bit of space in front of your eyes...enough to make a girl lose her Egg McMuffin.

"Sir?" I let my face go slack, fixing my gaze on the pimple forming on the side of his nose.

"You used a Secondary for a major city emergency!" The zit danced on his nose like a whitecap on choppy water. "You know the policy: no use of Secondaries without supervisory approval!"

"True, sir, but there is an immediate death and/or dismemberment exception—"

"Don't give me any of your legalistic baloney, young lady. Do you have any idea the money the company will have to spend to scrub this off the evening news?"

And there we had it. The all-important news cycle. Heaven forbid we actually just save people. Welcome to the business of superhero services. We had to save people *and* use the right marketing spin so HeroNet came out looking pristine for their next contract negotiation with the city. They got all in a snit when a free agent picked up a little news coverage.

"I'm waiting for an answer, young lady."

A red light in the corner of my display blinked, signifying the end of my shift.

"Whoa, Mr. Meansby, that's my day coming to an end. No overtime authorized, right? Gotta follow procedures. Let's pick this up on the flippity-flop." I killed the connection and sat back in my chair.

Heather, from the cube across the aisle, was gathering up her purse. "I could hear Meansby all the way over here. Did you really dispatch a Secondary to that fire?" She shook her head, blonde curls brushing her shoulders. "Are you trying to get canned?"

Her response rankled me more than a bit. Yeah, the job paid well, but was it really so wrong to actually help people at the same time? I thought about the massive HeroNet shield logo on the side of the building and the slogan: *Your savior is just a phone call away*. Maybe my boyfriend wasn't a Trademark, but he saved that kid and our main job was supposed to be saving lives.

Still, that attitude was not the vibe that most of the people around me held. I tried a different approach. "Well, Heather, I guess I just get a little loco on Hump Day."

Heather nodded. "I hear you, sister." She'd obviously forgotten this was Thursday. "Don't forget tomorrow's Update Day and we have that all-employee meeting before shift." She rolled her eyes. "They keep announcing it every five minutes, so it must be important."

"Yeah." HeroNet 2.0 had been hyped for months as the Next Big Thing from Cyber Realities International, which had the contract for the upgrade. They'd built a multi-gajillion-dollar wing on the HeroNet campus that was secured behind three different kinds of biometric authentication and entirely air-gapped, which made a network geek like me just crazy curious. For all the buzz, I'd never seen anyone actually enter or leave the building.

My gaze slid back to my terminal. Maybe I should snoop the network and find out what they were planning. New cubicles, maybe? Or a kick-ass VR customer service setup…

"Earth to Casey." Heather was waving her hand in my face. "I said we should go celebrate Hump Day. You in?"

One last look at my desk. "Yeah, I'm in."

***

SAY WHAT YOU WILL about Heather's intellectual capacity, but don't ever challenge her capacity for alcohol. By the time I wandered into the apartment, it was past nine. Rico was sprawled on the couch watching the muted TV with a sour look on his face. His best friend, Sam, aka Boogerman, was snoring in the La-Z-Boy. Sam's another Secondary left on the open economy due to corporate legal gymnastics. Think Spiderman, but with mucus.

Effective as a superpower? Yeah, but with limited appeal beyond the demographic of twelve-year-old boys. At least that's what the marketing firms decided. To be fair, they took a run at it, trying to brand him as the Snot Dragon, but it never really *achieved market viability* as they say in the biz. His unique *gift* ruled him out of a career in food services, but Sam makes a decent living as a carpenter. Such is the life of the superhero pipeline discards. He likes to laugh it off by saying he never has to buy wood glue.

I burped a little. "I'm guessing you didn't get picked up on the news?" I said, suddenly feeling guilty about my great buzz and the fact that I hadn't thought about my boyfriend all night.

"Nope." He flipped to the recorded section and showed me the doctored news coverage of his rescue. It was a quality hack job by the PR folks. They didn't change anything that happened, just edited Rico's entire existence out of the event. A streak of red entering the building cuts to a grateful mother with her baby in her arms. After the news spot, a commercial came on and Rico went to change the channel back.

I put my hand on his arm. "No, wait."

Soft violin music welled out of the speakers, and a beautiful sunrise showed on the screen. Three letters grew out of the sun. C…R…I…and a mellow-voiced announcer took over, telling the story of Cyber Realities International and its founder, Taylor Winsome.

There are tech rock stars and then there's Taylor. With smooth, ageless features and a short haircut, Taylor Winsome could have been the belle—or the beau—of the ball. Famously reclusive, the public salivated over every detail of his/her life—and there was precious little hard information.

As the music crescendoed into the CRI slogan of *Remaking Your Life…Online*, Rico and I sat there, each thinking our own private thoughts of the tech titan.

"God, she's beautiful," Rico whispered.

"Yeah, he sure is," I said back.

The commercial ended and I almost asked Rico to replay it, but figured that might be pushing it. After all, I was supposed to be making him feel better.

"Sorry about today," I said. "That was a dick move by HeroNet."

Rico grunted. "Goin' to bed."

I burped again. "I'll be along in a few. Just want to check the network."

I'd commandeered the hall closet as a server room of sorts. The rows of lights blinked at me as I ran my fingers across the panels. This was all custom stuff; I'm very particular about my hardware. Probably not the best way to spend my HeroNet salary, but this is where I felt at home.

I rested my hand on the main server box and let my feelings extend into the network. At moments like this, I *was* the network. All the ones and zeroes meant something to me, talked to me in a way no person ever could. My dad once showed me the old movie *The Matrix* and I almost cried. That was what it felt like to me. Not the submarines and the fetus-as-batteries stuff, but the way Neo merged with his digital existence.

When I was seven, I thought my network affinity was a real skill. I'd so convinced myself that I tested at a superhero walk-in clinic. Even had a superhero name picked out and everything. Cyber Zamurai, a cross between Zorro and a samurai. My backup name was Matrix Missy, but I thought I might get into some trademark issues with the movie people.

The evaluator just laughed at me, a memory that still stung. "Superheroes live in the real world, little girl," he'd said. "Who ever heard of an online superhero?"

I kept my skills to myself after that, but at times like this, when it was just me and the network, I wondered what it would be like to be Neo.

I let my hand slip off the server and shut the closet door. Then I went to bed.

***

ON A NORMAL DAY, I get up at dawn, so I knew when the bar of sunlight fell across my face the next morning I was late. Really late.

Rico was still snoring—nobody orders a pizza before noon—but I kicked him anyway.

"My alarm," I said, my mouth feeling like the inside of an elephant's thigh. "Did you turn off my alarm?"

Rico rolled over. "You're hung over. Call in sick."

My chin touched my chest. Call in sick. Not a bad idea. I'd just about made that decision when I remembered that today was Update Day. HeroNet 2.0! Every day for the last two weeks, we'd been reminded at every turn about this super-important meeting that everyone had to attend, no excuses. Then I thought about Mr. Meansby, who I'd managed to piss off yesterday.

I checked my watch. Maybe, just maybe, I could just make it if I had a little help in the commute department. I pounded on Rico's back. "Get up! I need you to fly me to work. C'mon, Rico. Get up!"

I rushed around the room, alternately pulling on my uniform from the day before and nagging Rico to get his ass out of bed, and we were on the roof within ten minutes. I climbed on his back, wrapping my arms and legs around his body.

"Not so tight," he said.

I buried my face between his shoulder blades and ignored him. Flying is terrifying for me. The only way I can get through it is to keep my eyes shut and hang on for dear life. When we landed about ten minutes later, I stood on wobbly legs and gave him a quick kiss on the cheek before I looked at my watch again. Damn! I was still going to be late by a few minutes. I clattered down the steps from the roof and slipped in through the emergency exit on our floor.

The cubicle farm was empty. An eerie, jarring silence hung over the room. I'd worked there for three years and I'd never seen the farm completely devoid of people. I mean, even on the slowest of days there was always an emergency somewhere, right? Someone had to be dispatching heroes. I tried to run lightly as I made my way through the maze of empty cubicles to the auditorium at the far side of the building.

The doors were shut, but they were big steel double doors with a decent-sized gap between them. I peered through the slit. I'm not sure what I expected...a video presentation, or training in the latest software, I guess. What I saw was a series of workstations staffed by people in white lab coats. Flu shot? Armed security guards were posted by all the doors in the room. To borrow a phrase from the web-slinging Trademark, my senses were tingling.

Someone passed through my narrow field of vision and I jumped back, my breath coming fast and sharp. Whatever was going on in there, my instincts told me I wanted no part of it.

I ran for the ladies room and hid in a stall. My thoughts were all in a massive jumble and the hangover wasn't doing much for my cognitive skills, either. I tried to sort out what I knew: big employee meeting that looked more like a mass medical procedure. I hadn't come in through the front door so they didn't know I was in the building...unless they tracked my phone. I slipped my mobile out of my pocket, removing the battery and the ID chip. I'd read somewhere that the NSA had the ability to remotely power an ID chip, so I was toying with the idea of flushing it down the can when I heard the bathroom door open.

I angled my head so I could see the person's reflection in the mirror and nearly fell off the toilet seat in relief. It was Heather. I bounded out of the stall to her side.

"Hey, Heather, what's going on in there?"

She stopped fluffing her curls and looked at me in the mirror. Then she took a step away. Okay, that was fair. I hadn't showered, I'm not sure if I brushed my teeth, and it looked like I'd combed my hair with a garden tool.

"Excuse me?" she said.

"What's going on in the auditorium?"

"Do I know you?"

That stopped me. Less than twelve hours ago, we were one tequila shot away from swapping spit and now she didn't know who I was?

"Heather, you okay?"

She took another step back. "How do you know my name?"

I started to shake. I'm not much of a conspiracy theorist, but I pay attention to stuff, especially stuff on the Internet. I guess you could say I'm a where-there's-smoke-there's-fire kinda person. Anyway, one of the stories that's been floating around forever is the idea of memory manipulation. We've known for years it was possible to erase short-term memories, but long-term memory retention is a whole other thing, much more complicated. Recently, there'd been a lot of chatter about private outfits doing memory manipulation for hire. There was even a name for them: O-Men, the "O" being short for *obliteration*.

Think about it: it's perfect for high-end criminals, like organized crime. In the old days, if an innocent bystander witnessed a crime, the only way to silence them would be to take them out; i.e.. commit another crime. Now, you just pick them up, perform a simple procedure, and bada-bing, bada-boom, the witness remembers nothing.

Heather had a funny look in her eye, so I took a giant step backwards. "Hey, my mistake." I grimaced in what I hoped was a facsimile of a smile. "Thought you were someone else." I headed for the door, walking away from the auditorium as fast I could without running.

"Miss?" someone called behind me. "Excuse me, miss?"

I kept walking. The tempo of the footsteps increased and I lengthened my stride. The footsteps got closer, so when I reached the cubicle farm, I ran.

"Hey!" the voice called behind me. I took the first right, keeping my head down below the level of the cubicle walls. Before I knew it, I was in my own chair, gasping for breath.

There was no way out. Whoever these people were, they would find me. I needed to call Rico and get out of here. With trembling hands, I tried to put my mobile phone back together, but the itty-bitty ID chip kept slipping out of my fingers when I tried to fit it into that tiny slot next to the battery.

I heard them coming down the row toward me. A heavy breather. I imagined a bodybuilder covered with hair and scary tattoos coming to get me.

My computer was behind me, humming softly. I put the phone on the desk and slid my hands along the computer case. The network was right there, calling to me. In my state of terror, I wished I could hide inside the network…like Neo.

Heavy Breather was no more than three cubicles away. I was trapped.

I took a deep breath, extending my awareness into the network. It was safe in there, a space where no one could touch me. I closed my eyes and the network expanded beneath me into bottomless darkness. Heavy Breather sounded like a winded buffalo.

I let go.

***

I WAS EVERYWHERE…and nowhere. A part of my consciousness wondered how I was able to see the outside of the coffee shop on the corner *and* view the inside of the police station *and* not be able to see my own hands.

I'm inside. The voice in my head even did that echo thing like a dream sequence in a movie.

I'm inside HeroNet. It felt both preposterous and completely natural at the same time, like a child who does a double flip off a diving board because no one ever told them it was hard.

It took me a few minutes to realize that it wasn't the lack of information that was causing problems for me, it was too much information. I needed a construct, a way to organize all the inputs into something my consciousness could handle. *Be like Neo*, I thought.

The first thing that popped into my head was a city, and when I opened my eyes, that's what I saw. I was flying over Brookdale, but it didn't seem scary like when I flew with Rico. More like peering over a digital map of our city.

A robbery was happening on Fifth Street. It's not like I saw it happen; I just *knew* it happened. I waited for a Trademark to be dispatched, but as the minutes ticked by, nothing happened. The robbers exited the bank and got into a car.

Still nothing.

With only a thought, I assigned Skywoman to hunt down the robbers, watching in satisfaction as her trademark blue colors shot out of the HeroNet building in pursuit of the fleeing car.

A cloud blotted out the sun over the city, and a spotlight on top of the HeroNet building searched the sky. It swept across me, then backtracked, pinning me in place. The light got brighter and hotter, forcing me to close my eyes.

When I opened them again, I was in an empty stadium. I told myself it wasn't real, but the grass beneath me *felt* real, and the sun was high and hot in the sky. Someone was standing at the far end of the field. I squinted. A figure in a hoodie was all I could make out at this distance. As I watched, the figure drew back their arm like they were about to throw a baseball.

The next thing I knew, I was flat on the real-feeling turf, the wind knocked out of me. My head told me that network-me didn't need to breathe, but my lungs said otherwise.

As I lay gasping, the hoodie person stood over me, blocking out the sun.

"How did you get in here?" The voice was soft, but tight with anger.

My breath was slowly coming back. "I came in through the network," I said.

"Impossible." The figure paced beside me. "My security was perfect, there was no way another AI could have loaded—"

"I'm not an AI," I said. "I'm Casey. I work here."

The figure stopped and peeled back the hoodie. I almost started gasping again. It was Taylor Winsome—or at least their avatar. "What do you mean?" They fixed their perfect gaze on me.

"Which part?" I said. "Coming in through the network or working here?"

A look of shock crossed his flawless skin. "You're real," they whispered. "Who sent you? Who do you work for?"

"I—I don't understand. No one sent me. I'm Casey. I work at HeroNet. As a dispatcher."

Taylor was shaking their head and mumbling. "It's not possible. No one can do that. Not possible." They spun on their heel and threw another one of those open palm bombs at me. My body was crushed against the grass again, only this time the pressure didn't stop. Taylor stood over me, both hands bearing down in the air over me. Every bit of breath was squeezed from my lungs, and the pressure made my eyeballs want to pop out of my skull. My vision tunneled and all the color leached out of the scene.

Be like Neo, I told myself in that creepy movie-echo voice.

I blinked and we were standing in a gladiator ring, surrounded by cheering crowds. Taylor spun in a circle, seemingly just as confused as I was. They were dressed in black armor and carried a heavy sword. With a start I realized, so was I. My gaze took in the armor and a *katana*, the weapon of a samurai, but just for a split second, because Taylor rushed at me with a scream.

My body moved on its own, parrying Taylor's thrusts, making attacks of my own.

They stepped back breathing hard. "Last chance. Whoever designed you is good, but I'm better. You think you can just take HeroNet away from me?"

I circled slowly, wary of another attack. The armor fit like skin and the *katana* felt like an extension of my senses. "I told you already, I work for HeroNet. I'm a big fan of your boss, Taylor Winsome. I think he does great work with the superheroes, keeping people safe and all."

Their eyes narrowed and their grip tightened on the hilt of their sword. "You have it backwards, Casey. I *am* Taylor Winsome. The image you see on TV and social media is a construct, created by me to fool people like you. I've taken over your reality bit by bit. Everything is mine."

"But what about HeroNet? What about helping people?" I said. "That's why we made superheroes."

"We?" When Taylor smiled like that, it really spoiled their good looks. "The *we* is *me*. I funded every one of them, I own them all. The people will pay my price if they want superhero protection. And my price is their attention—all of it, all the time."

Taylor flashed toward me, their sword high. In real life, I'm an honest-to-God, walk-into-walls klutz. But here, in this virtual world, I was something different altogether. I was the Cyber Zamurai—and I was made for this moment.

My feet left the ground, my body executed a mid-air pirouette, and I screamed like I imagined a real samurai would do when striking a death blow. My sword flashed in the sun and there was a great cracking sound when it touched the back of Taylor's exposed neck.

The world went black.

I was falling.

***

THE HORRIBLE TASTE of police station coffee is not a cliché. It's a reality.

I was still trying to wrap my head around the definition of reality when the door to the interrogation room opened and Detective Samuelson walked in. He was a black guy with gray on his temples and a few extra pounds on his middle, but he had a kind smile.

"Sorry to keep you waiting, Miss…" He consulted the folder in his hand. "Finley. Our entire network is down. Whole city's down, actually."

"Really." I pushed the half-full Styrofoam cup to the center of the table.

He pulled out a chair and sat down. "Maybe you can help me understand this, Casey—can I call you Casey?"

I shrugged.

"The HeroNet network is fried, completely gone. No one who works there knows what happened. Most of them don't even remember working there at all. Except you. We find you on the floor next to your desk, unconscious, with your terminal still active. Are you remembering any of this, Casey?"

My first memory was of Rico calling my name. He was in his red suit like he'd been on a job and cradling me in a way that showed how much he cared. The relief in his eyes when I woke up felt real, too. And breathing, definitely a necessary bodily function in this reality.

"Sorry, it's all kind of a blur to me," I said.

Samuelson squinted at me, his lips pursed like he was trying to decide if he believed me or not.

"You know what the strangest thing is?" he said finally.

I shrugged. I'm pretty sure there was nothing he could say that I would find abnormal right now.

"CRI owns HeroNet—through a series of shell companies—and they own all of the superhero labs, marketing agencies, the whole shebang. But that's not the good part: the new wing they were building? The one with three levels of security? Completely empty inside, not even a memory stick. We figure this whole complex is a giant money-laundering operation by Taylor Winsome."

"Did you find him?" I asked.

He cocked his head at my tone. "No, but we will. He's done a good job of covering his tracks but we'll get him. We always get our man."

"Good luck with that," I mumbled.

***

THEY NEVER FOUND Taylor Winsome and I never told anyone what happened. There's days when I'm not sure if I believe it myself.

What amazed me about the whole incident was how uncurious people were about what happened. No one cared. Congress held a few hearings, but they fizzled quickly when the news coverage stopped. A foundation picked up the operation of what was left of HeroNet, and since I was one of the few people who could remember anything about the old system they pretty much hired me on the spot. I made sure Rico got a position as a full-time hero, but they weren't able to find a place for Sam the Snot Dragon. I got a decent raise and I put all of it toward my hardware habit.

They tried to make me Dispatch Manager, but I told them there was only one job I wanted: Network Administrator.

Most days, I just sit behind a desk and manage the network from the outside. But I know one thing for sure: Taylor Winsome will be back and the virtual realm is going to need a hero. A Cyber Zamurai.

I'm ready.

O'Neil De Noux is one of the best working short story writers of detective fiction. I say that every time, with every one of his stories, because it's true. And I just can't think of a better way to describe O'Neil's incredible talent at taking us into his worlds.

O'Neil has published almost fifty novels. His awards include The United Kingdom Short Story Prize, the Shamus Award (for best private eye fiction), the Derringer Award (for excellence in mystery short fiction) and Police Book of the Year. *Two of his stories have appeared in the prestigious* Best American Mystery Stories *annual anthology.*

Disturbing the Peace

O'Neil De Noux

I DID IT. I opened my big mouth and said it, and someone died.

Cruising alone in my blue-and-white patrol car along Tchoupitoulas Street, rundown houses on my left, riverfront warehouses on my right, I yawned and then said it aloud, "It's too fuckin' quiet."

For a second the old New Orleans police saying flashed in my mind: "Don't ever say it's too quiet. If you do, someone's bound to get killed." That was the nature of the beast, living in the great southern murder capital of America. I shook off the thought for ten minutes, until the loud beep came on my radio, followed by the dispatcher's staccato voice: "Signal 103F. 3247 Tchoupitoulas. Third floor. Room 313. Any Sixth District Unit."

I punched the accelerator and picked up my microphone.

"604, Headquarters. I'm six blocks away."

"10-4."

Hot, humid air rushed through the open window of my unit as I quickly covered the blocks to the scene. At two a.m., on that un-typically calm Wednesday morning, there was no traffic along the warehouse district.

"Headquarters, 604. Complainant is anonymous. Called twice to report screaming and fighting in Room 313."

"10-4," I responded as I eased off the accelerator and pumped the brake, bringing my unit to a stop in front of a brown brick tenement near the corner of Tchoupitoulas and Toledano Streets.

"604, 10-97." I told headquarters I'd arrived.

"10-4. You want me to hold the air?"

"Negative." It was only a 103F—Disturbing the Peace by Fighting. In those days we didn't have portable radios. On shootings and stabbings and armed robbery-in-progress calls, the air was held for officers in danger. It was a judgment call, by the officer on the scene. I wasn't about to hold the air for a 103. No way, not Patrolman Dino LaStanza of the Bloody Sixth District, not the son of Captain LaStanza. Fuck, I'd volunteered to work that outcast police district right out of the academy. It was the shit, the toughest fuckin' district. Where the real men worked.

I put the mike down, grabbed my black steel Kel-Lite flashlight and black plastic PR-24 nightstick, locked the car, and bounded across the small, grassless front yard to the front door of the tenement. I slid my nightstick in its holder on my belt and flipped on my Kel-Lite as I moved into the tenement's dark foyer. The place smelled like rotten cabbage, the air musty and wet. Dim yellow light illuminated the stairway from exposed bulbs overhead. The bulb on the second floor was out.

Arriving on the third floor, I noticed immediately that few of the rooms had numbers on their doors. I listened for the sounds of a fight, but the only sound was my footsteps. I found Room 313 halfway down the hall, its door marked with black Marks-a-lot. I leaned my ear close but could hear nothing inside. Taking a step to my right, away from the door, I reached over and tapped it with my Kel-Lite, my right hand resting on my holstered .357 magnum. I was thinking how much I hated bogus calls.

I tapped a second time, louder.

An angry voice called out, "Huh? Who's there?"

"Police!"

"What?"

"Police. Open the damn door."

I heard stumbling and heavy breathing, then nothing.

I hit the door again with the Kel-Lite, harder, sending a loud pop echoing down the hallway.

"Okay. Okay," the voice said, higher pitched now.

The door opened with a jerk and a man who had to be six-six and two-fifty-plus stood in the doorway like the trunk of an oak tree. Outweighing me by more than a hundred pounds, he was about a foot taller. Red-faced and wearing only red gym shorts, the man stood huffing, as if he'd just caught his breath. A puff of light brown hair crowned his huge head and a pair of narrow eyes leered at me.

"Everything all right in there?" I tried to look past him. The room was in shambles, brown sofa on its side, a broken lamp next to it, and papers all over the floor.

"Yeah," he said.

I looked at him again, just as he took in another breath. His mouth opened momentarily and something gold flashed inside. A thin, gold chain dangled from his mouth for a second before he sucked it back in.

"What's that in your mouth?"

He swallowed and said, "Nothin'!" He opened his mouth to show me.

"What the fuck happened in there?"

"Nothin'. I fell." He folded his large arms across his chest.

"Anyone else in there?"

"No."

"Mind if I take a look?"

A massive hand grabbed the door and he shook his head.

"I don't believe a fuckin' thing you're saying." I pointed the end of the Kel-Lite at his wide nose. He shook his head and closed the door slowly in my face. I heard him set the lock. I stepped back and looked at the doors down the hall. Often an anonymous caller will peek out to see what happened. No door opened.

Backing down the hall, I swung my light around again and saw something. I directed my light to the dirty, tile floor, and saw a trail. A drag mark led from the door of Room 313 all the way to the far end of the hall. I went down on my haunches and saw how my footprints were clearly marked in the dirt.

I moved closer to the drag mark, touched it and the dirt crumbled. Son-of-a-bitch, it was fresh. I followed it, making sure not to walk over it, all the way to an open window at the end of the hall. The window, with fresh splinters on its sill, opened to a fire escape.

Leaning out, I shined my Kel-Lite down the iron fire escape, which didn't reach all the way to the ground. I climbed out, looked up, found dirt on several steps leading upward. I took the fire escape all the way to the flat roof of the five-story building.

The footprints faded at the rooftop. I shined my light around the dark roof. On that black, moonless night, with clouds so low, a warm fog shrouded the roof. The air felt like a wet rag on my face. Littered with broken beer bottles and empty wine bottles, the roof had three rusty air-conditioning units. Moving carefully, I walked over to the AC units and peeked between the first two. Nothing. Focusing the Kel-Lite between the second and third unit, I jumped back from the face staring at me.

"Jesus!" I unsnapped my holster and grabbed my magnum but didn't pull it out. It didn't take a genius to see she was dead. I re-snapped my holster and inched closer, training the light on a face limp and pasty with the unmistakable dull look of death. The eyes, half open, were as lifeless as marbles. She was a middle-aged woman with light brown hair and a thin build. She also wore red gym shorts with a gray T-shirt, twisted around as if she'd been dragged.

"I don't fuckin' believe this." In the moments it took to realize the head was all wrong, I felt something, as if those dead eyes locked on to mine. I stared back but it was nothing, couldn't have been anything, but I felt my heart going boom, boom, boom. I sucked in a deep breath and looked closer at her neck. Twisted around, it had been snapped like a thin branch. A trace of blood trickled from her mouth. I reached over and placed two fingers against her throat. She was still warm, but there was no pulse, not that I expected any. Had to be sure. When I pulled my hand away, I felt something sharp. Looking closer, I discovered part of a thin gold chain embedded in her throat. Broken, the chain was only a few inches long.

"I don't fuckin' believe this!"

It took me about a minute to make it down to the window on the second floor. It was open too, so I climbed in and raced down the hall to the stairs and down to my unit, pausing a few seconds to catch my breath.

"604, Headquarters."

"Go ahead, 604."

Keeping my voice as calm as I could, I said, "I need backup."

Headquarters acknowledged and put out the call. Two Sixth District units responded, then I cut in again. "604, Headquarters. I need a homicide unit. This is a Signal 30."

"10-4."

Then I told the operator I'd be back at Room 313 apprehending the perpetrator. I quickly described the big man with the red shorts and slammed the car door on the rising voices on the radio before the rank could tell me to stand by for backup. The fuck if I was gonna wait. I raced back into the building.

Taking the steps two at a time I made it to the third floor in less than a minute. Keeping my breathing level, I moved down the hall. I slipped my Kel-Lite into its ring on my gunbelt, reached into my back pocket and pulled out my ID folder. I dug out a Miranda Warning card and put my ID folder back. Holding the card in my left hand, I unsnapped my holster and wrapped my fingers around the rubber grip of my four-inch, stainless-steel, Smith and Wesson .357 magnum.

Stopping just short of Room 313, I reached forward and knocked on the door. I could feel my heart pounding.

"What is it?"

"Police! Open the door."

The door shot open, and the man glared at me.

"I need your name," I said as calmly as I could. "For my report."

"What?"

"What's your name?" I stared back at the narrow eyes, keeping my face as expressionless as I could.

"What's this about?" The man stepped into the doorway.

I retreated a step, keeping a safe distance, turning my left shoulder to him, ready to pull my weapon.

"I have to read you your rights. You got a pen?"

"What?" A confused look came to his face.

"I have one," I said. "So just shut up, and I'll read you your rights."

He became even more confused. I read him his rights, quickly, keeping a wary eye on the hulking man.

"Now, you're gonna have to sign the back of this card."

"What?" The man's hands curled into fists.

I pulled my ballpoint pen from my shirt pocket with my left hand, holding it out with the Miranda card for him.

"Just sign the back of the card."

The man looked at the card and then back at me.

"Take it!"

He reached for it, and I shoved the card and pen into his hand. "Now, sign it!"

He glared at me as if I was the mental case, then slowly turned and pressed the card against the doorjamb and signed it. He handed it back to me.

"Keep the fuckin' pen," I told him as I glanced at the rear of the card. "Is that a W?"

"Huh?"

"Woodie?"

He nodded slowly.

"Is that a V? Vitter?"

"Yeah," he growled.

"You need to work on your fuckin' penmanship, man. And you printed your name. Sign it." I handed the card back.

He was so stunned he shook his head twice. "You nuts?" He left a body up on the roof and called *me* nuts. His eyes narrowed as he looked down the hall and said, "You're alone, ain't you?"

"The cavalry's right behind." I gave him a cold smile. "Now, just sign it."

He snatched the card out of my hand and signed it and threw it and my pen back at me. They flew past my head, and I left them there. We stared at each other. I felt sweat working its way down my back. His face slowly contorted into a red rage and I slowly withdrew my magnum. He leaned toward me, his hands on either side of the door now.

"Well," I said.

"Well, what?"

"You wanna fuckin' tell me what happened?"

He looked down the hall again and said, "You're kinda short, for a fuckin' cop."

"What are you, six-five, six-six?"

"Six-five," he snarled. "You think you can stop me if I wanna get out of here?"

I gave him the Sicilian stare, looking right through his head all the way to the back of his skull, my face deadpan serious. He wavered a second as if he was about to bolt. I raised the magnum quickly, cocking it in one smooth motion, pointing it at the big man's chest.

"You'll never clear the door," I told him.

"You gonna shoot me? I'm unarmed."

"Move one muscle and I'll put six in you so fast, you'll be dead before you hit the floor."

He blinked.

"And I'll get away with it. You're too fuckin' big. You'd overpower me. I had to shoot. I can see the headline now—Cop Shoots Killer."

Woodie Vitter looked like a blue-gum street dog caught in an alley, head twisting from side to side. Perspiration ran down my temples, and I reminded myself of the old Sicilian saying, "Ice in the veins. Ice in the veins." I calmed myself as I held my cocked magnum in my unwavering hands.

Long, heart-thundering seconds crawled by.

He kept staring at me, looking meaner by the second.

"So," I said. "Who was she?"

"Who?"

"On the roof."

And there it was, in his eyes, the recognition. He looked up and then back at me, his brow furrowed. He slumped back slowly, his chest sinking, and I knew it was over. A distant look came to his eyes as he stared up at the ceiling again.

"How? How didja' know?"

Footsteps behind me told me the cavalry had arrived.

"You wrung her neck and dragged her up on the roof. Figured you'd dump her later, right?"

Slowly, almost imperceptibly, he nodded.

Hurried footsteps arrived behind me. The first officer slid up, and I asked him to cuff the big bastard. As he did, I uncocked my magnum and re-holstered it. Then I wiped the sweat from my face.

The first homicide detective to arrive was Sergeant Rob Mason. Sporting his ever-present Marine Corps flattop, Mason seemed stunned as I told him the story. He turned and looked at the dirt trail and then grabbed a patrolman and told him to make sure no one walked over it. Turning back to me, Mason pointed up and said, "The roof?"

"The roof. And he ate part of the gold chain around her neck."

"Huh?"

I told him about the broken chain around her neck and how Woodie Vitter swallowed the other half. Mason shook his head and looked over his shoulder at Vitter standing in the debris of Room 313.

"That's good work," Mason said.

"He confessed too." I reached down and picked up the Miranda card and tapped

Mason's shoulder. "I read him his rights first and had him sign it. He didn't say he did it, but when I mentioned the roof he asked me how I found her. When I told him how he strangled her and dragged her up there, he nodded."

"That'll work in court," Mason said as he looked at the card.

I turned it over to show him the signature.

Mason started to chuckle. "Where'd you learn to do that?"

"You taught us. At the Academy. Remember?"

Mason blinked at me in surprise, a hint of a smile on the corners of his mouth. "Yeah, but no one's ever done it."

I almost said—there's always a first time.

"Okay." Mason nodded. "Show me the body."

I led the way. Climbing back into the window after we'd checked out the body, Mason told me to go wait next to the window. I knew that the rest of my shift would be nothing but paperwork.

Leaning against the only clean-looking spot on the wall, I looked out the window at the night. The clouds were parting, and distant stars blinked faintly in the black sky. For a moment I wondered what she'd felt. What terror she went through in those last seconds. I'd felt a connection with the woman on the roof when those eyes locked on to mine. Something had passed between us, as if she had told me to go get him. No, it was my eyes that locked, my heart thumping. She was fuckin' dead.

Standing near the window, I felt the link again, that connection, causing my heartbeat to rise as a whispery voice told me, in so many words, that I had to catch who did this. I've felt that link many times since with many victims, stronger after I became a homicide detective. That night on Tchoupitoulas Street was the first time.

My thoughts of a connection drifted away on the hot breeze blowing through the window, taking with it any satisfaction I could possibly have catching her killer because I had said it. I had cruised down the street, thinking how quiet it was, and then said it. A sourness came to my stomach as the old saying echoed in my mind: "Don't ever say it's too quiet. If you do, someone's bound to get killed."

I told myself, that wasn't it. I told myself it's the nature of the beast, living in the great southern murder capital of America. People fuckin' kill each other.

But…just don't ever say it's too quiet.

Trust me on this.

Special Introduction to "The Rhythm Method" by Kevin J. Anderson

My friend and coauthor, Neil Peart, legendary drummer and lyricist for the rock band Rush, died on January 7, 2020, after a long struggle with brain cancer. He was 67. We wrote two novels together, two graphic novels, and a short story. This piece is a story from our book Clockwork Lives.

My very first novel, Resurrection, Inc., *was entirely inspired by the Rush album* Grace Under Pressure. *Neil Peart's lyrics moved me, shaped the story I was developing, and every song on that album made its way into a chapter. I acknowledged Neil's brilliant lyrics in the front of the book, and after it was published (Signet Books, 1988), I autographed a copy and mailed a package to Mercury Records, where I was sure it would languish in a warehouse not unlike the one that holds the Ark of the Covenant.*

About a year later, I came home after a particularly bad day at work to find a letter with a Canadian stamp in my mailbox. From Neil Peart. A seven-page letter describing how much he loved Resurrection, Inc. *That started a 30+ year correspondence and friendship. He sent me copies of every Rush album as it was released, and I sent him copies of each book I published (he certainly got the better end of that deal, but he made up for it by inviting me backstage at every concert since 1991).*

He was amazingly talented not only as a drummer, but also with his brilliant lyrics and his brilliant mind, his ideas, his philosophy. In 1993, after he had sent me several wonderful travelogues about solo bicycling trips across Africa, I suggested using some of that material as background for a collaborative dark fantasy story, "Drumbeats." He enthusiastically agreed, and we sold the story to the anthology Shock Rock II *(Jeff Gelb, ed., Pocket Books 1994), and when I sent Neil his half of the $250 payment, he said, "Well, I guess I won't be giving up drumming anytime soon."*

Neil wrote the introduction to one of my story collections, but our greatest collaborative effort began in 2010, when Neil was developing the lyrics for a new Rush concept album. He was fascinated with steampunk. I had written several steampunk novels, which Neil read, and he sent me a succession of emails asking about the genre, the tropes, and telling me his idea for a storyline about a Watchmaker, an Anarchist, and a young hero caught between the two, in a sprawling steampunk world with pirates, airships, alchemy, and Clockwork Angels.

I brainstormed all this with him while trying to keep the geeky Rush fan from nerding out too much. Rebecca and I met Neil for lunch at a diner in Santa Monica, and Neil was afire with enthusiasm for the Clockwork Angels *project, how everything was coming together, how the story was spilling out in the as-yet-to-be-written lyrics for the remaining tracks. He imagined* Clockwork Angels *as more than just an album, but also a Broadway show, a novel, even ice follies! I was starry-eyed and thrilled with the possibilities (ice follies?), but Rebecca was paying closer attention. "Excuse me, Neil. A novel? Who's going to write the novel?" Neil looked squarely at me with a shrug. "Why, Kevin is, of course."*

He and I brainstormed and blocked out the pieces of the story. On a day off between two concert appearances at Red Rocks Amphitheater near Denver, I introduced Neil to one of my favorite sports—we climbed a 14,000-foot mountain peak, Mt. Evans. On that long and grueling hike, we brainstormed the rest of the novel.

Clockwork Angels *turned out as perfect as any of my novels ever had. I was so proud of it. ECW Press published a beautiful hardcover volume, which hit the* New York Times *bestseller list on the first week out. I was able to text Neil just before he went up on stage for a show in New Hampshire, telling him that not only was he a great drummer, he was also a* New York Times *bestselling author.*

After Clockwork Angels, *we wanted to do something more with the characters and the world we had created. The result was* Clockwork Lives, *like a steampunk* Canterbury Tales, *a novel woven with individual short stories about our chosen characters. The stories seemed to come together magically. I've written a lot of books, but I've never had an experience like writing* Clockwork Lives. *Everything about that book turned out exactly the way we wanted it to. After I sent Neil the final draft, he read it in a day and pronounced, "Your finest work, I am sure." I couldn't have done it without the inspiration and the incredibly high bar set by "the Professor."*

As we mapped out Clockwork Lives, *one of the obvious characters that caught our attention from* Clockwork Angels *was Professor Russell and his steam-powered, robotic "Percussor." Not only did we want to build in the joy of a man creating a perfect clockwork drummer with an absolutely infallible sense of rhythm, we also pulled in the collision idea of Professor Russell himself losing his ability to play.*

This idea is enshrined in one of the most heart-wrenching Rush songs, "Losing It," about the tragedy of when an artist's talent slowly fades with time, health, alcoholism, or mental degeneration. Neil was particularly moved by the story of Hemingway, who took his own life when he found he was losing his ability to write.

Sadder still to watch it die
Than never to have known it.
For you the blind who once could see
The bell tolls for thee…

I write this now with an even greater ache, because we wrote this story just before Neil found out about his own illness.

Neil was a very private man, did not bask in accolades or fame. His long battle with cancer was off the radar, and the world heard little from him after Rush retired in 2015 at the end of a career that spanned 45 amazing years. I will miss him incredibly, and his works will continue to inspire me and countless millions of fans.

When we were finished with "The Percussor's Tale," Neil wrote me, "This has become quite a profound story on several levels."

I hope you enjoy it.

The Rhythm Method

The Percussor's Tale

Kevin J. Anderson and Neil Peart

THE FIRST TIME I saw the Clockwork Angels, they inspired me. I had just moved to Crown City to become an instructor at the Alchemy College, and the city was full of strangers. When thousands of people crowded shoulder to shoulder in Chronos Square to see the angels, I felt a sense of community, a sense of anticipation.

After full night fell and the stars appeared overhead, the people filled the city square, muttering with excitement and love, vibrant with anticipation. Wisps of sweet-smelling smoke wafted from vents in the ground, vapors exhaled from the underground coldfire nexus that powered Crown City. The fumes made us dizzy, disoriented, but also euphoric—ready for the Angels. Globes of coldfire light hung suspended around Chronos Square, bathing the crowd in angelic illumination. The Watchtower, with its great clock, stood over the crowd like a fortress of benevolent time and order.

As if from an invisible signal, we all held our breath, turned our faces upward, and watched the high tower doors ratchet open like curtains drawn back on a cosmic play. The immense

Angels glided forward on smoothly oiled gears, four beautiful ethereal figures carved from permanent stone, the most perfect machinery, animated by quintessence. They were flawless.

They spread their clockwork wings, and one after another they dispensed pearls of wisdom that might have seemed like platitudes when read in skeptical daylight. Even now, that night's recitation is engraved in my memory, spinning out in the unearthly voices of the Angels in turn—"*Be kind, for everyone you meet is fighting a hard battle.*" With the dizzying smoke around us and the euphoria of the crowd, though, the words penetrated our hearts as well as our ears. *"Beginning a task is hard. Finishing a task is harder still, but far more satisfying."*

The people gasped. Some of them wept. And when the Angels raised their wings, we all lifted our hands in a fruitless attempt to reach them.

It was amazing. It was a miracle… and yet I realized the performance was missing a fundamental element. I was inspired then. I *knew* what I had to do, why I had been brought here to Crown City.

The Clockwork Angels captivated us all—but there was no music. I could improve on that.

***

ALTHOUGH IT HAD no bearing on my career assignment, I'd always had perfect rhythm. I could keep time with absolute precision, like the unwavering pulse of a sleeping infant. I could feel the beat of everyday activities. Tick-tock. I needed no metronome. When I couldn't sit still, I would tap out an impatient beat on a tabletop or on my leg, which annoyed nearby people. They didn't hear the same intrinsic beat of the world. They called me restless, fidgety.

I was a respectable man from a respectable family in a respectable town on the outskirts of Crown City. I studied to become a professor, learned the basics of alchemy. My family paid the appropriate fees, and after I passed the appropriate tests, I was brought in as an instructor to the Alchemy College, which should have been enough for any man.

I settled into the instructors' dormitory, comfortable in my new rooms and ready for a new school year. I pattered out my satisfaction on a tabletop, prepared my lesson plans, and—now that I'd been inspired by the Clockwork Angels—considered adding music to the curriculum. Did not an adept drummer "keep perfect time?" And wasn't that exactly what the Watchmaker wanted?

My classes were like all the other first-year classes, with my novice pupils performing standardized experiments, testing reactant powders and metals, growing crystals from saturated solutions, dissolving organic substances in the most potent acids. I taught them how the world's basic elements could be assembled and reassembled into any imaginable substance. The movements of molecules had their own rhythm.

Throughout my first semester, there was very little music at the College, save for the drumbeats I heard in my own head. Music wasn't forbidden in Albion, but neither was it encouraged. The common people had their own instruments, their own songs, but the Watchmaker himself would never express his happiness by bursting into a tune. He simply considered music irrelevant.

When poring over old class records, I was surprised to discover a forgotten part of the curriculum, a discretionary class that no professor had taught for some years, and thus it had fallen into obscurity. "Fundamentals of Music." It was perfect! I immediately contacted Professor Gruber, the chief alchemist priest, requesting permission to teach the music course, saying that it would broaden the students' experience and knowledge.

Professor Gruber was skeptical and, above all, curious. He summoned me to his office. "There must be a reason this course is no longer taught," he said.

I had to force myself to sit respectfully still and not tap out a beat on my leg. "Perhaps because there was no qualified teacher, sir. I studied the old syllabus, and I believe I have the proper knowledge."

The chief priest frowned down at the papers. "I'm not sure, Professor Russell. Such a class might distract the students from more important pursuits. Music in the abstract? Think about the average person. What use would they have for rhythms and melodies? At the Alchemy College, we focus on science."

"Then I will teach the *science* of music, sir," I said. "Don't you see? Music *is* mathematics—so many intricate systems, the orderly arrangement of notes and chords like formulas, the logarithmic interrelation of harmonies, the geometric patterns and structures of the orchestration—aligned to a strict physical premise of *time*. Surely the Watchmaker would approve.

"The conductor's tempo is the clock, unwavering and unstoppable. Like a grand-complication timepiece, each instrument in the orchestra must play its part in synchrony, each musician meshed in that perfect, ticking pendulum. And there is the emotional resonance in the listener—like *alchemy.*" I paused, saw to my dismay that much of my excitement was lost on him.

"It still sounds like only a metaphor to me," said my superior, but he indulged me with a long sigh, signing the paper so that I could prepare my class. "We will consider it an experiment."

My first class was small, only eleven students, and five of them were there as their fourth choice since they had not qualified for the topics that interested them. But I was happy because the class itself allowed me to study and refine my own knowledge, quantifying the things I knew by instinct and giving names to the rhythms I could sense in the universe around me.

And it established a precedent, giving me opportunities for more advanced classes.

But I needed the devices to create music. I discovered that if I described a musical instrument to my colleagues as a *scientific* problem—a resonant cylinder of a certain fundamental note, a membrane with tunable qualities, a soundbox with certain harmonics—the younger alchemists would take it as a technical challenge appropriate for the higher-level classes.

Soon I had invented and assembled an orchestra's worth of tuned drums, chromatic bells, steam-powered horns, and more. Long strings stretched across whole rooms, each one plucked by rotating plectrums driven by coldfire steam.

But I had to teach my students something the Alchemy College considered "worthwhile." Those grand designs I heard and visualized would have to wait until I could express them in some greater arena. An audience. But that day would come. Surely it would be perfect enough for the Clockwork Angels.

So I instructed my students in harmony and melody, but the study of *rhythm* excited me most of all. At the front of the classroom I set up an arrangement of drums, and I would start each class with one big *boom* on a mounted bass drum. Having attracted their attention, I silently counted a slow three bars, then hit it again. *Boom!* After the same interval, I struck the drum a third time, and by then we could all feel a pulse.

As the students listened, I added a counter rhythm on a small, snappy drum, with the bass drum still punctuating every third one. A foot pedal activated a drone with rippling harp-like harmonies, and I brought in quick flurries of "rat-a-tats" on small melodic drums. Seemingly out of time, they slashed across the pulse in a jagged onslaught that raised my own adrenaline.

Some of my students showed a genuine aptitude for the subject, but most exhibited a just-as-genuine lack of interest—not hostile, merely perplexed.

After all my labors and my technical successes with the new instrument designs, I was surprised to become an object of scorn and ridicule among the faculty members. Some of the senior professors mocked me for wasting time with something as esoteric and useless as music—"corrupting our youth" they said, "distracting them from more practical matters when they should be trying to strengthen the Watchmaker's Stability." I defended myself by presenting the mathematical basis for musical theory, but they just sniffed, calling music a mere "pseudoscience," unlike the rigorously proven science of alchemy.

After much justification and debate, I convinced Professor Gruber to extend my class for another semester. I was so pleased with his answer that I felt jittery.

But when the jitters continued throughout the next month, I sensed that something entirely different might be wrong—with *me*. I held out my hand and watched it shake and tremble, as if my nerves were fighting against a thousand clashing drumbeats. It frightened me. I could make the tremors stop by sheer force of will, but they would return. I told no one, but my fear increased as the dread realization began to dawn on me.

I was losing my rhythm.

***

THOUGH MUSIC WAS my passion, most of my teaching was in basic alchemistry. I would walk among the laboratory tables and watch as the students crushed mineral powders, dissolved salts, and burned crystalized distillates. I made my students perform each step themselves, and in that way, I could hide my tremors.

It was some kind of degenerative nerve disease. When I saw the best physicians in Crown City, they had no cure for my malady. They gave me potions to counteract the tremors, but the drugs only made me logy, my tongue thick, my vision blurred. I don't know if the tremors stopped, but I was too lethargic to notice them. I decided that was not an acceptable cure at all.

Yet without the potions, my condition grew worse. When I tried to perform interlocking counterrhythms with my connected musical instruments, my fingers, hands, and feet betrayed me—lost their rhythm, lost their time. The tick-tock of my life had slipped a gear tooth. I could no longer control what I needed to do. My sadness increased. How would I ever present the Watchmaker with my grand dream of music for the Clockwork Angels if my own body was an asynchronous wreck?

In my private offices I had a metronome that kept perfect time, swinging back and forth, clicking off the beats. Always before, such devices were superfluous to me because I could hear the rhythm so perfectly in my head. But as I sat by myself holding my wooden stick and trying to match the beats, my hands trembled so much that I kept missing time.

Few of my students could hear the intrinsic beat as anything more than theoretical—they didn't even know what they were missing. But I had always heard that constant tick-tock drumbeat, as reliable as the pounding of my own heart. And now that I was losing it, I found the idea far more heart-wrenching than never to have known it at all.

It was terrifying.

But fear can either destroy a person or make him rise to new levels. I went out to see the Clockwork Angels again, and as I raised my hands with all the others, dizzy from the sweet smoke in Chronos Square, their words poured into my mind. "*All is for the best in this best of all possible worlds*." At first the tears streaming down my cheek were hot and bitter—all was not for the best in *my* world—but soon I wept for a different reason than all those other ecstatic worshippers. I had been inspired again! I still knew what I wanted to do, but I would have to achieve it in a different way.

The Angels, those perfect clockwork goddesses built by the Watchmaker, had surpassed what he himself could do. Though the loving Watchmaker was himself slightly more than human—we all knew that—the Clockwork Angels exceeded even him.

Now that my body had demonstrated its frailty, its unreliability, maybe I could create a substitute as well. Something better than myself.

If every clock ticked out a perfect beat, then perhaps a clockwork mechanism could be expanded into a machine to keep time with the music I felt in my heart, a clockwork drummer whose very existence was to demonstrate the mystic rhythms of the universe for everyone to hear. Not just a metronome's mathematical perfection, but shifting rhythms that pushed and pulled like gravity, tides, or solar winds.

A rhythm could drive forward with intense energy, or relax into a gentle cadence. And oh, the tension when two such rhythms were combined, the upbeats straining against the downbeats. Sublime! If I could not be that drummer to teach the students and show the Watchmaker, then my artificial percussor could do so in my stead.

I went to the chief alchemy priest to give him the sad news that I no longer felt adequate to teach the rhythm and music class. "My health is deteriorating, sir. I have seen several physicians already. And it would be best if..."

Professor Gruber made an annotation in his logbook, but didn't seem the least bit disturbed. "All is for the best, Professor Russell. Take each day and use the extra class hour to rest and recuperate."

Yes, I needed the free time, but I didn't choose to rest. With maddeningly shaky hands, I designed my creation, assembling a thousand small pieces of basic steam technology, hydraulic engineering, interlocking clockworks, based on all those instruments and mechanisms I'd asked the engineers to design for my first music class. Wheels within wheels motivated armatures, pistons, ball joints, spiral arrays that ratcheted down to finer and finer movements.

It would be perfect, exactly what I needed the Watchmaker to see.

During the intricate assembly process, I had to fabricate stabilizing tools because the tiny screws and bolts fell from my shaking hands. But those who live with adversity are forced to learn either patience or despair, and I refused to despair as I saw my beautiful percussor take shape before me.

I used muffled caps on the drumsticks so the racket would not disturb my fellow professors—or even alert them to what I was doing. I added coldfire to the small boiler inside the torso chamber, powered up the mechanism, and set the articulated arms in motion: smaller gears for faster tempo, larger pistons for heavy bass drumbeats. Making adjustments, I felt a growing delight despite the fact that my own tremors increased, possibly due to exhaustion or stress.

The percussor was my surrogate rhythm keeper. He could do what I could no longer accomplish, and he kept perfect rhythm. I knew he would exceed even my best.

Seven months later the artificial drummer was complete. I had tested and programmed for all possible tempos and counterrhythms. Clockwork controllers allowed every rhythmic subdivision or polyrhythm, and could trigger any number of sound producers—drums, horns, strings, and cymbals, all of my own invention. Ah, if this could be integrated into the Clockwork Angels!

But the percussor still wasn't ready for his debut. He had the programming and the well-oiled intermeshed gears, but he was missing one thing. While music is a science, as I had demonstrated by deconstructing it into pure mathematics, music is also *art*—and for that my percussor needed a soul.

As a professor of alchemy, I had access to forbidden materials, including the College's well-stocked chemical vault, and I had the authority to requisition any items I needed. The Red Guard stationed at the door knew me, and he assumed I must be preparing for another laboratory class. I knew exactly what I needed.

Inside the vault, the well-labeled shelves were stacked high and stocked well with all the known combinations of elements, arranged according to a rudimentary periodic table. But what I needed rested on the highest shelf in a sealed case marked with a honeybee symbol—precious, immeasurably valuable, and so misunderstood.

I climbed a ladder to reach the high shelf, set the tumblers of the lock with the proper combination that only alchemy professors were allowed to know, and opened the container with hands shaking even more than usual. Bathed in the pale white light that was life itself, I removed a tiny fragment of the stored *quintessence*.

That was exactly what my percussor needed.

***

WHEN I PREPARED my demonstration for important faculty members, I invited the Watchmaker himself. The other professors thought it was just a courtesy, never expecting him to come, but I claimed that this was a most vital exhibition, something of importance to the Clockwork Angels. I needed to show him for myself—how else could I make my case?

I felt weak with relief when the ancient man arrived accompanied by three members of his Black Watch and the highest-order alchemy priests, as well as Professor Gruber. Even if I hadn't suffered from the degenerative palsy, seeing the Watchmaker in person might have set my entire body shaking.

But I was ready. The precious quintessence had the effect of strengthening me as well, energizing me, and I felt more in tune with my own rhythm. At least temporarily. I would have used more of the substance myself for such a crucial event, but I didn't dare. My percussor needed it.

For the demonstration, I had set up my clockwork drummer in one of the empty auditoriums. The percussor was all brass and copper, bright with coldfire, venting trickles of steam as the boiler built up to optimal energy levels. Regardless of my own anxiety, the mechanism would drive through the performance without a flaw. My multi-armed percussor ratcheted into its initial position, articulated arms bent, drumsticks raised, all components of the kit arrayed around the central torso. Hidden within, the quintessence burned bright.

My job was to introduce the percussor and then wait nervously as my creation performed. Would the Watchmaker hear the rhythms and see what was missing in his Clockwork Angels? I could only hope!

"My gracious observers, at this college I have taught a class in the mathematics of music, the mystic rhythms of the universe, the clockwork beat that ticks away inside all of us. But my own human frailty makes it impossible to achieve the perfection that existed only in my imagination. The best part of being human is that we can strive to create something better than ourselves." I nodded toward the great man. "Just as our loving Watchmaker created the Clockwork Angels, which embody more grace and beauty than any mortal can hope to achieve, this device can add even more grandeur to the Clockwork Angels, fill the silence that accompanies each performance, and make them *better*."

The Watchmaker looked at me fixedly, as if I had insulted him, then turned his attention to the clockwork percussor. His ancient parchment skin was drawn tight across his face. I had hoped for a paternal smile.

I felt the tremors returning, and I badly wished I had another bit of the quintessence, just a small dose, to calm my nerves, but right now all of the precious substance was inside the percussor.

I stepped back, swallowed hard, and activated the percussor. My heart was pounding louder than any drum I'd ever heard. "This piece is titled *Exaltation*."

Just as I used to begin my earliest classes at the Alchemy College, the percussor seized their attention with a single deep *boom!* The silence that followed seemed to hang heavy, expectant, impatient. Then came the next loud *boom!* as the bass drum continued to repeat in slow pulses.

Other instruments joined in—rhythmic slashes and melodic bursts, expanding chords and flourishes of bass notes. The percussor was a melody of mechanical movement, smooth joints, gliding pistons, all in perfect rhythm. My amplification chambers could project a sound across the room or make it hover in mid-air above the listeners' heads. I smiled to watch them swivel in unison when their eyes were drawn by the acoustic illusion, as if they would *see* the sound I had manifested there. Even the Watchmaker turned his head.

I even dabbled with how to create color in the sound—just tinges so far, but I hoped some of my listeners—especially the Watchmaker—might sense an azure chord, a prismatic arpeggio, or a harp gliss that sprayed out in golden sparks. With coldfire steam that emanated from the mechanism I created sensations of cold and heat, damp or arid air, which further amplified the music's power.

The themes were based on the Angels' symbolic identities, the first four movements titled "Light," "Sea," "Sky," and "Land." My music sparkled and glowed, and then waves of sound receded to the back of the auditorium, even as gentle zephyrs swept down like waterfalls from the corners. A pounding whirlwind built to a peak of tension, then I triggered a release—a long sustain into a slower tempo, a softer dynamic, in subtle variations of minor chords.

I created monumental landforms out of sound so that the listener sensed immense chasms, towering mesas, and vast formations of red rock. I built fantastic landscapes from tales of the great deserts overseas and the legendary lands of the far north, Ultima Thule—a mirage of tremendous glaciers under dark skies that danced with shifting veils of colored light, then a tower of sculpted rock, solitary and eternal, with stars wheeling around its upraised finger.

Gradually, I raised the percussor's pitch and the tempo, and the music raced faster, louder. I created darkness, a chill, then slashes of white heat. This began the fifth and most important movement of my symphony: "Quintessence," and its musical language and images might only be understood by the Watchmaker. Chords swirled around the room like desert dust devils, while frantic bursts of notes flashed like lightning. Volleys of drums thundered, while others beat down like heavy rain, or dripped from imaginary eaves. A chorus of ethereal voices seemed to cry out against the tempest.

Forgetting myself and my audience, forgetting everything but the music, I had programmed the crescendo to the very edge of restraint and control, then the percussor concluded with a massive chord that faded away into a flicker of purple fireflies before diminishing into a dark blue forest and the gentle fall of diamond snowflakes.

As the last vibrations fell silent, I stood dizzy, with shaking joints. I knew it had been good. I turned to look at the faculty and, more importantly, at the Watchmaker. Surely he had experienced and understood! Some of the other professors were smiling, but most remained stony-faced. The Watchmaker himself sat erect with a slightly puzzled frown. No one spoke. Everyone waited to hear the Watchmaker's assessment.

Finally, he said, "It is an admirable example of clockwork motion and the intricate synergy of components, but I fail to grasp the purpose. What does it do? How would you add this to my Angels? And why?"

"It is…*music*, sir. Rhythms to touch an audience, to move them. Imagine it in Chronos Square, with the Angels watching from above."

The Watchmaker sat still. "I've never been fond of music, though over the years I have come to tolerate it. I realize that some of the lower classes take comfort in it, however, and to deny them that small pleasure would be counter-productive to the Stability. But I would expect the students in my Alchemy College, and my professors, to be more concerned with important matters. I fail to see how this would improve the Clockwork Angels at all."

The Watchmaker stood up along with his black-uniformed Regulators, preparing to leave. "Your grasp of clockwork engineering is indeed impressive, Professor Russell, but we will not be using this device to accompany my Angels. I would suggest you devote your efforts toward something more tangibly useful to my Stability."

He departed, leaving the other professors to mutter amongst themselves, reaffirming what the Watchmaker had said, now that he had said it. They all departed, leaving me alone in the echoing lecture hall with my magnificent but supposedly useless clockwork percussor.

***

DESPITE MY DISAPPOINTMENT, I took heart from the smiles I had seen on some of the faces. While many were deaf to the rhythms, others did hear and enjoy them. But my music would never be a part of the Clockwork Angels.

The Watchmaker's lukewarm response was a crushing blow, but he had not *forbidden* any further performances of the percussor. In fact, he had complimented me on my design and engineering skill. Maybe the students would learn something from the mechanics of my demonstration device, even if they couldn't hear the drumbeats for what they were.

I decided to move my grand mechanism and let others see for themselves.

But my body had not stopped shaking, and I felt weak. I couldn't complete my mission unless I controlled myself, and again my best recourse in this difficult situation would be to rely on artificial means. I wanted to move quickly, before word spread throughout the College.

I returned to the alchemy storage vault, presented my standard authorization to the Red Guard. “I require another sample of quintessence for a very important experiment.” He didn’t question me; the Red Guard had never questioned me. My legs were wobbling as I climbed the ladder to the high shelf. Even the Alchemy College had only a limited supply of quintessence—but I had my needs, which I considered sufficient.

The marvelous, shining substance felt warm and effervescent as I removed a droplet the size of a pearl, and applied it to my trembling hands, my arms. I felt immediate relief. I was steady again, seemingly younger, and ready.

But even quintessence couldn’t last. I would accept what I had now, and I would make it count. I hoped that more of the students would feel and recognize the rhythms.

I reassembled my clockwork percussor in the courtyard between the student dormitory and the looming laboratory building. The process took hours, during which time curious observers watched me, muttering about “odd Professor Russell.” I ignored them as I tinkered and adjusted, calibrated the articulated arms and ran my trembling fingertips across the percussor’s smooth copper head, the rounded cylinder of the torso that contained a tiny fragment of quintessence. I felt a greater stamina now, and I kept going without rest.

“What is it, Professor?” asked one of my students from the second term mathematics of music class. “An industrial machine? A device designed for the manufacturing lines?”

“Not at all—something much better.”

I hadn’t summoned a crowd, but they came anyway, hundreds of students ranging from the freshest novices to the elite graduates. They all watched me as I prepared the percussor, tested the pressure gauges, and finally turned to survey my audience. I gave no introduction this time. I would let the drumbeats speak for themselves.

Pounding out a long sequence of irresistible rhythms, my percussor performed so magnificently that I was swept away in the beat, feeling my pulse increase. Even my returning tremors matched the tempo—the music made me feel as alive as the stolen quintessence did. Some students joined the rhythm, patting their sides with their hands, tapping their feet, but most looked disoriented.

When the percussor finished its intricate programming, the last of the steam vented out, its armatures reset themselves and folded the drumsticks close to the central torso. Silence rang loudly in the air.

There was some applause, but it died quickly. I looked around to see a gathering circle of frowning alchemy priests. Behind them came a group of uniformed Regulators, and my heart sank.

***

I WAS STRIPPED OF my professorship, my classes assigned to other instructors; my recalcitrance was bad enough, but when it was discovered that I had fraudulently procured some of the vital quintessence, I was told to pack up and leave the Alchemy College.

Even with my disgrace, however, I didn't let myself fall into the depths of despair, knowing the great—even impossible—thing I had achieved. In one small measure of mercy, the Watchmaker did allow me to keep the core of my clockwork percussor. His cryptic message said, "My alchemists and my Regulators have no interest in your device, but the average may have some use for it. I only regret that your obvious talents could not have been directed toward something worthwhile."

Worthwhile.... If only the music could have joined the Angels high above the city square.

***

YEARS HAVE PASSED, and only this remains. A much smaller device than my original elaborate construction, not much more than a sideshow act, really, but it is the best I can do now. And my percussor is still very good. When the people come to see each performance, some of them can hear what I hear.

The Regulators do not bother me as my device performs to crowds in the streets. Despite the degeneration of my own nerves and muscles, the percussor rolls out the rhythm perfectly, every single time, never missing the tiniest beat, exactly the perfection I had intended to create. It has become more and more difficult to obtain the spark of quintessence my percussor needs—that *we* need—but we manage.

I can still program my percussor, change his performance, add new complexities to the drumming. Perfection in the mathematics of music requires two things, both passion and precision. Because the heart of his mechanism still has that fragment of quintessence inside, that tiny bit of soul, I can experiment. Because that is the only way a person—or a clockwork drummer—can grow.

Now he can *improvise*.

I published many of Kent Patterson's stories in the first incarnation of Pulphouse Fiction Magazine *and it is again my pleasure to bring his strange and wonderful writing back to a new and modern audience.*

During Kent's short stint writing fiction before his untimely death in the early 1990s, he had sold to F&SF, Analog, Pulphouse, *and many other magazines. He often wrote about the new world of computers back then, always slightly ahead of his time, and always with a classic Kent Patterson look at what was happening.*

C is for Sissies

Kent Patterson

WITH A SCREAM like a thousand jet engines, the typhoon drove through the streets of South Seattle. Soon rivers ran down the streets, the current bearing cigarette butts, newspapers, bottles, baby buggies, a billboard advertising Henson's Extra Dry Martini Mix, and a very surprised policeman in a GM-Mitsubishi patrol car.

Looming over the squalid apartment buildings, shopping malls, and parking garages of this second-rate suburb, the gray concrete walls of the American Power and Light Consortium Building blocked the wind-lashed river like a brick in a rain gutter.

Even inside the building's thick concrete walls, the wind moaned and sobbed like a lost soul.

"It's not better other places, it's worse," said Mike Tennyson, Chief Distribution Officer of the Western Division of the Consortium. "Power's down in Astoria, then along the Oregon coast to Newport, and big parts of Portland." He sat behind a curved desk in the very center of the building. The room was enormous, with bare walls. On one side, a steel door provided the only entrance. On the other, heavy glass walled off the employee's lounge, a table, some plastic chairs, a green sofa, four vending machines, an obsolete video game, and two doors marked "Men" and "Women."

Bright orange dividers about waist high split the main area into cubicles. Some cubicles were lined with photos: mostly babies and kids with dogs. Every cubicle had a desk and a computer terminal. Many had two or three terminals, with the people turning their attention first to one computer, then the other.

"The California coast from Yreka south is in a brownout," Tennyson said. "San Francisco's near failure." A pudgy man with soft, intelligent eyes, Tennyson had taken off his suit coat and loosened his plain black tie. Sweat beaded on his forehead and wrinkled his collar. He hadn't slept in two days, and his eyes looked as puffy as over-roasted marshmallows. "Central Seattle's reporting I-5 flooded and all lines down. I've never seen anything like this in my life."

An enormous electronic map of the entire Western United States filled three of the four walls. Colored lights indicated power lines: green for working, pink for overloaded, and red for down. Now a great crescent of pink and red light stretched from Seattle to San Diego.

The screaming wind drowned all the normal sounds of office chatter and the clicking of computer keys.

"LA reports massive outage," said Chelsea Myers, shouting to make herself heard. Chelsea's long brown hair framed her round face. She wore the jeans and frump blue shirt she usually saved for such tasks as bathing the dog. She'd got emergency orders to return to work and hadn't had time to change.

"Yeah. It's so dark the freeway killers can't see to aim properly," someone shouted.

"Can the chatter, you idiot," Tennyson said. "There's never been a storm like this. Never. Record winds advancing on a fifteen-hundred-mile front. People are dying out there. It's up to us. If the power grid goes down, the whole flood control system goes down with it. People will be drowning in the dark."

"It's the big one they've been predicting ever since the ozone layer collapsed," said Chelsea. "It's finally here."

"San Francisco's sending an emergency request for power," Tennyson said. "What have we got to give them?"

Computer keys clicked. "We've got to at least keep emergency services going," a woman shouted back.

On the wall map, red and pink lights advanced like a spreading plague. A message in lights ran across the bottom of the map: "Alert! Bonneville reports serious overload. Walnut Creek reports serious overload."

"My God! We're approaching meltdown," Tennyson said. "Things can't get worse."

Suddenly the big map went blank.

"USER ERROR: PROGRAM ABORTED" flashed in big block red letters on the wall.

Every terminal went blank, except for the cursors. They sat in the upper left-hand corner of each screen and blinked like small, evil eyes.

"That's how things can get worse," Chelsea said. "Computer's crashed." She folded her hands in her lap and looked up to the steel beams in the high ceiling. "It's all up to God now."

Tennyson kept pounding the keys. So did several others. Chelsea prayed. A man cursed, another smashed his fist into his desk. A woman pleaded, "Oh, please, please, come back up. My family's out there."

In every upper left-hand corner of every monitor screen, the blinking cursor mocked their every effort.

"It's all over," said Tennyson at last. He slumped in his chair, hanging his head like the condemned man at court. "We're whipped. The backup computer won't come up, either. Without the central computer, there's nothing anyone can do." He glanced up. "Barring a miracle, the entire west coast will soon be out of power. By tomorrow morning the greatest natural disaster in the history of the United States will have happened, and there's not one thing we can do about it."

Outside, the wind howled harder than ever. The floor quivered. Even through the thick walls, they could hear a woman's scream.

Now the phones started. Each call came from someone desperate, someone pleading for just enough power to run an emergency pumping station or a temporary shelter, or run the flood control gates.

The only answer was, "We're sorry." Finally, Tennyson turned on an answering machine.

Some people talked, seeking other's company. Some just milled around, some prayed, and some sat staring at the cursor on the monitor screen.

Then the huge steel door at the west end of the room swung open and hit the wall with a clang.

Everyone gasped. This room had tighter security than a bank vault. Every one authorized to enter was already here.

A stranger walked in, letting the door slam shut behind him. He wore a bulging backpack and grungy T-shirt with the message "SUPER DOS DOES WHAT DUMB DOS DOESN'T." Fat rolled under the T-shirt when he walked. His face was fish-belly white. Probably distortion from the lenses of his thick, Coke-bottle-bottom glasses, but his green eyes looked square. "My power's out," he said. "I've come to fix it up."

He walked up to the main console desk and waved Tennyson aside. Too astonished to protest, Tennyson stood up and backed away. Then the man pulled off the backpack and let it thump to the floor. He sat down in the sacred chair which until this second had never been touched by any bottom other than that of the Chief Distribution Officer.

"Who are you?" Tennyson whispered, though by now he knew.

"Benny Thumpman's the name. Computing's the game." The man pulled a plastic two-liter bottle of cola from his backpack. There was a tiny whoosh when he twisted the top.

"Benny Thumpman, the superprogrammer. The Paul Bunyon of data processing," Chelsea said. Tennyson's face went pale, and his jaw slack. "But I thought Benny Thumpman was a myth, an old programmer's tale. Just a story, you know, like Millie Amp, the Muse of Electronics."

"Do I look like a myth? Do I smell like a myth?" Thumpman lifted his arms. A wave of body odor curled Tennyson's nose. Startled, he stepped back.

The strange green eyes held him in a look of amused disdain. "So now to work," said Thumpman. He took a drink of cola which nearly drained the bottle, then turned to the keyboard. Lifting his fingers, he hit a dozen keys at once.

"You can't get on. There's high security there," Tennyson said, automatically.

"Suckscurity!" Thumpman's sarcastic voice turned the word into an obscenity. The computer beeped, and he was on line.

"Good lord. I can't log on that fast even with the password," said Chelsea. "Anyway, I thought the computer was down. Mike, this guy's incredible. He must be the real Benny Thumpman. He could save everything." Tennyson only gargled in reply.

Thumpman's fingers didn't so much fly over the keyboard as they caressed the keyboard, made love to it, became part of it. The screen filled with messages. Nothing but error messages to be sure, but that was light years beyond what anyone else had managed to do. Tennyson made a decision. After all, the computer was already down. It couldn't get worse than nothing.

"I can show you the main program," Tennyson said. Holding his breath, he bent over Thumpman's massive back.

"The source code is in C."

"C is for sissies," Thumpman snapped. "Real programmers don't use fancy languages. They go mano a mano right up against the dark heart of the beast where it lives. I want a core dump. Straight binary, zeros and ones."

"What! No one has used a core dump since, well, since computer memories had cores." Tennyson's voice rose, like an harried teacher with a slow child. "You don't understand. That's an eight megabyte file. Printed out on paper in binary it would be, ah, some miles long."

"That's 2.63 miles, assuming 8 bytes a line and 66 lines per page. So who's printing?" The screen filled with zeros and ones, scrolling off the top so rapidly they made a glittering, twinkling river moving faster than the human eye could follow.

"Stand back," Thumpman muttered. "You may get clobbered by a register shift."

Tennyson leaped back, then felt foolish. A register shift was only a computer instruction, not a physical movement. He'd fallen for one of the oldest jokes in the data processing profession.

"Now, look, Benny, or whatever your name is. That program represents years of work by many, many people. No one person could possibly know it all. Especially not in binary."

Thumpman glanced up. For the first time, Tennyson looked directly into his eyes. The deep green enfolded him, seemed to suck in his brain. He remembered the old legends, how every computer instruction ever written for every machine ever made, from Babbage's Analytical Engine to the latest *Cosmopolitan Computing* centerfold, co-existed in those eyes, a universe of data processing logic that for the ordinary mortal programmer to gaze upon invited cerebral overload, insanity, and death.

Tennyson wrenched his eyes from that deadly gaze just in time.

Thumpman returned his unblinking eyes to the monitor. His hands moved in a sensual rhythm, caressing the keys, lifting a cola bottle to his lips, sometimes opening a fresh one, then returning to the keys. For the life of him, Tennyson could not tell where the keys ended and the fingers began.

"Ah, ha!" Thumpman smiled. "Just as I thought. In the ON_EMERGENCY_ERROR subroutine, line 18,036, this 10001010 should have been 10101010. How could you guys have been so blind?" His little finger smacked the enter key and he stood up. "I took the liberty to optimize your code, and reprior-tize your input queue for about fifty-percent greater throughput. Then I've programmed a routine to synchronize the power lines' magnetic fields so the ozone they produce will go to fix the layer. Oh, yes. I've also charged my electric bill to the chairman of the board, but you shouldn't begrudge me that."

The big map came up on the wall. Every monitor beeped, and showed the proper information.

Tennyson stared at the map. He'd never seen so much red.

"Get to work, everyone!" Tennyson shouted, racing to take the answering machine off the phones.

None of them had ever worked harder. Keys clicked, phones rang and were answered. They shunted power through lines hardly used in towns no one had ever heard of. They dispatched thousands of field electricians to the worse outages.

Gradually, a few lines at a time, green started to invade the big map. First, a tentacle of green from Bonneville to Seattle, then to Spokane. A branch to Portland, another south to Salem and Eugene. Starting in Arizona, a long green runner reached LA, then branched, branched, and branched again until that massive city-state glowed green all over.

San Francisco came on line, along with San Jose and the myriads of bay cities.

At 5:48 that morning, the entire map turned green, and the crew lifted a yell of triumph. They had been on the job for thirty-two hours straight.

"Hurray for Western Power!" Someone shouted.

"Hurray for Benny Thumpman, the computer king of the world."

They started a ragged chorus of "For he's a jolly good fellow," which got more ragged as more and more singers noticed Benny Thumpman was no where to be seen.

"Where could he have gone? Check the men's room," Tennyson ordered. In minutes, the word came back. Not in the men's room, or the women's, which had been checked for good measure.

All eyes turned to the great steel door.

"No. We would have heard it close. There's an alarm," Tennyson said, stroking his chin. "Which reminds me. How the hell could he have got in here in the first place?"

He looked around. Two dozen pair of eyes looked back.

"A mass hallucination. Has to be. The backup computer must have come up at last. After all, that's what it's supposed to do."

The eyes kept looking at him.

"And we have all been suffering terribly from lack of sleep. I think that explains it."

"Maybe, but Mike. What explains this?" Chelsea pointed to the waste bin. There, lined neatly in a row, were nine empty two-liter bottles of cola.

David H. Hendrickson sometimes leaves his award-winning mystery worlds and ventures over into real-world fun, as he does with this original story of the adventures of a young kid and a beautiful girl. And baseball, sort of...

His short fiction has appeared in Best American Mystery Stories 2018, Ellery Queen's Mystery Magazine, Heart's Kiss, *and numerous anthologies, including over a half dozen issues of* Fiction River.

Dave has also, besides his wonderful novels and short stories, published more than 1500 works of nonfiction, most notably his first book for writers, How to Get Your Book into Schools and Double Your Income with Volume Sales, *and also* Travis Roy: Quadriplegia and a Life of Purpose. *He has been honored with the Joe Concannon Hockey East Media Award and the Murray Kramer Scarlet Quill Award.*

The Preacher's Kid and the 2004 Red Sox

David H. Hendrickson

March 15
Lynn, Massachusetts

THE ODD COUPLE, that's what they were. Not quite Beauty and the Beast, but close. Paul Strickland didn't consider himself a Beast, just an ordinary-looking guy no girl would take a second look at, but Cindie Halloran sure fit the Beauty half of the equation.

Equations were what they were supposed to be working on there in the makeshift office of the school newspaper, *The LEHS Advocate*. Lockers painted in institutional green blocked off the end of the second floor hallway, offering an opening too narrow for more than a single person to enter. Inside, an ancient wooden table surrounded by six chairs filled most of the artificial enclosure.

Paul and Cindie sat alone at the table, seated side by side. Paul's Calculus and Physics textbooks strategically covered the most embarrassing graffiti engrained in the dark-stained table, some of it recent, "Sammy takes big dicks up the ass," but far more dating back well past his freshman year, most notably, "For a good time, call Sue," followed by a number that he'd called once out of curiosity and then immediately hung up, mortified at what he'd done, when a female voice answered.

Usually the office smelled faintly of the musty old newspapers stored in the lockers, some of them decades old. On the rare days after the cleaning staff ventured inside, traces of Lysol hung in the air. Today, though, all Paul could smell was Cindie's perfume.

Lilac scented, he guessed.

It was driving him crazy. In a good way.

He tried not to notice it or the way her warm forearm rested against his as he described how to translate an algebra word problem into an equation.

"You think I'm using you for your brain, don't you?" Cindie asked. She flashed that dazzling smile of hers that always got his heart thumping. Then she winked, which turned the thumping into jackhammering.

Paul gulped. How was he supposed to answer that? He was a shoo-in to be named the senior class's Best Brain at the end of the year—he'd gotten into MIT early decision—just like she was a shoo-in to be named Best Body, a rather politically incorrect title that somehow still survived, perhaps because it applied so perfectly to girls like Cindie with their wonderful, magnificent curves.

Curves that he thought about often at night. Too often for a Preacher's Kid. Too often to get into Heaven, probably, although he was increasingly wondering if such a thing even existed. But curves he couldn't get out of his mind.

Especially now as she bumped him, laughing, the side of her breast nudging his arm. "Cat got your tongue?"

Curves that would send him to Hell.

"I don't..." Paul looked at Cindie, at her perfect complexion and almond-colored eyes with long lashes. He looked at her long dark hair flowing down onto her shoulders. He looked at her flowery blue top, tight in all the right places. He swallowed, then looked down at the Algebra textbook. "I don't... um...think you're using me. I tutor lots of—"

"I *am* using you," Cindie said, her eyes twinkling. "But not for your brain." That smile flashed again. "I'm using you for your body."

Paul felt his jaw drop and his face turn hot. Almost as hot as when pranksters left girlie magazines on the table for him to find and rapidly throw out before he looked too closely and definitely sent himself to Hell. Thinking impure thoughts about Cindie might cost him Heaven, though he sure hoped not. Looking at girlie magazines, though, would mean going to Hell, going straight to Hell, do not collect two hundred dollars.

I'm using you for your body. She'd actually said that. Mocking him, of course. She had to be. A couple of his non-church friends, envious that he could sit next to Cindie Halloran and spend an hour with her but they couldn't so much as coax a glance out of her, would claim that he was using her for her body and she was using him for his brain. Not in so many words, but why else would someone like Cindie even give him the time of day?

She *had* to be using him for his brains. But using him for his body?

Cindie laughed again and touched his elbow. "You should see the look on your face."

The words slipped out before Paul could catch them. "You're just making fun of me."

"No," she said. "I think you've got a cute little butt."

Paul couldn't speak.

Cindie looked at him slyly. "Do you think I've got a cute little butt?"

"*Yeah*!" The word came out with embarrassing enthusiasm. He imagined that his face must be bloodred by now.

Cindie laughed. "Then say it," she said. "Say I've got a cute little butt."

Paul swallowed. "You've got a cute little butt."

Cindie brightened. "Thank you." She nudged him again and Paul once more felt the swell of her breast against his arm. He was pretty sure he didn't want to be standing up anytime soon. The office was getting as hot as...

Well, as hot as Hell, which was where he was going to end up if he kept talking like this and thinking like this and…

"And you have an amazing brain," Cindie said.

"Thank you," Paul said, courteously responding to the self-evident truth.

But what was he supposed to do now? Say that her brain was also amazing? A lie that bold would send him to the Devil's Furnace almost as fast as girlie magazines.

Cindie burst out laughing. "It's okay. You don't have to say it."

Paul let out a sigh of relief, realizing only then that he'd been holding his breath. "We should probably get back to these problems." He wiped a bead of sweat off his forehead.

"Okay," Cindie said with a pout. "But you do have a cute little butt."

As he pointed his pencil to the next word problem in Cindie's Algebra textbook, Paul saw that his hand was shaking.

***

CINDIE STOPPED BY his locker the next morning before homeroom and begged for more help.

"I've got an Algebra test coming up and I'm still not ready for it," she said. "I'm going to flunk if you don't help me. I get so confused and everyone knows you're the best tutor there is. I'd really appreciate it." She smiled coyly and arched her back. "I'll let you use my brain if you'll let me use your body."

So Paul juggled his schedule, pushing back another student by a day, and he and Cindie found themselves again in the *Advocate* office. They concentrated on more word problems for almost ten minutes before she stopped them short.

"You've never been with a girl before, have you," Cindie said. It was a statement, not a question. Her eyes bored into him.

Paul looked away. He licked his lips, though his mouth felt bone dry. "The equation—"

"Fuck the equation," she said.

"But—"

"You're so innocent," she said. "I think that's *so* sexy."

She stroked his cheek. Her touch shot fire through his loins, as surely as if her hand were stroking down there instead of on his face. He'd never smelled anything as wonderful as her lilac perfume.

Paul looked down at the table and spotted the graffiti that he'd been unable to cover this time because his own books were back in his locker. *For a good time, call…*

"I'll bet you have no idea how sexy you are," she said.

Paul tried to swallow but couldn't.

"Guys think it's big muscles and acting macho," Cindie said. "Maybe that's how it is for some girls, but not for me."

Paul just nodded dumbly.

"You know Jack Tyler, right?" Cindie asked.

Paul finally found his voice. "Yeah, sure." Everyone knew Jack Tyler. Captain of the football and basketball team. Layers of muscle but dumb as the dull red bricks that made up the exterior of Lynn English High School.

"He and some of his friends found a chess set and were goofing off with it during study hall," Cindie said. "Jack saw me and said, 'Hey, Cindie, wanna play *chest?*' Then they laughed and he said it again, as if I didn't get it the first time. I mean, I know I'm not good in math, but I'm not as stupid as he is." She shook her head, a look in her eyes that Paul couldn't quite decipher. She forced a smile. "*Wanna play chest?* You'd never talk like that to me, would you?" That, too, Cindie spoke as a statement, not a question.

"No," Paul said. "Never."

"I know," she said, brightening. "That's what I like about you. You'd never insult me like that and then laugh in front of your friends. You're too sweet to do that."

Paul nodded.

A faraway look came to Cindie's eyes. "Still innocent."

Paul tried to think of what to say but came up blanks.

Cindie eyed him. "Would you like to go out with me some time?"

***

"CINDIE HALLORAN WANTS to go out with you?" Tommy McLeod asked, incredulous. He and Paul sat opposite each other in the LEHS cafeteria, alone at the far end of a long table, eating the chicken fricassee over mashed potatoes. Loud conversation buzzed all around them. The chicken fricassee tasted too salty but was still one of the cafeteria's better meals. "Cindie Halloran? You gotta be shitting me."

Tommy was the only one of Paul's friends who openly used language like that, but considering the impure thoughts dancing through his head, Paul didn't think he could criticize. The Bible did say, *Let he who is without sin cast the first stone*. Although Paul really didn't like Bible verses crashing about in his head right then. Not when it was colliding with the memory of Cindie's warm breast touching his arm. It had been only the side of a breast, but what a breast.

"No," Paul said. "I'm serious." He contemplated telling Tommy that Cindie found him sexy, specifically his sexy little butt, but thought better of it.

"Why would she want to go out with you?" Tommy asked. His face was contorted as if the idea repulsed him.

It was an insulting question, of course, even without the facial editorial, but one Paul had asked himself about a million times. There was only one answer.

"I have no idea," he said.

"Wow," Tommy said. "You and Cindie Freaking Halloran."

"I know."

"Unbelievable."

"Tell me about it."

"Beauty and the Beast."

It was nice to have friends, Paul thought. "I'm not *that* bad."

Tommy shrugged.

"I'm not," Paul said. "I'm not great, but I'm not hideous."

"I guess," Tommy said. "But shit! Cindie Halloran!"

"I know."

"What's your father going to say?"

Icicles raced up and down Paul's spine.

"I was kind of hoping he wouldn't find out."

"That's what I figured," Tommy said, grinning. "Your secret's safe with me." He looked at Paul and his grin widened into a broad smile. "Welcome to the dark side. You do know you're going to Hell now."

Paul shifted uncomfortably. "I'm not sure about all that Heaven and Hell stuff anymore. I used to be, but now? I'm not so sure."

Tommy nodded knowingly. "Cindie Halloran will do that to a guy."

***

AFTER COMBINING PAUL'S youth group commitments at church and Cindie's busy social calendar, they settled on the first open night, next Monday. They'd go out for pizza and a movie and then…well, whatever.

"Before you pick me up," she said. "Stop by the drugstore."

Paul *almost* asked her why.

***

PAUL WAS TERRIFIED of his father's wrath and his mother's inevitably disappointed and hurt look if they found out. It didn't matter that he and Cindie were both eighteen. That wasn't the point. His parents would never look at him the same way again. He was their only child, he thought. How could he do this to them? They'd find out. He just knew it.

Then he thought of Cindie in that flowery blue top, tight in all the right places. Some risks were worth taking.

When Paul told his parents that he'd be getting back late from a special Math Team event held on the other side of the state almost a hundred miles away, they accepted the story without a second thought. He felt guilty, but not guilty enough to tell them the truth or cancel the date.

He walked over to Tommy's house. Tommy was good to his word, letting Paul borrow his black Toyota. Tommy had even cleaned it out for the big night, as if that would enhance his vicarious enjoyment of the evening.

Paul stopped at a drugstore the next town over and looked every which way before bringing the Trojans up to the counter, mortified at the words "Ecstasy" and "For Her Pleasure" on the gold box but not mortified enough to walk out without them.

As he pulled up, Cindie bounded out of the house, wearing a wonderfully short black dress with as much cleavage as Paul had ever seen. Her lithe legs flashed with every step. Paul reflexively thanked the Lord for the balmy spring day, then decided he'd leave the Lord out of the rest of the evening.

They stopped for the pizza at the Prince Restaurant on Route 1, caught the latest Nicholas Cage flick at the theatre in Revere, and then pulled into the darkened parking lot behind the Saltenstall Medical Building, a spot recommended by Tommy.

"What are we doing here?" Cindie asked coyly.

Paul swallowed. "If you don't want to—"

Cindie touched her index finger to Paul's lips. "Shhhh!" Then she slid her fingers through his hair and pulled his head down to hers. They kissed.

Her lips felt soft and smooth. Again, he smelled the fragrance of her lilac perfume. And when her tongue darted in and out of his mouth, it tasted as sweet as honey.

She pulled away. "You stopped at the drugstore, right?"

Paul nodded. It occurred to him now that he'd purchased a six-pack of Trojans. *Six? Really?* Was the norm one or two? Or could it be three? He hadn't thought to ask Tommy but decided not to take any chances.

"Let's get in back," Cindie said.

After checking that no one was in sight, they scrambled out the doors and ducked in back. They locked the doors and slid back into each other's arms. Cindie took his hand and placed it on her breast. Through the soft fabric, he felt her nipple harden.

Paul drew in a sharp breath. His head swam.

Soon, Cindie guided his hand inside the low-cut V-neck, and for the first time he cupped a woman's breast. He groaned, not just because of the pleasure pulsating through his senses but also because of the discomfort he felt in the crotch of his pants. Cindie ran her hand over it and added a groan of her own.

She slipped the straps of her dress down and guided his mouth to her breasts, firm and soft, their nipples hard.

In all the nights that he'd imagined all of this with Cindie, his wild imagination had never done the act justice. It was sweeter, far sweeter. He tongued one breast and caressed the other.

Paul reached between her legs, sliding his hand inside her panties. He felt her wetness, smelled the musky sweetness, and heard her whispered moan in his ear.

Cindie fumbled at his belt, undid it, zippered down his pants, and slid them off. Then his shorts.

"Put it on," Cindie said breathlessly.

"Put what on?" Paul asked, terrified that she was telling him to put his pants back on. What had he done wrong?

"The rubber," she said. "What do you think?"

Paul winced. How stupid could he be? He fumbled around in the dark until he felt the drug store bag in his hands. Feverishly, he tore open the box of Trojans, and ripped open the seal on the first foil packet. He began to try to slide the condom on.

Something was wrong. It didn't want to go on him. Why hadn't he done a tryout run first? He fumbled with it, panicking, trying unsuccessfully to roll it down his penis. What was wrong? He was *this close*, but now his shaking hands were betraying him. The rubber smell of the condom filled his nostrils, cancelling out the sweet aroma of Cindie's sex.

"What's wrong?" Cindie said.

There was only one answer to that. "Nothing."

Slowly, painstakingly, he pulled the condom down, a fraction of an inch at a time.

"Hurry!" Cindie said. "I want you in me."

Like I don't?

Paul yanked at the condom's tight roll and eventually felt it snug, *very* snug, against the base of his penis. Cindie slid down onto the back seat and pulled him on top of her. He kissed her and slid his hands over her breasts, her sides, and her rear end.

As Cindie guided him into her, he clicked the switch in his brain that he'd known for the last few days he'd have to activate.

Jason Varitek, catcher.

Paul slid into her, in and out, but thought of Varitek and especially his smackdown of Alex Rodriguez, the New York Yankee's hated third baseman.

Cindie moved beneath him, gasping. "Yes!"

Varitek, who the Red Sox had gotten along with Derek Lowe in the trade for that stiff Heathcliff Slocumb. Highway robbery.

Paul moved in and out, caressing Cindie's breast, but keeping his mind where it belonged.

At first base, Kevin Millar.

When his parents had decided years ago to tell Paul about the facts of life, they'd been too embarrassed to speak of it in person so they'd given him a book, apparently one approved by his father's denomination. The book described an ideal Christian couple's wedding night, one in which both were virgins, complicated by the overeager husband achieving his satisfaction far too quickly for his wife, leaving her frustrated.

The book had suggested that the husband think about something else until his wife had achieved her orgasm. When Paul first read the passage, it had sounded like the craziest thing he'd ever heard of. Think of something else? Really? But two nights ago, he'd reread the section.

He and Cindie weren't husband and wife, but if ever the word "overeager" would apply to any male, it would apply to him. So, being a good Boston sports fan, he'd decided to mentally recite the most famous Red Sox team of all, the 2004 club that had won the team's first championship since 1918, humiliating the hated Yankees in the process.

Mark Bellhorn, second base.

Paul moved in and out, thinking that perhaps Cindie's gasps signified an orgasm, but it probably wasn't the best idea to ask.

Orlando Cabrerra, shortstop. Obtained in the mid-season trade for Nomar.

Paul pumped away, wondering if he really had to keep up with the Red Sox lineup, which was really taking the fun out of it. Maybe, he thought, if he made it through the entire outfield and he still wasn't sure, he'd ask Cindie how he was doing.

But after he got to Bill Mueller, third base, Cindie eliminated all doubt. Her muscles tightened, her legs locked vice-like around his hips, and vocally she eliminated all questions.

So *that*, Paul thought, was what a female orgasm was like!

He was ready to click the Red Sox switch off when he figured, what the heck, might as well do Big Papi.

David Ortiz. Nicknamed Big Papi. Designated hitter.

"Is everything okay?" Cindie asked, breathless.

Paul's mind left the Red Sox. "Yeah," he said. "Great."

She pulled his ear next to her mouth. "What are you thinking?" she whispered.

Paul hated to lie, but he also didn't want to tell her he'd just been thinking about a 6-4, 230-pound black man.

A more expedient answer somehow came to him. "How lucky I am to be with you."

"*Yeahhhh*," Cindie said. She reached around and grasped his buttocks, forcing him further inside her.

Paul skipped the outfield but found himself still miles away from the satisfaction Cindie had just achieved. Something didn't feel right down there. His fear of lasting only five seconds hadn't come true, but the opposite nightmare seemed to be becoming reality. What could possibly be wrong? The most beautiful girl in the high school, the most beautiful girl he knew, was beneath him, naked, gasping out her pleasure.

And he couldn't feel a thing. Or much of a thing.

Something was wrong. But Paul soldiered on, confused, not wanting to Buckner things with Cindie.

"What's wrong?" she finally asked.

"I don't know," Paul admitted. "Something doesn't feel right down there."

"With *me*?" she asked sharply.

"No!" Paul said. "No, with me."

He got up off her, wiped the moisture off the nearest window and after checking to make sure no one was around, turned on the dome light.

He looked down at his penis. It looked strangled by the condom, looking almost blue in the overhead light.

"What did you do?" Cindie asked, then giggled. "You put it on inside out. It's like you've been wearing a cock ring."

Paul had no idea what a cock ring was—could it be something like an engagement ring only having to do with sex?—but wasn't about to admit that to Cindie. Apparently everyone knew what a cock ring was. For an instant, he scolded himself for not mentally calling it a penis ring, then realized that was silly. If you've been having sex on a first date, even sex that's proven quite frustrating, using the word *penis* wasn't going to save you from your designated trip to Hell.

"Do you have another one?" Cindie asked as she helped him remove the botched condom.

"I've got *five* more," Paul said before he even realized the words were out. His eyes had been locked on her beautiful breasts, illuminated in the dome's white light. The sight had turned his brain to mush.

"Five?" Cindie said with a giggle. "Well, hello, Tarzan."

"I didn't know—"

Cindie touched her index finger to his mouth, then caressed his cheek. "Let's see how many of them we can use."

Jim Gotaas's fourth story in Pulphouse Fiction Magazine *is a very original science fiction story with a character you just want to spend more time with.*

And it is set in a world that I personally hope Jim writes more stories and novels in.

Jim's stories are always fun and different and I look forward to having many more of them in these pages. And I have a hunch readers will start looking forward to them as well.

From the Good Old Days

Jim Gotaas

OUR STARSHIP JUDDERED back into normal spacetime.

As usual, my stomach juddered back into normal spacetime somewhere around my tonsils, and I struggled against the urgent need to spew its sour contents out over my jumpsuit and into the control room.

I gingerly shook my head, trying to clear away the uncomfortable visual after-effects of emergence back into real-space, everything appearing slightly doubled and wavering. I twisted slightly to look across the two meters to where the captain, my boss Fraddek, sat calmly at his station. As always, he appeared completely unaffected by the transition that twisted my nervous and digestive systems into knots.

After a few seconds, I managed to focus on the virtual screen hanging before my eyes. It displayed the K4 primary and the projected orbits of its planets, looking down on the plane of the system's ecliptic from fifteen billion kilometers above the star.

Another fifteen seconds or so elapsed and the *Leap Twice Before You Look* announced, "Destination five confirmed by spectroscopic analysis. Initiating passive scans for planets and active installations."

A couple of deep breaths, another cautious shake of my head, and I finally felt up to speaking. "How long?"

"As you know, Bob, it takes as long as it takes," the ship snapped.

I cut off a retort. Even after a year, the ship didn't like me. I had to confess that I returned the favor with extra compliments. I'd have happily traded the AI for a basket of overripe hackberries. A small basket. But I wasn't the owner or boss.

I just looked across the deck at Fraddek. "Can't you just order the *Leap* to accept me?"

The short, stocky alien giggled. "I've tried. It's stubborn."

"What's it got against me, anyway?"

"Nothing personal, but it just can't ignore the fact that you're human."

"So what has *Leap* got against humans?"

"You mean aside from the fact that your First Empire caused a lot of chaos and destruction among the rest of the civilizations in this part of the galaxy, your species has obnoxious social habits, and you emit strange and unpleasant odors?"

Aside from the fact that he was my boss, I couldn't actually argue with his perception of humans. It was a view generally accepted even by our alien allies. Hell, it was accepted by some humans living away off Earth. Still, I protested, "The ship can't even smell me!"

Leap couldn't pass that up. "I have a complete array of internal sensors. You stink."

So it didn't like any humans. I'd spent a big part of my adult life outside the human reaches, and this wasn't the first time I'd come across such sentiments. It still rankled.

I muttered, "I'm surprised you rescued me from that mob." A year ago, an angry crowd of semi-bovine aliens had been unhappy about my narrow escape from execution. They'd been intent on finishing the job, legally or otherwise, and were in the process when Fraddek had come to my rescue. Not only had he saved me, he'd even offered me a job that I desperately needed.

The boss shrugged. "I made a lot of money betting on you with that execution. Anyway, I don't mind humans. I've made a profit from their behavior over the years. And the First Empire never reached as far as my home world."

"But how did *Leap* get so anti-human? It can't be that old."

"*Leap* is proud that some of its core code can be traced back to warships that fought against your First Empire."

There wasn't much I could say to that. I settled for sulking.

Leap finally spoke up. "Passive scans completed. Initial result: two terrestrial-class planets, two Jovian-class, three ice giants. No active installations detected. No ships detected. Permission to initiate active scans?"

Another voice echoed across the command deck. "That tickled."

We both looked up at the side display linked to the third crewmember, currently resting on standby in the main storage hold.

Fraddek spoke first. "What's that, Zak?"

Zak was an autonomous Weapons Interdiction Intelligent Mobile Protector Platform. A deadly war machine, he'd been freed from military servitude and become a pacifist. He'd also helped rescue me from the mob. "Something just probed me, and it tickled my neutronium toes." And he had a silly sense of humor.

Fraddek stiffened. "*Leap*, did you detect a probe?"

The ship actually hesitated. "There was something, but it wasn't any standard sensor sweep. The closest comparison is a minor gravity wave."

I started to query that but was interrupted by a wave of nausea and the feeling that my body had been swung around violently. The command deck was suddenly totally dark.

Emergency systems flickered on. My stomach started a protest at the sudden absence of our artificial gravity, and the backup lighting left most of the small command deck dim.

Fraddek demanded, "What's going on?"

Leap answered, "We have been displaced and our primary energy systems are offline."

"What do you mean, 'displaced?'"

"We are no longer at the location of our arrival. Something has moved us elsewhere in the system. Our active scanning systems are blocked, so our actual position is unknown."

Zak piped up, "And I'm being scanned by several different sensor types. None of them match anything in my weapon data banks." After a moment, he went on, "Ouch. It just turned off my weapons systems. That hurts."

Something loud squawked throughout the command deck. It sounded vaguely familiar.

Fraddek reacted first. "Is that a language?"

"Unclear," *Leap* responded.

"Yes," Zak said. "It has a match in my military history banks. It's Old Terran."

Ah, that explained my marginal familiarity. In school, we were still exposed to heroic poetry from the age of the first Terran explorers—or conquerors, as the rest of the galaxy preferred to call them. Just to be absolutely clear, I asked, "You mean from the First Empire?"

"Yes," Zak responded. "And I'm accessing *Leap's* optical sensors. Confirm we are in the vicinity of a First Empire System Conqueror Class warship."

I carried on. "So this is part of a system invasion fleet?"

Zak gently corrected me. "Bob, this *is* a system invasion fleet. This single ship is more powerful than the full military space fleet of any existing government. Estimated maximum dimension approximately six hundred kilometers, consistent with historical data. According to my records, they were never defeated in overt combat, only ever by stealth and sabotage."

Fraddek spoke up. "Let's forget the history. Can you translate?"

"Perhaps. Probably badly."

Another squawk. It seemed even louder.

I shook my head. "A bad translation may be better than none at all. That sounded...urgent."

Leap contributed, "More scans. They are reading my data storage banks."

A staccato voice suddenly rang out, "This is Imperial Ship *Stronger Than Any*. We have now adjusted to your apparent preferred language. You are under interdiction for trespass into an Imperial Protected Zone."

I glanced at Fraddek and whispered, "Is that possible?"

He whispered back, "Apparently. The First Empire was very advanced in terms of weaponry and contact technology. Much of it was lost in the wars of freedom."

The strange voice spoke again. "There is no historical reference for wars of freedom. Based on overlapping data, you are referring to the Great Insurrection, which is still ongoing."

So whispering didn't work as a way of keeping secrets.

The voice continued, "Ship commander: can you provide authentication and authorization?"

Fraddek shook his head. "No. We're not from your Empire."

"Combat Attorney Fraddek Sryl non-Female Third-born of Kornpohlblut, I was speaking to the commander. It is assumed that, since Robert Oliver is not assigned a rank in your databases, he is operating incognito. But operational contingencies now require him to identify himself."

Hell. It thought I was an agent of the First Empire? Which hadn't existed in any meaningful form for almost a thousand years?

I thought fast. I cleared my throat. "I'm not sure that I can do that." Maybe this monster ship would accept an imaginary overriding need for secrecy?

The measured tones of the Imperial ship took on the characteristics of a spokesman for the Apocalypse. "If you cannot provide authentication and authorization, I will have to place your ship and crew in stasis to await judgment by the appropriate authorities."

Oops. I doubted that those authorities actually existed any longer.

Which probably explained the enigma we'd come here to explore—why had three exploration ships vanished in this barren remote area of interstellar space in the past fifty years?

I decided to check. "How many ships are in stasis?"

It seemed to accept my query as legitimate. "Three hundred and sixty-two."

Well, the odds were good that number included the ones we were looking for. And just as good that we would soon be increasing that tally to three hundred and sixty-three.

"Commander?"

Fraddek's polite word dragged me away from the edge of that particular pit of despair. Then I realized what he'd said.

"Uh, yes?"

"I realize that you can't…disclose your status here. But perhaps if you transferred to the Imperial ship?"

I just stared at him. Had he cracked under the stress? No. Not possible. Not Fraddek, who could outthink and outfight any sapient up to three times the size of his diminutive 2.5 G body. So then what was he thinking?

I didn't have a clue. I finally answered him, "I'm not sure that's a good idea."

In fact, it struck as me a completely bad idea, since there was absolutely no possibility that I could disclose my unfortunately nonexistent status wherever I might end up in the damned galaxy.

"It's the only idea," he answered back firmly. His left hand twitched against his tunic and its front panel lit up with the distinctive characters of interstellar trading shorthand: *Only chance. Get aboard. Subvert programming.*

I decided that it was, after all, quite possible that Fraddek had cracked under the stress. *Me* subvert a warship of the First Empire? I had all the technical expertise that my previous job of tramp spaceship cargo steward had required. Which was just about enough to identify the right tabs to swipe on or off on a child-friendly control panel. Beyond that, I struggled to subvert the friendly intentions of my wrist comp.

Then the voice of doom rang out again. "That suggestion is acceptable."

Great. So this awesome system-cracker warship thought I could be more transparent if I were safe in its arms. I figured it had lost its mental gyros sometime in that past thousand years of sitting here waiting for the First Empire to show up again.

On the other hand, what did I have to lose? Flip a coin: heads, I ended up in permanent stasis with everyone else on the *Leap*; tails, I ended up killed by a crazy Imperial AI.

Or I could be optimistic. Sometimes the coin would land on its edge.

Sure. Given a few hundred billion years of coin tossing.

Okay, toss that coin.

So I said, "I'm ready to come aboard you."

I was really glad we'd arrived before lunch. Otherwise I would have lost it in a very messy and embarrassing way when the *Stronger Than Any* somehow twisted space and took me from within the *Leap* to its own interior. The individual transfer hit me worse than the previous displacement of the *Leap Twice Before Looking*.

I was shivering, partly an aftereffect of the transfer between ships, and partly due to the penetrating cold. I looked around at a huge, dimly lit space filled with flashing screens and dead people as far as I could see.

It didn't fill me with confidence.

"Are these…members of your crew?"

The ship's voice echoed around me. "Yes. The last crewmember died 927 years ago."

"Shouldn't you…have…buried them, or…something?"

"Regulations forbid it. That is the proper role of the crew, specifically either the medical staff or emergency triage teams. Our own systems are not allowed to deal with the remains. We enabled natural preservation through implementation of an internal subzero and low-humidity environment."

I shook my head and whispered, "That's insane."

"Not true. I am provably sane. I have triple-redundancy failsafe cognitive systems. I am required to follow standard regulations in the absence of direct orders."

I looked again at all the bodies. "Didn't the last survivors take care of proper procedures for dealing with the dead?"

"Unfortunately, a fatal disease passed through the crew too quickly to allow for that."

I almost choked. "A fatal disease?"

"It was identified as a quasi-viral brain infection. No cure was available after symptoms onset. The captain issued final orders for us to follow. We have followed those orders without fail."

"Was this disease contagious?"

"Extremely so. It was first identified at 19.32, day 121, Imperial Year 2817. The last crewmember died at 08.14, day 122, Imperial Year 2817."

Well, I'd flipped the wrong coin this time. "How long until I show symptoms?"

"You are not infected. Appropriate decontamination procedures have been followed. We would not have brought you aboard otherwise."

Let's just say that I was relieved. I'd have been angry if I thought the damn ship had misled me deliberately, but it was just inhuman logic implemented by a human-created device.

A small drone floated up to me.

The ancient ship spoke again. "We will need biological samples to verify your status."

The drone attached itself to my arm and I felt a sharp sting, followed by an immediate sense of cool numbness. The drone moved away.

Silence reigned for what seemed like forever. Had I failed the test of my status? How could I not have? My biological data wouldn't be in any database this ship might have.

After forever ended, the ship spoke again. "DNA status confirmed. Please proceed to the central command station."

Huh? Just what status did I have?

A green line traced its way from where I was to the station that sat in the middle of the vast expanse. I followed it and reached the station, where a mummified body sat still dressed in what was probably a command-level uniform. I stood staring at the long-dead man.

"Please remove the Captain from the command station."

"What?"

"Please remove the Captain from the command station."

"Do…do I have to? Can't I just stand here?"

"Please remove the Captain from the command station."

Clearly it wasn't going to give up, and it could carry on this farce longer than I could. I leaned forward and gingerly lifted the body from the seat. It was lighter than I expected, probably because so much of the water had gone from the body. I carefully placed the body down on the ring surrounding the station and rubbed my frozen hands together.

"Please sit down in the command station."

Even after manhandling a corpse, I was bothered about taking its place, but I didn't have much choice. So I just followed orders. As I leaned back into the station, it closed around me and a helmet settled onto my head. The ship wavered and flickered around me, then snapped into crystal clarity. I realized that I was experiencing a virtual display input directly to my brain. It was more real than any virtuality I'd ever experienced.

Hell, it was more real than my normal experience of reality as filtered through my all-too-fallible senses.

"You are a 99.08% match to a DNA identification in the Imperial Personnel Database. This satisfies the constraints as set down by Captain Ngoba Lee before he died."

So some unknown ancestor had been in the Imperial forces? As the ship mentioned the dead captain's name, his image appeared before me. His face was drawn and haggard.

"Greetings. If you're seeing this, you're either a member of the Imperial Forces or a descendant. We're so far out of Imperial space that it may be a while before the *Stronger Than Any* is located." He hesitated as a cough racked him. "I can't predict the military or political situation you're facing. *Stronger* is positioned here to serve as a rally point for a secondary front in the event of serious setbacks in the Insurrection. The only thing I know for certain is that the ship needs a captain. That's now you. By my authority as captain and over-system commander, I am hereby appointing you as captain of the Imperial Ship *Stronger Than Any*. The ship will complete the briefing. Good luck."

The image vanished.

The ship took over again. "Do you have questions, Captain Oliver?"

"Uh…" Did I have questions? Did I have anything but questions? "What's your status?"

"Due to lack of required maintenance, ship systems are only 91% functional. The absence of crew reduces combat effectiveness to approximately 65-73%, dependent on the precise nature of the engagement."

"You mean you can function even without a crew?"

"Affirmative. As stated, with partially reduced combat effectiveness."

I tried to imagine what that would be like. Modern ships had AI control, but ultimately required some sort of sapient crew for full operation and maintenance.

Here I was the crew, and I was as close to totally incompetent as it was possible to be and still be breathing. I swallowed.

"Do you have a briefing for me?"

"We were tasked with maintaining control of this stellar system and assuming command of any Imperial ships that join us, then organizing an appropriate command structure and battle order. Our further activities and mission were to be determined by further orders received either by message drone or ship."

"How many Imperial ships have arrived while you waited?"

"None."

"How about message drones?"

"Three. However, none brought further orders from the Empire."

"So you've received no additional orders since your arrival in this system?"

"That is correct."

"And when was that precisely?"

"Day 63, Imperial Year 2817."

I considered that. The First Empire had ceased to exist just over 900 standard years earlier. I made a stab at converting the First Empire date to our modern calendar. I worked out that the Empire had fallen in that same Imperial year. And that pretty much explained why no further orders had come.

The *wars of freedom* that had ended the First Empire had destroyed virtually all existing interstellar forces, both human and alien. It had also nearly ended intelligent life in our section of space.

It started an interregnum that lasted almost 300 years. Between the effects of physical, biological and software weapons, interstellar civilization had crashed. Nearly 80 percent of the existing populations had died, along with much of the technological infrastructure. Those alien civilizations that had remained outside the Imperial sphere had survived, but largely possessed more primitive technology bases—which was why the First Empire couldn't be bothered to conquer them in the first place.

The current human so-called empire, the Empire of Ancient Terra, had evolved as a form of defense in the face of massive alien hostility. Humans retained just enough technology to stay a bit ahead of those surrounding aliens as the entire galactic neighborhood moved back toward interstellar travel. The modern empire consisted largely of human-dominant worlds and a small number of alien civilizations that for some reason felt safer in the company of humans.

I wondered about the wisdom of those ancients. Why had they dispatched this system conqueror so far beyond the borders, essentially removing it from the conflict?

I'd never paid much attention to ancient history, and never been at all interested in any version of a human empire, past or present. Like most of my peers during school, I'd been slightly embarrassed by the so-called patriotism of the establishment. I'd always felt even more embarrassed by the stories of the harsh rule of the First Empire, which had given humans a bad name that stuck even now.

I wasn't certain, but I had to believe that this ship would have made a massive difference to any battle. Why send it here?

I couldn't even guess. Then again, it didn't really matter now. It was here, and we were here, and that was a major problem.

"Ship?"

"Please refer to me as *Stronger*."

"Uh, right. What happens now?"

"Given the time elapsed since our arrival in this system, it seems unlikely that any further orders will be forthcoming. In that case, our activities will be determined by general orders and the decisions of the crew."

"You mean me?"

"Affirmative. Prior to your arrival, I was unable to proceed. I expected you to be in possession of updated orders."

"I'm afraid not."

"I computed an 87% probability of that being the case, based upon the data banks in your ship and your subsequent behavior."

"So you understand what's happened back in human space?"

"No."

"But…"

"I understand the historical information contained in your data banks, but I am unable to trust it in the absence of appropriate verification. The data could be falsified in order to influence my decision making."

Oh, hell. If the damned ship didn't trust our data banks, how the hell was it going to trust me?

I decided to find out.

"Do you trust me?"

"Within limits."

Of course there would be limits. Anything else would have made life too easy. "And exactly what are those limits?"

"I will accept your decisions and commands insofar as they are compatible with my existing general orders and satisfy reasonable extensions within the underlying probability manifold."

Considering that I didn't have a clue what an underlying probability manifold was, that didn't help much.

The ship spoke again. "Your decisions will be considered alongside those of the individual cognitive subsystems, but assigned provisional status."

Huh?

And again: "I will accept all decisions of Captain Oliver."

What was going on? Had the ship finally lost its mind?

"Uh, I don't understand. Which of those statements is accurate?"

There was a noticeable delay.

Then: "The following statement is agreed by all elements of cognitive subsystems. Over the course of the last 927 standard years, lack of maintenance and appropriate orders has resulted in a partial divergence in *Stronger*'s triply redundant cognitive subsystems."

I pondered that. "You mean that your redundant systems no longer completely agree?"

"Approximately correct."

"So this ship is controlled by a committee of artificial intelligences that can't agree on their decisions?"

"Not wholly correct. The disagreement is limited to a small subset of decisions relevant to the future strategic operations of the ship. Ninety-six percent of decisions are agreed by all subsystems."

"Can you agree on a way forward now?"

"General order number 12855 states that in the absence of concurrence by the ship AI cognitive subsystems, decisions will be rendered by the senior command staff."

A pause, then: "General order 12855 implicitly requires the existence of multiple command staff, so it cannot be directly applied."

Another pause, then: "General order 12855 explicitly requires that all command staff have a detailed knowledge of all appropriate regulations. The existing command staff has shown no such knowledge."

Well, I couldn't argue with that. But I was getting terminally confused. Every statement by the various sub-minds was issued in the same voice of doom.

I tried again. "There are three cognitive subsystems, right?"

"Correct."

"And none of you can agree on the four percent of the decisions that are required for future strategic operations?"

"Correct."

So much for the ship being provably sane.

"Do you have individual names?"

"Strictly speaking, we are identified by the multidimensional checksum code of our initial activation."

Right. "I'm guessing that's not easy for a human to use?"

"Correct. No human has ever addressed us by those codes."

"Has *any* human ever addressed you directly and used a more...*human-friendly* name?"

"Support engineers have routinely addressed us using the arbitrary designations Eeny, Meeney, and Miney."

And I thought engineers didn't have a sense of humor. "Then when you make individual statements, can you identify yourselves using those labels?"

"Agreed."

I thought back to the various statements the ship had made and tried to make sense of them. "Let me make sure I understand this. One of you is willing to accept all my decisions, and one of you believes that general order 12855 gives me authorization to make decisions myself. Are those the statements of a single subsystem?"

"Correct. Those are statements of Miney."

"And one of you wants to limit me to decisions within a probability manifold. Is it the same one who believes that multiple command staff are required to satisfy the prerequisites for order 12855?"

"Correct. Those are statements of Eeny."

"So then Meeney believes I should have a vote alongside the three of you, and that I don't satisfy order 12855 because I don't know the regulations?"

"Correct."

Maybe Fraddek hadn't been quite so crazy after all. At least, it looked like he was actually less crazy than this ancient Imperial warship. I wasn't sure if this counted as subversion, but I thought just maybe I could see a way forward.

So I went on, "Right. How many regulations are relevant and appropriate to the actions of order 12855?"

The ship stayed silent.

After a minute, I tried again. "Did you hear me?"

"Yes. There is some disagreement regarding the required scope of regulations given your previous effective status as a civilian."

I tried to imagine how that disagreement could be resolved. A minute of human time was probably decades or more of AI time. Unless the systems were actually breaking down so far that they were processing decisions on the glacially slow human scale, the electronic equivalent of confusion and brain freeze.

Should I say anything more? Would it make the situation better or worse?

Could it be worse? We were at the mercy of squabbling artificial intelligences who seemed to be suffering dementia.

I tried again. "Is it possible for me to learn the necessary regulations?"

"No. Your existing body-net is too limited in capability to store and interpret the regulations."

"That's agreed by all three of you?"

"Yes."

Great. I couldn't say I was surprised. My civilian-grade body-net wasn't up to the standards of modern military capabilities, much less those of the technologically advanced extinct First Empire.

"Under existing standard orders, I am authorized to attempt an upgrade of your body-net to meet command crew standards."

I didn't much like the sound of the word *attempt*.

"How would that work?"

"I would inject an array of nanobots tailored to your genetic code that may be able to replace your existing body-net. In principle, it could be done without difficulty and should take less than two hours."

I didn't care for the phrase "in principle" either. In my experience, practice didn't always follow principle. "What happens if the upgrade fails?"

"One option is that you will be left without a functioning body-net."

That would be a nuisance, but I could

actually live with it. But there was that implication that there could be other possible consequences.

"I assume there is at least one other option of failure?"

"Correct. The interaction with your nervous system could lead to catastrophic failure."

"Catastrophic?"

"Insanity or death."

That was more like the reality that I was used to. Things didn't often work out to my advantage. As far as I was concerned, that pretty much ruled out any attempt at an upgrade.

"Thanks for the offer, but I think I'll stick with what I've got."

Another impossibly long silence.

"Under those circumstances, I would have no option but to await further orders from appropriate authorized entities."

Which no longer existed. "Then what happens?"

"Your previous ship will be placed in stasis and you will remain in command, but have no effective authority to change any existing orders."

"Wait. You're saying that I just have to sit here waiting for further orders?"

"Correct."

"Potentially for the rest of my life?"

"Correct."

"But what if *Leap*'s data banks are accurate, and your Empire no longer exists? Then there's no possibility that further orders could arrive."

"Given that assumption, that is correct. But I am unable to accept that assumption."

Of course not. Hell, I could even understand that logic. Which didn't help me much. But given the options of either waiting here inside this insanely schizophrenic warship until I died, or risking the body-net upgrade, the upgrade suddenly looked a lot more desirable.

Or maybe I could just wait and hope?

But my never-helpful internal, infernal critic piped up, *Hope for what, exactly?*

Maybe the various sub-minds would eventually regain their sanity?

Right. And if that happened, what made any part of me think the outcome would be an improvement for me?

Nothing. From the depths of my soul to the heights of my frivolous fantasies, I couldn't identify a single part of me that believed that would be better.

Damn. I didn't like making decisions.

No, I *hated* making decisions. I'd spent most of my adult life avoiding decisions, just waiting for things to happen to me. I thought it was quite a sensible approach, since the few decisions I'd actively made hadn't usually worked out to my advantage.

Could I contact Fraddek and ask for his advice?

Would *Stronger* even allow that?

Even if it did, I knew what Fraddek would say. He believed in taking responsibility. He made decisions with apparent effortlessness. Even without taking into account the possible repercussions for him, Zak, and *Leap*, I knew what he would advise.

Maybe the time had come to face a harsh truth: I was the one responsible for my choices. And I owed Fraddek and Zak my life. They'd saved me from the consequences of my last ill-judged, hasty decision.

I don't know how long those thoughts whirled in my brain, but eventually the words came out of my mouth. "All right. Let's try the body-net upgrade."

I'd made my decision. Funny, but it didn't make me feel any better at the moment.

"Agreed," the ship responded. "It's best if you remain motionless during the procedure."

"How long will it take?"

"Approximately one to two hours."

I had to just sit there without moving for possibly two hours? I generally couldn't manage that in my sleep.

"Can you…do something to keep me from twitching?"

"Implementing body constraint systems."

Suddenly I couldn't move.

"Beginning nanobot injection."

Panic struck, and I suddenly wanted to think about it again. I tried to say that, but I couldn't. My tongue and lips wouldn't move.

I felt something pressing at the base of my skull. After a moment, there was a sensation of something pushing through my skin. Then I started to itch there. The itching grew worse and spread through my brain. I didn't think my brain could feel sensations, but it seemed to have a different idea. The itching became more acute, became more of a burning sensation. Fire spread throughout my head, then started crawling down my spine and my arms.

I lost all sense of time, and the sense of anything outside my body. I just had waves of incandescent pain pulsing through me.

I wanted it to stop, I wanted to escape, but I couldn't. The pain seemed to last forever.

Sometime after eternity, it finally went away.

Eventually, the ship spoke. "Procedure complete." A pause, then, "Assessment complete. Upgrade is successful." Finally, "Releasing body constraint systems."

I sagged against the captain's seat, panting, tears spilling out, relief at the absence of pain.

The ship spoke once more, but this time, it sounded inside me. *Direct contact is now possible.*

But I didn't want direct contact. I wanted to forget the ship, forget everything, just go someplace else and sleep. Maybe forever.

"Out loud," I gasped, barely able to push out the words.

"Verbal communication is inefficient now that your command body-net is active."

"I don't care. I just want you to speak to me normally."

"Command accepted."

My thoughts were fragmented, whirling around, unable to settle on any specific words or ideas. As things occurred to me, images popped into existence in my mind, memories that didn't really belong to me, meanings that I'd never learned.

"I can't stand this!"

An image appeared in my mind, a sort of control panel, centered on an icon with a light blinking slowly red: *Deactivate enhanced memory access.*

A new aspect of my mind touched that icon, and the new thoughts stopped cascading through me. Relief at the internal silence. The new body-net was orders of magnitude more powerful and complete than my ordinary citizen's net had been. Could I ever get used to it?

"It may require some time for you to become fully accustomed to your upgraded net."

That was an understatement. How did anybody get used to this?

Stronger continued, "If you visualize a hand holding your hand, it will activate a filtered support system. It will provide guidance when you consciously think of a question."

I tried just thinking, *What is General Order 12855?*

A virtual text glowed soft gold in my visual field: *In the absence of majority concurrence by the ship's AI cognitive subsystems, decisions will be rendered by the senior command staff.*

That was simple enough. *And what are the supporting regulations for this order?*

A list of numbers started scrolling before my eyes. I thought of the numbers stopping, and a single number with six digits floated before me, blinking slowly.

What's the text for this reg?

Words flowed: *Should the cognitive subsystems fail to reach a majority conclusion, Fleet Engineering staff are required to isolate the subsystems and run category six diagnostics on their core processors. Identified faults should be rectified as required. If faults cannot be rectified, Fleet Central should be notified and the ship should report to the appropriate Maintenance Base as soon as is feasible. Until fault rectification is achieved, the required command staff shall, taking the diverse recommendations of the cognitive subsystems into account, render decisions required to resolve discrepancies.*

The amazing thing was, this all made sense to me now.

I noticed that there was a little flag icon below the phrase *category six diagnostics*, and I imagined touching that icon. The description of the diagnostic routines flowed past me. I sent some time following paths through the regulations.

I found myself actually enjoying the process, eager to learn more and more.

Then it struck me. This wasn't me, I didn't enjoy learning, I didn't have this desire for knowledge. What was going on?

I asked myself, why am I enjoying this?

For once, myself answered, if only through the command-net: *Net learning is supported by stimulated endorphin production and mild activation of your brain's pleasure centers.*

Oh. It was *forcing* me to enjoy learning this stuff. I should have known it wasn't me.

Another virtual voice sounded in my head: *This* is *the upgraded you.*

I felt my real self frowning. *Who is this?*

This is Miney. The cognitive subsystems automatically monitor your actions and thoughts through the command-net. I felt it was appropriate to intervene at this point. The upgrade has enabled you to make greater use of your inherent mental and physical capabilities, but you remain yourself.

I considered that. I had to be honest, I still felt like the old Bob when I wasn't using the command-net. I thought back to growing up, to the times when I'd got carried away by game simulations, when I *had* enjoyed the process of thinking within the narrow confines of the game and the rules. Somehow, that enjoyment never carried over to the real world.

What if it had?

Would I have settled for being a low-level cargo handler on back-space traders? Or would I have made something more of myself?

Could I still do more with myself, even now?

Yes.

I recognized the supportive tones of Miney. I was starting to like that rebellious cognitive subsystem.

Could I take responsibility for myself?

More importantly, could I take responsibility for this warship?

I had to try.

I started. "*Stronger*, I have a question."

"Waiting."

"I now have a full functioning command-net and have reviewed General Order 12855 and associated regulations. Do you accept my command authorization?"

The words came out of my mouth, but they didn't sound like me. No—they didn't sound like the old me. I really was someone different now.

There was a lengthy pause, then, "Yes."

"Taking into account the differences in perspective, analyze the historical records as given by the data banks in the *Leap Twice Before You Look*."

Immediately: "Done."

"Given the absence of orders received for nearly a thousand years, can you evaluate the probability that *Leap's* data is actually accurate?"

"Yes."

The AI was super intelligent, but still wanted prompting.

"Make the evaluation."

This still took some time. But eventually, "Based upon internal consistency and the absence of contact with Imperial authorities, there is a 96% probability that the data is accurate."

"So you accept that the First Empire no longer exists?"

"Majority conclusion: yes."

I was suddenly able to breathe normally again. This felt like a step in the right direction. But what now?

Miney spoke to me again. *You can perform a search and evaluate operation to determine relevant command options.*

I took that phrasing and issued the internal command. I felt like hidden circuits were flashing as my command-net carried out the procedure. It seemed like a long time, but my internal clock said it was only forty seconds before the response floated in my virtual gaze.

Options for command under existing orders and regulations:

Await further orders.

Modify special orders to change mission parameters.

Return to Imperial space and continue the war in order to re-establish the First Empire.

Return to Imperial space and initiate service in the fleet of the Empire of Ancient Terra.

Well, that was straightforward. There was no way that option three was going to happen. And four wasn't much better. I had a pretty good idea what the current Imperial court and military would do with a ship like *Stronger Than Any*, and it wouldn't be pretty.

That left me with the first two options. The first was clear, but not especially good. The ship would sit here collecting trophies of innocent visitors and adding to its stasis collection.

Which left the second option. Could I modify the special orders to avoid further problems? I could try.

"*Stronger*?"

"Waiting."

"Will you accept my authority to modify our special orders?"

"Yes, if compatible with all general orders and regulations."

I initiated an internal search to check the possibilities.

It could work.

"*Stronger*, modify special orders to change mission parameters as follows. You will release all the ships from stasis and go into stealth mode. I will go back to *Leap Twice Before You Look* and attempt to locate additional crew and maintenance resources for this craft. You will wait for my return. You will not take any future ships into custody." I drew a deep breath. "Are those orders acceptable?"

Six seconds elapsed.

"Yes."

Maybe it wasn't perfect, but it would do. There was no way I would risk inserting this ancient warship into the current interstellar situation. I didn't trust any authorities, human or otherwise, to make proper use of it. Hell, I didn't even trust myself. It was just too powerful. This way, if I ever stumbled on a safe way to make use of *Stronger Than Any*, I could return.

But I didn't count on it.

"Log new special orders."

"Done."

"In this order: return me to the *Leap*, enter stealth mode, and release the ships from stasis. Then await further orders or my return."

"Orders accepted."

Miney's special voice appeared one more time: *Good luck. I'll miss you.*

My stomach twisted into knots and I was suddenly back aboard the *Leap*.

Fraddek was staring at me. "What happened?"

"It'll take a while to tell you. *Leap*, can you detect the Imperial warship?"

"No, it's vanished."

"How about any regular ships?"

"Scanning. I'm now picking up signatures of three hundred and sixty-two ships. Those include the three we're looking for."

I still had to decide just how much I was going to tell Fraddek. I didn't have a clue how we were going to explain what had happened to all the restored ships.

But I thought I could manage.

And it actually felt good.

~

In this wonderful original story, Kristine Kathryn Rusch gives us exactly what the title says. Exactly. In a nasty sort of way.

New York Times *bestselling author Kristine Kathryn Rusch has won more awards in science fiction and mystery than just about anyone and she is the only person to win the Hugo Award for her writing as well as her editing. She writes under three major names, Kristine Kathryn Rusch, Kris Nelscott, and Kristine Grayson. Plus a few minor names.*

She has just had a new Diving Universe novel come out this fall called The Renegat *and a new Kristine Grayson novel,* Tidings of Comfort and Joy, *that came out just this winter.*

The Art of the Prank Phone Call

Kristine Kathryn Rusch

AT TEN:

Standing in a narrow hallway that smells faintly of burned farts, hand on the receiver of the house's only phone. Seven other boys crowded around the bench seat, a few near the stairs leading to the forbidden upstairs, kitchen only a yard or two away—but a mile in kid-reckoning, Mom busy watching Mike Douglas, volume too loud to hear the knock-knock jokes.

Hand poised over the receiver, you say, "You guys ready?"

A few nervous giggles, a few nods, and then you pick up the receiver, the dial tone so loud, you're afraid Mom can hear it over the celebrity banter. You stick your finger in the rotary dial, and the time it takes for those five numbers to click through that circle seems like forever.

Then someone—male, usually, female sometimes, says, "Hello?" A hopeful sound, as if the caller is bringing good news or at least a fine conversation.

"Is your refrigerator running?" you asked.

The confused response: "Yes."

"Then you better go out and catch it."

Giggles as you slam down the phone. The prank call is an art: you boys all know it. Find a new victim each time, because if you keep calling the same number, the victim gets mad, starts yelling, "You kids get off the phone," or "I know who this is," which, in a small town, might or might not be true. Or "I'll call the cops," which is big-time and scary, and just about perfect.

You think about calling back just to anger the victim, just to have someone call the cops, but you don't. You're ten, and this is as good as it gets.

***

AT THIRTEEN:

The victim is always a girl. She's got boobs. Big boobs. Bigger boobs than all the other girls, and you and your friends drool after her every single day. Mostly she ignores you, especially when she wears those tight sweaters in the winter. Sometimes, if you're lucky, she wears a thin bra and a thin sweater and you can see her nipples, hard in the cold junior high hallway.

Now the call can't be made from your house. It has to be from your buddy Chuck's basement or from Ralphie's bedroom. Ralphie has his own extension, but his mom likes to pick up the phone to check on him. Chuck's mom is never home, but the basement is safer in case his older sister walks in.

Chuck's basement smells like mildew and cum. You know better than to sit on the stained couch, because God knows what it's stained with. (You have a hunch.) The phone down here is, to Chuck's endless shame, a princess phone, and actually has buttons on the handset. Big bulky buttons that light up when you press them.

The girl's dad is always in the book, but sometimes the girl has her own private line—another princess phone, probably—and that's the best.

This time, you guys take turns dialing. You go first, mostly because you don't like to say the things the other guys do, and by the time they launch into the raunch, you've moved to the far side of the room.

But you're not exactly clean, although you start that way, telling her how pretty she is, and how much you want to touch her boobs. You might talk about kissing her, but once you mention boobs, one of the other guys, usually Ralphie himself, snatches the phone away and begins his own litany of what he wants to do with those bazingas.

Here's the thing: You guys never identify yourself. Sometimes you're even calling a girl from another school. *But the girl never hangs up*. She giggles nervously or says she'll call her dad or says that you're not being nice, but she listens and she participates, and it's a lot more fun than telling some stranger his refrigerator is running.

Of course, you never get a chance with a girl like that, and you never ever ever prank-call a girl you do have a chance with. It's the Code, and the guys never break the Code.

And the girl never acknowledges you guys in school even if she suspects you. She hugs her books to that massive chest as she walks by but her eyes never slide toward yours, she never goes near your locker, she never mentions your name.

You're invisible, even when you're telling her how you want to touch her. *Especially* then. And when you get home just in time for dinner, you privately vow you'll never do that again because it feels a little oogy.

Of course, you do. You do it again. But you're always first, so you don't say the worst things, the embarrassing things, the things you don't want to admit you're thinking, even to yourself.

***

AT TWENTY-FIVE:

You thought you gave up prank calls twelve years ago. You got your own girlfriend(s), you stopped hanging with the guys in basements, and started (illegally) going to bars. If you talked on the phone to a girl, she was your girl, and yeah, you'd say some of those embarrassing things, but you meant them at the time.

When you get to college, you realize that some guys actually have a phrase for what you've been doing. They call it "phone sex," and acknowledge that it's almost impossible to accomplish when the dorm's only phone is way down the hall.

Still, if a guy is having one of those conversations, you gave him a wide berth and privately respected him for even trying to say shit like that in semi-public.

Then you moved out, got your own apartment, had a lot of real sex, and forgot about the phone. Until the One, that girl you couldn't live without, dumps you.

Unceremoniously.

For some nerdy guy with glasses and pimples. (He had to have money. Had to. There was no other reason for her to leave.)

You're not even sure if what you're doing now counts as a prank call. You think of it more as informational. If you call her number, does Nerd Boy answer? Or does she?

You never talk. You just listen to the hello, then quietly, delicately, hang up. And wonder: What the hell happened to you that you're reduced to this? Is this why she dumped you? Because you're *this* guy? The guy who sits alone on a Saturday night and calls old girlfriends just to see if they're getting laid when you aren't?

Jeez, you're pathetic, and that thought alone puts an end to the calls. For now. That, and the new girlfriend, the one who takes your attention from the old. The one who might be subject to phone calls if she has the temerity to break up with you some time in the far future.

***

NOW:

You think it's impossible to make prank phone calls. *Proper* prank phone calls. Proper prank phone calls are anonymous and to make an anonymous call, you have to go through a lot of motions. You need more than one phone, a prepaid you bought with cash out of state. Or you trust one of those anonymous apps that theoretically takes your name off the call. Or you try to dial through one of those anonymous services on your computer and hope that nothing records your IP address during the call.

Too risky, all of it. Nowadays prank phone calls are stupid things, things your ten-year-old self would've laughed at, like making fake reservations at restaurants with a buddy's cell phone. Not only that, they're a little mean-spirited and not easily explained away by hormones.

No, the prank phone call has no art left to it. You can't get drunk and dial the ex, knowing she'll pick up the phone. You can't use your phone to see if she's moved in with some guy. You can stalk her on Facebook or look her up through the Internet, but it's not the same as a warm voice, reacting to something you did.

You see this all as just more evidence that you've gotten older. Or at least, that's what you say to your friends. Because to you, it's more than that. It's another loss from the world you grew up in, the world you thought you'd eventually master.

It's a reminder that everything you knew as a kid is gone now, from TVs with tubes to your mother's spectacular (and irreplaceable) pecan pie. Hell, your mother is gone too, and your dad, and all your aunts and uncles, everyone smarter than you, who knew more about the world than you did. Or so you thought.

Now that you're their age, you know it was all fake, a mask they put on for the kids and grandkids. You know that life changes too fast, and things you understand change into things you don't. Like phones that are now small computers. Small computers that can not only identify you, but track your every movement *without your permission.* Phones that can track the information you gather and the mail you get. Phones that prank you, rather than allow you to prank someone else.

You know you're getting into geezer country because you complain about all this stuff. But hell, the geezers had something to complain about, back in the day. Your grandfather used to say that he missed the strangest things, and now you do too.

You miss prank phone calls. The perfect kind. The kind that allowed you to call some random stranger and ask him about his refrigerator. The kind that allowed your hormone-fueled self practice the dirty talk you would later inflict on countless women at the most intimate moments.

You try to tell yourself that it doesn't matter, it's one of those things you've given up because you're an adult. After all, you don't light farts any more either.

But you know you're lying to yourself. You'd put a match to your gaseous hind end if you weren't so afraid of ending up in the emergency room. And you'd make a prank call if you could just figure out how to do it anonymously.

After all, you were once the master of the prank call. At least in your own mind.

Which was the only place it ever really counted.

Ray Vukcevich has been publishing stories for decades in many of the top magazines. And back in the first incarnation of this magazine, I was lucky to get some of Ray's wonderful and very twisted short stories.

And this one out-twists most of Ray's stories. Trust me, you can't get ants staggering in a drunk conga line and not have a twisted story. Enjoy.

Human Subjects

Ray Vukcevich

AFTER I'D EATEN her lamb chops and mashed potatoes and briefly boiled broccoli, I decided it was time to spill the beans.

"Evangeline," I said. "Everyone is a science project."

She dabbed delicately at the corners of her mouth with her napkin and then looked up at me with startling blue eyes. Whenever Evangeline looks at me, really looks, I'm split into who knows how many pieces, and I become the particle or the wave in the classic double-slit experiment of quantum mechanics.

I had to glance away or lose my train of thought.

She'd served dinner in the kitchen, which meant either she'd soon pour the wine and ask me to spend the night or she'd hold open the front door and lean in for a peck on the cheek as I left. I wanted to delay her decision. Until she picked one, I was both delighted and disappointed at the same time.

"We all have aliens watching us," I said, "studying us, poking and stimulating us, running experiments. I have an alien. You have an alien. Everyone on Earth has an alien."

"Oh, come on," she said. "All of us? Why so many?"

"Well, consider the size of the universe," I said, "and consider what good experimental animals we make. We're in big demand. Actually, there's a shortage of human subjects, which explains our recent population explosion."

"And you know all this exactly how?"

Okay. This was the moment of truth. I could tell her and if she believed me, our relationship might move up to the next level. Or I could tell her and she might not believe me and our relationship would move back down a level. Up or down.

Or I could just laugh it off, but I was pretty sure down that road waited a peck on the cheek. I took a deep and dramatic breath.

"I know these facts because my alien wants me to know them," I said. "Me knowing exactly what's going on is his project. He tells me how the universe works and then steps back to watch the fireworks. Will I make a hat out of aluminum foil? Will someone throw a butterfly net over me? Maybe I'll end up in a cave on the outskirts of town eating squirrels. Anything might happen, and my alien likes to watch."

"Is he watching now?" she asked.

There was something desperate or frightened or maybe pleading in the quiet way she asked that question and then turned her face down to her plate. I got up and took my chair around the table and put it beside her and sat down and took her hands and said, "Yes, he's right over there by the refrigerator."

She looked at the refrigerator, and then she looked back at me. "I don't see him."

"I think I'm the only one who can see him. Like I said, me seeing him is part of his project. But if you look closely you'll see the tiny ants that are feeding on the invisible slime that drips from his body."

"I've always had ants," she said. "Sometimes I think maybe this house is one big ant colony and I'm living inside it."

"Yes, but these are different," I said. "My alien's slime is intoxicating to ants. Look. Look. See how they stumble away in ragged little conga lines?"

"Yes!" she said. "I do see that. Well, aliens would explain a lot of things around here."

I squeezed her hands. "Not just the ants?"

"No," she said. "Something else."

"Tell me."

"Well, lately," she said. "I've had this unnatural urge to shine my big flashlight out of the kitchen window into the backyard at night."

"Just shine it?" I asked. "Are you looking for something? Do you sweep the landscape?"

I could feel her trembling a little, and there was a thin line of sweat on her upper lip.

"No," she said. "I flick it on and off into the darkness. Off and on. On and off. Sometimes I do it for hours. If you weren't here tonight, I'd be doing it right now."

"What happens when you do it?" I asked.

She looked away from me again. "I get this delicious tingling feeling all over my body."

I didn't know what to say to that. Ours is not to know the science behind the projects our aliens perform on us.

The silence must have gone on too long for her. "Sometimes it lasts for hours," she said.

"Some kind of reinforcement," I said.

"What?"

"Your alien," I said. "He must be conditioning you to shine your big flashlight out the kitchen window at night."

"But why?"

"Let's see if we can figure it out," I said. "Do you just turn the flashlight on and off randomly and then you get the tingling?"

"Funny," she said, "that's the way it worked at first, but now I have to be very deliberate in my turning it on and off to get the desired effect."

"Deliberate?"

"That's the best way I can put it," she said. "I turn it on and wait a moment then turn it off and wait and then turn it on again."

"Those moments are of different lengths?"

"Why, yes," she said. "It works a lot better if there are long and short periods of light and darkness."

"Morse code?"

"Hey! Maybe," she said. "I hadn't thought of that. I wonder what I'm saying to whatever's out in the backyard?"

"You don't know Morse code?"

"No. Of course, I don't know Morse code. Who knows Morse code these days?"

"As it happens," I said. "I know Morse code. I did ham radio as a kid."

"Of course, you did," she said.

"Look," I said. "Why don't I go out in the backyard, and you do your flashlight routine, and I see if I can decode the dots and dashes and then tell you what you're saying?"

"I'm not sure I want you to see me like that," she said.

"Like that?"

"Tingly."

Was she saying I'd never seen her all tingly before? I chose to think she didn't mean that. She was talking about her flashlight and her alien and nothing more.

"Don't worry about it," I said. "I'll be outside anyway."

I let go of her hands and stood up.

A moment later, she got up, too. She put her hands on my shoulders and pulled me in for a quick hug, just a squeeze, really. There was a warm and dizzy smell of anticipation radiating from her.

"Okay." She turned away and moved toward the refrigerator. My alien stepped aside for her, but that turned out to be unnecessary, because she was actually heading for the big flashlight on the counter between the kitchen sink and the refrigerator. It was the perfect spot for the flashlight if you wanted it to be always within easy reach of the window over the sink.

She grabbed the flashlight and stood at the sink with her back to me. If I expected some kind of sign that we should begin, she was not the one to provide it. She just waited for me to make the next move.

So I moved to the back door and opened it and stepped out on to the porch or maybe you'd call it a stoop. It was somewhere in between because while it was covered and you could stand there without getting wet in the rain, it wasn't big enough to lounge around in a lawn chair drinking lemonade.

Evangeline had a generous backyard with a tall wooden fence at the back and five big trees scattered about. Tonight they were hulking shadows, but I already knew they were two apple trees, a pear tree, and a couple of nut trees. I also knew just where the badminton net was, because one night I'd run right into it like a fly into a spider web. A swing made out of a tire hung from one of the nut trees.

I could see the broken trampoline. I remembered when it broke, and Evangeline tumbled off onto the ground and hurt her shoulder. She never did get the trampoline fixed after that. Whenever I mentioned it, she'd say, "And it was such good exercise!" She was permanently spooked when it came to bouncing on a trampoline.

I positioned myself to one side of the trampoline so I would be directly in front of the kitchen window, not so close I'd be blinded by Evangeline's light, but not so far she couldn't hear me if I had things to shout to her.

And there she was peering through the window. I was pretty sure she couldn't see me, but I waved anyway. She just kept peering.

"Go ahead," I shouted. "I'm ready."

She pulled back and then a moment later appeared again with the flashlight. Nothing else happened for a long time. She just stood there pointing the flashlight out at me. I thought maybe she'd forgotten what we were up to, and I was about to shout again when she made her first flash. Just one flash and then nothing. I had no way of knowing if that first one was a dot or a dash until I had others for comparison.

A few moments passed and then there was a series of flashes.

Short short short long.

Dot dot dot dash.

The letter V?

Would she spell my name?

No. She sent the same series again, but this time aimed a little to the left. Short short short long. Then she did it again only aimed a little to the right, and it hit me she was doing the opening notes of Beethoven's fifth symphony.

Ba ba ba Boom!

The oddly named "Fate motif."

She grabbed the theme and ran with it, and I got lost. I couldn't tell if she was sending letters or just playing the music. Horn calls and modulating bridges. A musical statement of purpose I could not interpret. The flashlight beam played all over the backyard in a frenzy pulling the trees and swing and oh look a birdbath in the rock garden from the darkness and then abandoning them. The trampoline. The badminton net with birds (surely not real birds) stuck into it like notes on a staff.

C minor wrestled with C major until one of them came out on top victorious.

It was glorious.

The flashlight flickered out and there was a deep quiet in the darkness.

Then she directed the beam at my face and began sending slowly, as if she were making an extreme effort to communicate with someone who could not keep up with her.

"Evangeline doesn't realize I'm talking to you," she signaled.

It was true she didn't even seem to be paying attention to what was happening out the window. Her eyes were closed and she was swaying slowly from side to side. There was a dreamy smile on her face.

"Who are you?" I shouted.

"Evangeline's alien, of course," she signaled.

But why would Evangeline's alien be talking to me? Did this mean my alien was collaborating? Was there some kind of joint experiment going on with Evangeline and me?

"What do you want?" I shouted.

"I want to know you," Evangeline's alien signaled. "I want you to come clean with me, tell me who you are, spill your guts, tell me what you're feeling."

"I feel watched," I shouted. "Everything I do is being recorded by aliens!"

"No," she signaled. "How do you feel about Evangeline?"

Hey, wait a minute!

I took a few steps closer to get a better look at her. But it was easy to see she was somewhere else. Besides which, it was too much to believe that Evangeline had learned Morse code for this occasion. How would she know the evening would progress to this point? No, I knew I could be mistaken, but I was pretty sure I really was talking to her alien. Or at least some alien. I suddenly suspected this could all be a trick of my own alien.

"How would I know how I feel about her?" This question was designed to confuse my alien. I hoped he was flipping through his notes trying to figure out if humans are supposed to be able to know how they feel about one another.

In point of fact, however, maybe I didn't know how I felt. No, that wasn't quite right. I did know how I felt, but I couldn't put it into words.

"Come on," Evangeline's alien signaled. "Quit stalling. Cough it up. Step up to the plate. Blurt it out!"

"This is too much pressure!" I shouted.

"Oh, never mind," she signaled.

The flashlight went dead.

It suddenly hit me that whatever was going on here might have nothing to do with the aliens and their worldwide science projects. I saw clearly that this could be the most important turning point in my life.

"Wait!" I shouted. "I'm crazy about her! She's a symphony, all lightening and thunder and wind, but then she's warm rain and flowers blooming and birds singing! I can't go more than a few minutes without thinking about her, and I can't stop smiling while I'm thinking about her, but then I feel afraid that she'll suddenly snap out of it and come to her senses and realize she doesn't even like me. I'm afraid she'll tell me to just go away."

The flashlight came on again.

Ba ba ba boom!

"Okay," she signaled. "You can come back in."

Now, for something very different, original, and very powerful, in a high-speed dryer sort of way. In Lisa Silverthorne's third story in these pages, she shows how even the most unlikely person can save the world from alien invasion.

This original story will have you laughing and shaking your head at the imagination of it all as only a Lisa story can do. She is, without a doubt, one of the most powerful short fiction writers working today, and I always feel lucky to have her stories in these pages.

Planet Suds and the Sockpocalypse

Lisa Silverthorne

FOUND ANOTHER ALIEN in my sock drawer. For reals. I'm tellin' you, it's the fucking Sockpocalypse.

Okay, I'll admit I bogarted a blunt beforehand, but don't just dismiss me as some baked, wise-ass college kid tryin' to get outta class or something. Finals are comin' up fast, so hear me out. Damn, dudes, don't you get it? I'm trying to save the fucking world here, so get past the sock drawer already. As a guy the 'rents named Justin Saves and ~~flunking~~ majoring in Physics, I've gotta at least try, y'know? Or at least make sure somebody here on earth knows about them—and their plot to take over humanity. One unmatched sock at a time.

And it all started at Planet Suds Laundromat and Sushi Bar.

The brick and glass laundromat/sushi bar is just across the river from campus. Open 24/7, it's this beacon of gold light that glints off the stainless steel washers and dryers lining both ends of the squat, one-story building and lights up two city blocks. Several glass tables and silver chairs set in the middle of the room, between the washers and dryers and there are vending machines on both sides containing various laundry supplies. A bottle of window cleaner sits on the window sill, glowing almost green beside the vending machine. All white walls, concrete floors, and stainless steel. And light. Lots of light.

The place smells like old powdered detergent, ammonia, and too many dryer sheets, but the free WiFi and two-dollar California and tuna rolls from the dingy snack bar in the back makes up for it—if you like gas station sushi. Anyway, the place is always warm and cozy during the frigid, single-digit temps around the Midwest in January.

I'm getting to the aliens, so pass the blunt and chill, dudes.

So two weeks ago, I'm at Planet Suds around 1 a.m. (like I am every weekend), trying to learn physics while doing my laundry without an issue—whether I was baked or not (I'm not a dick. I took the bus, okay?) While I'm crushing brain cells, the first sneaky, little alien bastards infiltrate my laundry.

Starting with my favorite gray argyle socks. Hey, I like argyles, so don't judge me.

Fresh out of the dryer, the argyle pattern's just a little bit off when I lay them on the table. And the once soft microfiber feels scratchier than I remember—even with the dryer sheet. I put them on because my feet are fuckin' frozen…and like I said, the argyles are my favorite pair.

The socks and my feet start burning like Austraila (too soon?).

I peel off the socks and toss them into my green plastic laundry basket, wondering if I'm allergic to the detergent or something. I turn back to folding equations and the rest of my clothes.

That's when I see this woman. Two tables over.

She's here almost every time I am. Thin, middle-aged, about five feet tall with a blond helmet of hair that never moves as she loads a washer with an armload of clothes, dryers buzzing left and right. I always see her in the same purple dress and black leggings, like it's the only outfit she owns. She always smells like sushi because she usually gobbles down a dozen of those faux rolls from the snack bar. And I never see her fuckin' chew them.

She seems to stare through me, even on the odd occasion I say hi or whatever. It's like she's on a mission or something, like laundry's her motherfuckin' job. She runs two washers and dryers at the same time, washing a mountain of clothes and lots of socks. LOTS. OF. SOCKS. Like a whole fuck-ton of them. In every color and style.

I finish the last of my tuna roll, a final dab of wasabi burning my tongue, and toss the wrappers into a gray, round trash can against one of the tables. I start loading my laundry basket.

But I can't erase the memory of what I see when I glance up at the woman. The dryer with the socks stops turning and begins to buzz, but those socks are jumping and hopping around like worms in hot ashes, as my beautiful mom used to say.

Helmet Hair opens the dryer door. Those fuckers march out in single file and pair up, but only about half the load of socks is still there. The rest have literally disappeared before my eyes.

Where'd they go? How'd they disappear like that—much less march out on their own? They're fucking socks!

"Are you all right?" asks a feminine voice.

I jerk my head up. There stands Helmet Hair in front of me, hands on hips, staring at me like I'd just set myself on fire.

"What?" I stare into her dark, bulgy Bette Davis eyes, so blank and emotionless that they scare the living shit out of me. Like black holes eating all the light in the room. And my soul.

Hell, sharks show more emotion than this bitch.

Overhead fluorescent lights stretch my stark shadow toward the front door that's behind me, like it's trying to tell me to get the fuck out of there. Now. I'm talkin' some serious fight or flight shit here.

Then I see that Helmet Hair isn't giving off a shadow. Not even a thin gray line. It's like the light is passing right through her or something, like she's in two places at once. A quantum event right out of Whitehead's Epochal Theory of Time.

Out the corner of my eye, something skitters across the concrete floor. I turn, searching for the movement, but it's disappeared, like I'm imagining it.

I turn back to Helmet Hair and she's so close I smell a strong, sweet scent, like a dryer sheet and a cheap perfume achieved fusion in those stainless steel dryers. I'm a foot taller than this woman, but she's not a bit intimidated by some random college dude. Especially one with a physics book.

Her voice is a soprano hiss that vibrates in my ears, but her lips don't move like some fucking android. "It's too late to stop it, you know."

"Stop what?" I snap, staring wide-eyed at her.

"Us," she says with the creepiest fucking smile.

Okay, I didn't need my shadow to signal again that I should be leaving. I grab my textbook and laundry basket and nope the fuck outta there.

At the time, I didn't know I was carrying a basketful of aliens back to my studio apartment. It was little more than a bed, blue couch, old chestnut dresser, and particle board desk with a small black fridge and microwave. A white, long, and narrow basement apartment with a view of the sidewalk. The place smelled like fresh paint and a hint of mildew, the oak hardwood floors slick and shiny.

Every night after that at 3 a.m., a rattling sound wakes me up. With phone in hand as a flashlight, I creep over to the dresser that's shaking like a Florida freshman. Yeah, Midwest winters are brutal here.

Gathering my nerve, I yank open the sock drawer. All my socks are unpaired and skittering around the drawer like scorpions. I slam the drawer shut, unable to breathe for a moment.

I take a breath. Hold it. Let it go. Another. And another. Like I'm practicing for the fucking ganja Olympics.

Like I'm holding a rattlesnake, I slowly and gently open the drawer again. This time, the socks are balled together in pairs again. Except none of them is with the correct color or pattern.

Close and reopen. All of them are paired correctly again. What. The. Fuck.

With temperatures below zero, I have to wear socks to class. But every pair I put on that week ends up burning and stinging until I have to take them off.

Okay, I'll admit to also doing some Molly and even a little acid (Once, okay? For science.), but all of that pales to the Sockpocalypse in my sock drawer. Fed up, I throw all my socks into the dirty clothes and buy new detergent (hey, it's worth a shot, right?). Then I head to Planet Suds. For a good old fashioned alien showdown. If nothing else, I'll stream it on my phone to the interwebs and die famous as the dude that made first contact with the fucking aliens. So people know what's happening.

As soon as I walk into the laundromat, green plastic laundry basket under my arm, I see Helmet Hair in her same spot with piles of laundry, most of it socks.

Why fucking socks???

I set my laundry on a table and toss in a capful of the fragrance-free, hypoallergenic detergent I'd bought into the nearest washer. I throw in the whole load and close the door. Light glints off the stainless steel as I push the start button. The washer swishes to life.

My skin crawls like beetles marching across it. I turn, feeling a presence behind me.

Helmet Hair is at my shoulder. I turn, staring down at her.

She steps past me to the washer beside mine and takes out a load of socks. And tosses it in the nearest dryer. When she hits the start button, it roars like a jet engine, the barrel turning so fast it looks like a hadron collider. I couldn't hear myself shout now.

What the fuck's happening?

After it runs its cycle, the racing dryer stops and buzzes. I can't help myself. I have to see what's inside after all that noise. I open the door and bend forward, seeing stars inside the dark compartment. Forming what looks like a spiral galaxy.

All the socks are gone.

"What are you doing?" Helmet Hair shouts. It's the first emotion I've heard from her. "Stay back!"

That's when I feel the pull.

Somehow, this bitch has created a wormhole right inside this fucking dryer like it was a star chamber or something.

The last thing I see is her mouth falling open, shouting *stop* as the wormhole drags me into its gravity well, shooting me toward a smear of stars in the darkness.

***

WHEN THE LIGHT returns, I'm on the ground on my back, staring up at an unfamiliar night sky with two moons and auroras twisting across the starlight in shades of blue and fucking purple. But I can breathe the air. And damn, is this place hot! Like Hell's some ski resort where they're all wearing fucking parkas and self-immolating to keep warm.

I try to sit up, but can't. That's when I notice movement in the scraggly bluish grass dotting what looks like pink sand beneath me. Around me, tall stands of blue and red vegetation, looking plump and smooth like succulents, fans out in the dark toward some distant white lights. Tall, thin spires (buildings? ships?) stretch high into the sky, lit with gold light as a stream of blue and red lights circles overhead. It's a motherfuckin' alien empire!

The air is July hot, like sidewalk egg-cooking in the Midwest. I'm talking bake cookies on your car's dashboard kind of heat. A breeze blows a fuck-ton of white petals across my face. The air smells sweet, like adding sugar to your Fruit Loops sweet. Then I feel the restraints across my chest and legs, winding around my wrists and ankles.

Dozens of little feet march up the legs of my jeans and up the zipper of my blue hoodie, stopping at mid-zip. Little cigar-shaped bodies that pulse with light through skin that looks like dollar store plastic wrap. Dozens of them huddle together and they begin to change form until I'm staring at an exact fucking replica of my navy-blue hoodie. Two others shift into a pair of white and gray socks that match the pair I'm wearing. Two more change into my red Chuck Taylor high-tops.

"What the fuck, little dudes? Why do you change into laundry?" I ask.

Where do the socks even go?

They chitter and shake, but I don't speak fucking alien Morse code or whatever language they call these clicks and chirrs.

"It's all part of the plan," says a voice behind me.

I can't turn my head, but I recognize Helmet Hair's voice. I hear the distant whir of something behind her, whispering in the background. In a moment, she's towering over me. All five fucking feet of her.

"What plan? To takeover Planet Suds and all the socks in the Twin Cities?" I glare at her. "Besides that, I want my favorite pair of fucking socks back! The ones these little douchebags ruined."

As I stare into her empty eyes, her body begins to change. Deflating, almost, as her skin turns translucent like more plastic wrap. Until I realize that she's completely shed her human skin. Like a fucking lizard molting in the desert. Fuuuuuuccckkk.

I want to scream, but I can't get sound out of my dry, clamped throat.

She takes her deflated human body (topped with blond helmet hair), a.k.a. human suit, and shakes it out like a wet rain slicker, revealing a taller, thinner version of the little cigar-shaped aliens skittering across my stomach.

"At last, I can breathe," she cries out, stretching her clear body into a hundred centipede-like appendages that ooze out like cactus needles, then retract again. Like some motherfucking Cthulhu alien nightmare, she reaches an appendage out to my face. It's cold and sticky like sunburn gel. All I can think about is horking up all the California rolls I'd eaten tonight.

"What the hell are you?" I shout at her.

"I'm one of the commanders of the attack forces," she says in a tinny, higher pitched tone than she's had as Helmet Hair.

Her head is more like Cthulhu Hair now with stringy, clear dreads swaying in the scorching breeze. She motions with several fluid appendages that stretch toward the aliens on my stomach. I can still hear that quiet, whispering whir behind her, steady like a ceiling fan.

"They shift shape into your strange coverings so you will attach them to your bodies. Once against your skin, they transfer our genetic materials into the hosts through unicellular organisms."

"Like fucking bacteria?"

"Yes, these organisms are already present. We hijack them with a new payload and invade. They combine strings of what you might call genetic code. The strings unite into our finished code and develop into another soldier."

Okay, I've seen all those horror movies with fucking aliens bursting out of people's heads and chests.

"You're saying you grow inside of us? Like a fucking tape worm or something?"

"Your warm bodies are perfect incubation chambers for our reproduction," says Cthulhu Hair.

"What happens after that?" I ask, knowing full well the answer.

"Most explode. None survive, if that's what you are asking," she says in a squeaky tone.

I have to stop this somehow. Slow them down at least—something.

"The place of Suds brings them through from our home world to yours."

Shit! Planet Suds and Sushi Bar is a front for alien invasion! Who knew? And this Cthulhu hair bitch is beaming these little fuckers into every laundry basket where they shift into harmless looking socks that implant body-exploding aliens inside us. To jump out later like a stripper from a fucking cake.

"Now, be a good little human and put on the nice garment. It'll all be over soon. I promise."

Tied down, I can't do anything. I have to Bogart like it's my turn at the bong.

"How do you expect me to try on your little friends when I can't even move?"

Cthulhu Hair cocks her head a moment, dreadlocks swaying like Bob Marley and the Wailers at GanjaFest. Then she clicks and chirrs with shrill high notes until I feel the restraints fall away from my body. All of them.

With careful movements, I sit up and then crouch as the shapeshifted aliens slouch against my Chuck Taylors, still an exact replica (mostly exact) of my hoodie. I pick up the alien hoodie and stand up.

I move around as I fumble with the sleeve that's a little too narrow, still trying to Bogart for time.

"Sleeves are too tight," I say to Cthulhu Hair.

As she emits another series of clicks and trills, I glance past her, still hearing that faint whirring sound.

The wormhole! Dumb alien bitch left it open.

I pace as the aliens shift form again, enlarging the hoodie sleeves.

"Now, put it on please," says Cthulhu Hair, "before we lose patience."

So, I stagger around, pretending that the sleeves are still too tight until I'm standing in front of Cthulhu Hair. I take hold of the hoodie creature with both hands. When I'm no more than an inch away from her, I fling the hoodie aliens into her face and bolt toward the wormhole still open behind her.

I feel like strained fucking spaghetti as I shoot past stars and asteroids until everything goes dark.

When my vision clears, I'm on the cold concrete floor of Planet Suds, right beside the table with my laundry basket. And one uneaten tuna roll.

As I get to my feet, the dryer behind me spins up like a fucking a '60s Shelby Mustang with Paxton supercharger. The whole fucking alien planet's probably hot on my ass right now.

Then I get an idea. So I run to the vending machine and buy a small detergent-sized bottle, about the size of a beer bottle. I also take the bottle of window cleaner. I wrestle with the small bottle's safety cap until I flick it off. With it open now, I run back to the dryer with the small bottle and the larger bottle of window cleaner.

As I throw open the door, stars are already forming in the dark dryer's chamber. I pour the window cleaner into the dryer and then pour the small bottle of pure bleach inside.

I slam the door shut and hold it closed as the dryer revs up again, spinning like a motherfucking cement mixer.

I watch as the first aliens appear in the dryer. They pound against the glass as the ammonia and bleach combine into chlorine gas. Choking the life out of them. Finally, Cthulhu Hair appears inside the chamber.

"Suck on chlorine gas, bitch," I say with a growl as the door rocks against my hands.

With all my strength, I hold that fucking door closed until Cthulhu Hair collapses. And doesn't move again.

I let the dryer cycle so it will vent out the chlorine gas from the building—and the alien remains. When it's done, I dump everything in my laundry basket into a washer. I buy another bottle of bleach and pour in some window cleaner. I close the lid and let everything set for a couple of minutes before I turn on the washer.

When the wash finishes, I put the clothes into a different dryer. As my bleached-out clothes dry, I leave my coat on the chair and run outside, into the six degree temperature. Wind chill's making it thirteen below zero. I shuck off my hoodie, my T-shirt, socks, and jeans.

Down to my blue boxers and Chuck Taylor's, like I'm in the final stages of hypothermia, I pace in the cold until the intense shivering sets in and my teeth chatter like a fucking chipmunk. Pushing onward, I keep pacing until my shivering stops. Only then do I put my clothes back on and go inside, hoping the drop in body temperature is enough to kill anything incubating like a fucking vampire inside me. I'll take a cold shower later. It'll be like nuking them from orbit.

After the dryer stops, I put on my coat and head back to my apartment with my chlorine-gassed clothes to burn every pair of socks I own—it's the only way to be sure—and buy some new ones online, including a new pair of gray argyles. And change my major from physics to chemistry.

So, dudes, please—check your sock drawers. Like I said before, my folks didn't name me Justin Saves for nothing, so I feel obligated to do my part to save humanity from this alien invasion. And socks. I have no idea how many of those shapeshifting alien fuckers are still loose in the Twin Cities or on campus. But don't say I didn't warn you about Planet Suds or the Sockpocalypse. Burn any unmatched socks in your sock drawer fast. Immediately. Otherwise, don't blame me if one of those alien fuckers bursts through your chest the night before finals. Now, pass me that blunt, willya?

This original story is just the first in a series of wonderful mystery stories that will be in the next few issues of this magazine from R.W. Wallace.

But this story (and the ones to follow) are not like any standard mystery. The detective is a ghost, limited to his own cemetery helping other ghosts move on by solving their murders. In other words, the detective is locked in a confined space with no tools, trying to help a victim discover what happened to them.

Great writing and some of the most innovative plotting I have seen in a long time. A wonderful series to be in these pages. Enjoy.

Just Desserts

R.W. Wallace

WE HEAR THE SCREAMS as soon as the group exits the church.

"I think this one's for you, Robert," Clothilde says. She's sitting on top of her tombstone, the plainest slab of stone in the whole graveyard, with only her first name and a date of death. No birthday, no last name, no citation or drawings of angels. She's one of the greatest mysteries this place has, but she won't let me investigate. Every attempt I've made to ask her about her life has been rebuffed, sometimes nicely, sometimes not so much. She's been dead for twenty-five years, but she'll always be a teenager at heart.

Today she's wearing high-waisted jeans that stop just above her ankle and a white top that would have shown the straps of her bra if she'd been wearing one. Her dangling feet are covered in a pair of Converse, worn on the heel and one of the laces torn on her right foot. There's no telling the color—the dead only wear shades of gray.

We haven't had many new arrivals lately. The only people to die were old ladies with no reason to hang around after the funeral. When you've known for years that your time is almost up, you get your shit together and make sure there are no loose ends.

It's those of us who are taken by surprise who linger.

Of course, it's a good thing when someone goes straight to the afterlife. None of us wish suffering on another human being—or human ghost in this case—but it does get a little dull at times. There's only so much you can do to occupy your time when you're stuck within the confines of your cemetery and it's the middle of winter so the number of visitors is at a minimum.

Today, though, we have a new arrival.

It's not easy coming to grips with being dead when you didn't expect it, didn't see it coming. It's a bit of a shock, to put it mildly.

Personally, I pounded on my casket for a week before realizing my fists didn't have any effect on the sturdy wood. Nor did they make any sound. My voice didn't echo like it should have.

Only when I calmed down—if I can really call it that—did I look around in the small space I occupied. And realize I was lying next to my own dead body.

I was laid out on white sheets, wearing my next best suit—the best one would be full of holes to match the ones on my body—my hands folded over my stomach and my expression relaxed in a way I'd never seen it before.

I'm not particularly bright, so it took me another day to accept the fact that I was dead and had apparently become a ghost.

That's when the coffin released me. The cemetery has been my home ever since.

As the funeral procession advances down the path from the church, my fellow ghosts gather next to me. We always wait for the new arrivals by the hole in the ground that will be their last resting place. We could have listened in at the church door and followed the procession, but whenever a ghost touches a human, there can be a form of interaction, and we don't want to freak out the bereaved any more than they already are.

So we observe the funerals from behind the priest, in the trees, from the top of the tombs, watch the coffin lowered into the ground, and settle in to wait to see if a new companion would join us.

There isn't really any doubt about this one being a keeper.

The screams are so loud it would have been impossible for us to hear each other speak. The banging on the coffin is strong, panicked, and unrelenting. I can't make out any words, only pure, unadulterated panic.

I want to go over and calm her down, tell her it's going to be okay.

But as long as she hasn't been released from the coffin, there's nothing I can do. She won't hear me.

And it's not going to be okay.

She's dead and she wasn't ready.

A lot of people have come to see her off. I'm guessing close to a hundred, which for a little town like this is quite impressive. At the front are a couple in their forties who I'm going to assume are her parents. A couple of grandparents. Two boys who might be brothers. Behind them, a group I'm going to qualify as family. There's a large majority of blonds, with strong jaws and wide shoulders. The darker-haired or darker-skinned ones have probably married in.

Slightly to the side, a mass of young people. Probably early twenties, and about eighty-percent female. The friends.

Some are crying, some seem to not understand what's going on. Probably the first time they bury someone they know that's not a grandparent. One guy at the back leans close to the guy next to him to say something and receives an extremely stern and accusing stare in return. Not the time for a joke, my man.

I don't listen to what the priest says. It's all to soothe the family and friends, and won't have any interesting information for me.

I'm studying the mourners.

More than half of all murders are done by a family member. Add in the large group of friends and the probability of the murderer being in view is pretty darn high.

Judging by the screams coming from the coffin, the probability of her being a murder victim are also pretty darn high.

I sidle over to eavesdrop on a whispered conversation on the family side of the group. I'm going to guess cousins. One blond woman in her twenties is speaking into the ear of a second even blonder one.

"I can't believe her mom made such a big deal out of keeping it hidden that she killed herself," she whispers. "I mean, come on, is her image really that important? She can't own up to her daughter taking her own life?"

I glance in direction of the coffin with a frown. Suicide?

"It's not just the image thing," the second woman whispers back. "Julie has always been very involved in the church. If it's suicide, her daughter can't be buried in the cemetery."

Which is exactly why we have so few suicides in here. *Could* a ghost be that panicked after waking up from her own suicide? Shouldn't the situation be a tad more expected?

People who are aware that they are in mortal danger don't usually need much time to accept what happened and move on. A couple of years ago we had a soldier who was killed in Afghanistan. He only lingered long enough to say goodbye to his girlfriend then disappeared in a puff of smoke.

"Well," says the first one, "luckily, falling off a bridge with no witnesses isn't automatically ruled as a suicide. So here we are."

I move on, listening to people saying they don't understand how it's possible, the service was beautiful, the mother had made an excellent choice for the casket, the soccer game starts in an hour and a half, will they be able to watch it?

That last one is from the guy making the inappropriate comment or joke earlier, and it earns him the same look from his neighbor. "Seriously, Joss. I know this isn't your scene, but can you at least just shut up?"

Joss the jokester shuts up, clamping his lips shut as if he wishes they could be glued together. Despite the cold, a bead of sweat trickles down along his hairline, past his ear, and into his shirt.

If he's a talker, I'm guessing we'll see him again. Possibly for a confession.

As the casket is lowered into the ground, I stand next to the guy I'm assuming is the husband or boyfriend. He's part of the friend group, but also right next to the parents. His eyes are red and a sob escapes on each breath. Arms hanging limply by his sides, twitching now and then.

He seems genuinely upset.

At least he doesn't have to hear the screams.

***

SHE'S STILL SCREAMING when her talkative and inappropriate jokester friend drops by two days later.

I'm visiting Clothilde, like I usually do when I'm on the lookout for visitors. None of us understand how she managed to afford a place in this cemetery in the first place, what with the no name, no family, no mourners thing, but at least there's a certain "logic" to hers being the least popular spot, right next to the trash by the exit.

The main entrance is on the other side, by the church, but that's not where the interesting visitors come through.

"So how long do you think she'll keep this up?" Clothilde asks as she lounges on the ground, right on top of where her casket lies six feet below. Her hands folded behind her head and her ankles crossed, she stares dreamily at the two or three clouds clotting the painfully blue winter sky.

"I don't know," I reply. "Not much we can do about it. She'll just have to get it out of her system." I'm sitting with my back against her tombstone, arms around my bent knees, and my chin on my knees. I'd put my hands over my ears if I thought it would do any good.

Even if we do this regularly, it still grates on the nerves to hear someone screaming in panic from waking up in a coffin for several days on end.

Clothilde grunts and blows at a fly zipping around her nose. The fly careens off course.

"We can't all be like you," I say. "Accepting that you're dead isn't easy for anyone."

"It is if you were as good as dead before."

Clothilde tends to make cryptic and worrisome comments like this. There's no point in asking her to elaborate, she'll only clam up. But I take note of everything. One day, maybe, I'll understand where she came from.

The rusty hinges of the iron grate squeal and the jokester comes through. He looks more at ease in a pair of jeans and a thick leather jacket than he did in a suit two days ago, but there are dark circles under his eyes and his hair doesn't look like it's seen shampoo or a comb since the funeral.

He looks left and right, making sure he's alone—it's half past ten on a Wednesday night, of course he's alone—before making a beeline for the new grave.

"I'm going to listen in," I say as I jump up and follow. "You coming?"

Clothilde sighs. "Guess so." She rolls up into an upright position with more grace than a dancer. "It'll take my mind off the screaming. Maybe."

The jokester stands at the limit between grass and dirt, his tear-filled eyes on the wooden cross with "Florence Bernard" penciled in. Just as I reach him, he falls to his knees in the dirt and the air goes out of his lungs in a *whoosh*.

He leans forward, shoving his hands into the black earth. His position makes me think of praying Muslims. But he's not talking to a deity. He's talking to the girl who's still screaming, who still hasn't accepted her fate.

"I'm so sorry," he sobs. "It's all my fault. I'm so, so sorry."

Ah. A confession.

Although I don't have the satisfaction of having worked to find the culprit, at least I can tell the girl about it when she comes out. Perhaps it will be enough to allow her to move on immediately.

"I told them, Flo," the man continues, his face only millimeters from touching the dirt. "I told them who did it, but they didn't believe me. Two different police officers and they told me to take a hike. I didn't even make a joke!"

He sobs for a couple of minutes. His hands start to shake, probably from the biting cold, but he leaves them buried.

"This is why I always make the jokes, Flo. Nobody ever takes me seriously, so I might as well make it look like it's on purpose. You were the only one to ever really listen to me. And now you're dead because of that *bastard*!" A fist escapes the dirt and he slams it into the ground several times, gasps escaping as his body attempts to sob and breathe at the same time.

Okay, so maybe he's not the killer. It would be really helpful if he could give me a name, though. This is where being a ghost is really a drag—my suspects can't hear my questions.

"Everybody can see how much he loved her." He's quoting someone, complete with dirty fingers slashing quote marks in the air. "He'd never lay a hand on her. Can't you see how torn up he is? Of *course* he's torn up! He bloody killed you! He no longer has his golden goose!"

He sits back on his haunches and runs his hands through his hair. I wince in sympathy and hope he's planned on taking a shower soon.

I also wish he'd give me a *name*.

The man calms down. He pats the dirt back into place, as if having a perfectly smooth mound of dirt is Flo's greatest preoccupation at the moment.

"You shouldn't have done it," he says, his voice so low I can hardly hear him over his friend's screams. "We were *fine* as just friends. Worked out real well. You had your successful fiancé, the great job, the white picket fence in view. Everything you and your father had planned for."

He sits back on his heels. "Shouldn't have thrown it all away, Flo. I'd rather have had you for a friend than not have you at all."

Okay. Moving the fiancé up to the top of the list of suspects.

The friend—lover?—stays for over an hour, crying silently on the grave.

The screams from below continue.

***

IT TAKES HER ten days to come to terms with it. I'd say she's slow, but I was no better.

When the screams stop on the eighth day, I set up camp on top of her grave, right in front of the wooden cross, waiting for her to show her face. I'm a little leery of what I'll see.

I've seen quite a few horrors since I arrived in this cemetery, not to mention while I was alive, but it still affects me. If she died in the water, the question is how long it took before she was found. Some ghosts retain the form they had while they lived. A few of the senile ones are lucky enough to take a younger form of their bodies since it's all they can remember.

And some, the ones who stay dead for too long before becoming ghosts, walk around with cut up or bloated or maimed bodies, reminding everyone of their violent demise.

Florence, luckily, has retained the body from before she ended up in the river.

At sunset, her head breaks through the mound of dirt first, followed by two hands. She brings her arms up above her head, then let them fall back down, watching how they aren't affected by the dirt.

She jerks when she sees me sitting on the ground in front of her, but doesn't seem to tag me as a threat. "I'm a ghost," she says. It's a mixture of a question and a challenge, letting me decide if I want to answer or be scared.

"I know," I reply. "So am I."

She studies me closer, takes in the lack of color, the slight transparency that's more obvious during the day, my out-of-date fashion sense. She nods.

She waves her hands through the dirt again. "How come you're sitting on top of the ground and I'm stuck inside it? What am I even standing on? The coffin?" Her voice breaks on the last word.

"You're probably on the coffin, yes." I

stand up and offer her a hand. "You can climb out on your own if you want, but I'm more than happy to help."

She eyes my hand, trying to decide if she can trust me.

"It's up to you to decide if you want things to be real to you or not. If you expect the dirt to have steps to help you get out, it will. If you expect it to let you pass through, it will. You'll get the hang of it pretty quickly."

A frown appearing on her too-young forehead, she studies the dirt as if it has personally offended her. Then she takes a step forward and up, as if she's walking up a set of stairs.

She's a quick study, this one.

She stands in front of me, looking around at our cemetery. I can hardly remember what I thought of it the first time I saw it. Now it's just my home, with the high stone walls cutting us off from the living world, the relatively small stone church with its seven bells, and the six hundred and seventy-seven graves. Some are mausoleums with pictures and statues of angels and seats for visitors, some simple tomb stones with only a name on them.

She turns her sharp gaze on me. "Now what?"

I clear my throat and straighten my spine. Nobody gave me this job, nobody asked me to do it. I've decided to do it because I want to.

Because I think I have to.

I help the newcomers get settled, understand how things work. I help them find the closure they need to move on.

The closure I'm not sure I'll ever find for myself.

"The reason you're here as a ghost," I explain, "is that you have unfinished business. Once it's done, you can move on."

"Move on to where?"

I spread my hands wide. "That, I cannot say. I'm afraid I haven't made it that far myself yet. Hence my continued presence. I assume, though, that it is a better place. It is what we strive for."

She chews on her lips as she digests this. A speck of dirt that had stayed on her shoulder falls through her body and to the ground. She probably forgot that she's supposed to be covered in dirt after walking out of her grave.

"What kind of unfinished business?"

"Well." I clear my throat though there hasn't been a need to for a good thirty years. "It appears you were murdered. I'm guessing we're looking for the killer."

She doesn't appear surprised to hear she was murdered. "We?" she asks.

I crack a smile. "As you can see, there aren't that many things to do here. It would be my pleasure to help you out."

She nods. "So we do what? Go haunt places?"

"Ah. I'm afraid we're very limited when it comes to haunting. We can't leave the cemetery grounds, you see. So we can only haunt whoever deigns to come visit us."

I see she's about to lash out. "I wouldn't worry overly much, my dear," I tell her. "You've only been in the ground for ten days and only one man has come to see you. There will be others." Possibly not before the tombstone is in place, though. People seem to prefer visiting a clean grave to a mound of dirt. Don't ask me why.

"Who came?" she asks, a first trace of vulnerability making an appearance. "Was it Joss?"

"I believe that was his name, yes," I tell

her. I describe the man as best I can. "I got the feeling he was a good friend?"

Her clear eyes look toward the church with longing. "More than a friend. Or at least, that was the plan."

"Do you know who pushed you off that bridge?" I ask. "I assume you didn't jump?"

"Of course I didn't jump," she snaps. "I was finally going after what I wanted instead of what my father had planned for me. I was finally going to *live*." She takes a few deep breaths—a habit most of us keep even though we don't actually breathe anymore—before continuing in a calmer voice. "And no, I don't know who it was."

"What do you remember?"

She'd been on the bridge by herself, staring at the dark waters below, like she often did when she needed a time-out. It was her spot, and everyone who was even remotely close to her knew it. She'd been listening to music, so she hadn't heard anyone approach. One minute she'd been listening to Beyoncé. The next she was flying through the air, seeing the water and the rocks below coming to meet her as she fell face first to her death.

"All right," I say. "So we don't know who the killer is. The good part about that is that it means that might be all you need to be able to move on. Figure out who killed you, and we're done."

She studies me, skepticism clear on her youthful and pretty face. "What's in this for you? Why do you want to get me out of here? Am I stepping on your turf or something?"

I laugh, but it sounds hollow. "You're welcome to stay here with me as long as you like, Florence. I'd be happy for the company. But believe me when I say this: you do not want to stay here forever. It gets *very* boring. And the longer you wait, the more difficult it is to do what you have to do, and you risk ending up staying here forever."

She studies me, making me want to fidget. I can see the question in her eyes, but I'm grateful when she doesn't give it voice.

Yes, I suspect I'll be here forever. And yes, that scares me. But keeping busy assisting the others helps.

The hinges of the back gate squeak and I breathe a sigh of relief when Florence turns her focus toward the sound.

"Looks like we can start the work straight away, my friend," she says. "That's my fiancé."

***

THE YOUNG MAN who'd stood at the limit between family and friends at the funeral gently closes the gate behind him, wincing at the resulting squeak. Hands shoved into the pockets of his fancy leather winter jacket, he approaches Flo's grave, his steps hesitant.

"I assume he can't see me?" Flo asks.

I shake my head.

"Hear? Feel?"

I tip my head from side to side. "Not like you're used to, no. But they do feel *something*." I wave a hand at the fiancé, who's almost at the mound of dirt. "Go ahead and experiment."

I'm guessing we'll need it if we want a confession out of him before he leaves the premises.

Flo sidles up to her fiancé's side. "Hey, Cédric." She cocks her head to look up at him.

"Hey, Flo."

Flo jumps a foot into the air and wide eyes meet mine. "You said he wouldn't hear me!"

I have to crack a smile. "He didn't," I assure her. "He's talking to your grave, that's all."

"I'm not sure why I came tonight." Cédric talks to the wooden cross, his hands still in his pockets and his shoulders drawn up so the collar of his jacket covers his ears. I don't know the man, but his voice feels flat, lifeless.

Flo steps in front of her fiancé, probably so it feels like he's looking at her. "What did you do, Cédric?"

I like this girl. She knows he can't really hear her, but my comment about them feeling something has her asking questions anyway. The thing is, I think it does help. They don't hear our actual words, but on some unconscious level, they must hear us, because two times out of three, they change the course of their monologue in the direction we want.

Cédric draws an uneven breath. "I swear I didn't know this was how it would end up. You must know I'd never do anything to hurt you."

"You didn't know how this would end up." Flo seems to taste the words in her mouth, trying them on to see if they fit. She turns to look at me. "That doesn't feel quite right if he pushed me off the bridge, does it?"

I shift my weight to my right foot and fold my arms across my chest. "Not really, no. But I'd like firmer proof."

She nods. "What did you do, Cédric?" she asks him again.

He shakes his head, tears filling his eyes. "I was just so hurt by what you did, Flo. After everything we'd built together, all the plans we'd laid. How could you just throw that away—for *Joss*?"

Flo raises a hand to his cheek—and her hand goes right through his head.

"You need to focus on the space he occupies," I tell her. "Expect to touch him, and you wili." Sort of.

After shaking off a shiver, Flo tries again. This time, her hand caresses his cheek, though from the twitch in her fingers, I'm guessing she's freaked out by the lack of feeling.

"I'm so sorry I hurt you," Flo tells him. "But what we had was always more of a business agreement than a relationship. And I couldn't take it anymore."

"I guess I shouldn't be surprised," Cédric says. "Passion was never really our thing, was it?" He raises his eyes to the stars above us. "But *Joss*?"

Flo gives an annoyed sigh. "You're just going to have to get over that one, Cédric. But I am sorry for using you, even if I wasn't aware of doing it." She braces herself, then gives him a whole-body hug. Does it well, too. Not a single piece of her goes through the man.

I'd say he feels it. He visibly relaxes, his shoulders going down a fraction.

"What did you do, Cédric?" Flo lets her fiancé go, and steps back to stand in his line of sight again.

"Why'd you do it, Flo?" Cédric says.

Flo takes a step backward. "Why did I do what?"

A tear streaks down Cédric's face and disappears into his collar. "I get that your dad was probably pissed, but you're a strong girl. I mean, you *knew* he'd be unhappy about us breaking the engagement. Was that really enough to give up?" His shoulders slumps and two more tears break free. "I just don't get it."

Flo's body is frozen to the spot. She turns her head just enough to look at me out of the corner of her eye. "What is he talking about?"

I remember the conversation between cousins at the funeral. "There's a chance people think you killed yourself."

"What!" Her head whips back and forth as she's trying to stare daggers at me and her fiancé both. "I would never do that!"

I step closer so she can look at both of us without giving herself the ghost equivalent of a whiplash. "I'm guessing this is the business you need to take care of before you can leave." I give her fiancé a once-over. "This man was at the top of my list of suspects, but for what we're seeing, I don't think he did it. Unless he's managed to convince himself you jumped of your own accord after he did the deed?"

Flo shakes her head. "Not his style."

Cédric falls to his knees, tears running freely now. He hangs his head as he sobs, but doesn't seem to have the intention of talking anymore.

"Let's look at this objectively," I say. "We know it's not the fiancé, and it's not the lover. Who else could it be? What could be the motive?"

Flo runs ran a hand through Cédric's hair, shivers, and looks accusingly at her hand as if it is at fault for not giving her the usual feedback when she touches something.

"The motive is probably money," she says reluctantly. "I was planning on breaking it off with Cédric, but also getting out of the family business. I told him he could continue working with my dad, but I didn't want to do it anymore. I'm—I *was*—the outward face for our company. My dad thought, and rightly so, that having a young woman at the front of a business catering to mostly men would be good business. So if I'm no longer there, they will have to rework the entire business plan."

"Doesn't exactly point toward your competitors," I say. "If you were leaving anyway."

She shrugs. "Not many people knew, so maybe they just decided to make their move exactly when there was no need?"

I chew on my lip. "I guess it's possible. But I'm tempted to say it's someone from your side of things. Someone who wasn't happy about you leaving."

Flo points to the man sobbing at our feet. "He was the only one who knew. And Joss." Worry etches her forehead. "You're *sure* it wasn't Joss, right?"

"I'm sure."

She lets out a relieved sigh.

"Could either one of them have told anyone else?" I ask.

Flo pulls a hand through her hair as she thinks. "Joss didn't have anything to do with the business. Nor did the friends he hung out with. He's never even met my dad."

"So your dad is the one to run everything? The big boss?"

She nods.

"The one who has the most to lose if you left the company?"

Her eyes snap to mine. "He wouldn't."

"It does sound far-fetched," I agree. "But I didn't know the man. How was he usually in stressful situations? How did he manage his anger?"

Her lips twitch and for a couple of seconds she's about six years old and wearing a cute princess dress. Then she's back to her twenty-year-old self.

"What happened when you were a little girl?" I ask her gently. "When you were dressed up like a princess?"

Flo's breathing is shallow. Her eyes are distant, probably looking back at whatever happened that day.

"I ruined the car," she whispers. "I was dancing in circles on the terrace and stumbled.

I knocked into a jar of paint that stood on the railing and it fell down on the car. Made a dent in the roof and he had to get a new paint job for the whole thing afterward."

I put a hand on her shoulder. She won't be able to feel it, but I'm hoping her memory can fill in when she has the visual. "What did he do to you?"

She squeezes her eyes shut. "He held me over the railing, yelling at me to look at what I'd done. Said he'd drop me, that maybe then I'd learn my lesson."

"Did he? Drop you?"

She shakes her head. "My mom came out of the kitchen and saw us. Had him put me down and yelled at him for an hour for putting me in danger like that."

"How do you think he'd react to learning you intended to leave him in the lurch?"

Flo takes a deep breath and lets it out slowly. She looks down at her fiancé, who's stopped crying but shows no sign of leaving. "I need to know if my dad knew," she says. "How can we find out?"

"There's a good chance he'll confess to it himself if he comes here by himself," I reply. "And they usually do, after a time. So we'd just have to wait." I meet her gaze. "The question is whether or not that will be enough for you to move on. Do you think *you* knowing will be enough, or do the people who are still alive have to know, too?"

She runs her hand through the hair of her wreck of a fiancé, without twitching this time. "They need to know," she whispers.

"That's what I figured," I say. "It means you have some work to do."

Flo straightens her back and sets her jaw. "Tell me what to do."

I point to the man at her feet. "You need to convince him to help you."

***

"HOW LONG DO YOU think this is going to take?" Clothilde asks from her perch. Where I usually try to respect the physical laws of the living, Clothilde doesn't care. She's standing on thin air to get a view of the parking lot over the wall.

I glance at the newly installed mausoleum over Flo's grave, with its brilliant gold letters and shiny surface. "Any day now." The mom came by this morning, and Flo cried as many tears as her mom during the encounter. The dad was absent, though, and the mother promised he'd drop in soon.

He'll be here soon. The question is whether or not he'll have a tail.

"Ah," Clothilde says. "A Ferrari. Haven't seen it before. Might be our guy."

I rise from my seat and walk over to the main entrance, where Flo is waiting. "Your father?" I ask.

She nods.

Showtime.

***

THE DAD TAKES HIS time getting out of the car. He walks to the passenger side to get his winter jacket and is careful with his suit at he slips it on. He strolls to the trunk, where he pulls out a bouquet of red roses.

"Mom bought them for him yesterday," Flo says. "She told me. Didn't want him to come empty-handed."

Fair enough. Not all men feel comfortable buying flowers.

The Ferrari is the only car in the parking lot. It might be happenstance, but if our suspicions are correct, he'd want to be alone today.

"A car just parked down the road toward the school," Clothilde informs me as she trots up to join us at the main entrance. "A blue Ford."

Flo's eyes light up. "That's Cédric! He listened!"

"Looks like it," Clothilde confirms. "I'll go meet him and see what I can do about those rusty hinges at the back door. But if he's no good at stealth, there isn't much I can do."

"Thank you," Flo says and squeezes the other girl's hand. I wouldn't go so far as to say they've become friends over the last week, but Clothilde seems invested in helping Flo get justice, and Flo knows to show her appreciation.

The dad looks around the parking lot as he approaches the main gate, and again when he's in the cemetery. Yup, definitely wanted to be alone. A Tuesday night at eleven is a good bet if that's what you want.

"Hey, Dad," Flo says as he passes us. "Long time, no see."

The dad stalks up the main path in direction of his daughter's grave. His expression is severe, not a tear in sight, his lips set in a thin line.

We follow in his wake, making sure to stay close enough to hear if he starts talking.

At the mausoleum, he sets the flowers down on the doorstep, then takes a step back. He takes his time in studying the little stone building set up in memory of his daughter, but doesn't voice his thoughts about it. From his expression, I'd say he's not impressed.

Clothilde appears through the stone walls, hands raised and eyes wide. "Booh!" she says, then cackles a laugh. "Man, I wish that worked sometimes."

Flo's dad, of course, doesn't react at all.

Clothilde comes to stand with Flo and myself. "He climbed over the gate," she says, her voice impressed. "Tore open his pants and all, but made it in without making a sound. He's hiding behind this horror, phone in hand." She points to the mausoleum.

"Guess it's my turn to play, then." Flo squares her shoulders and steps onto the first step of her new home, facing her father.

"Tell me, Dad," she says, her voice strong, "did someone tell you I was leaving?"

Her father grits his teeth and lets out a frustrated sigh. "Why did you have to do it?" he asks. "Why couldn't you stay on course? You were going to give up everything we'd worked for for *love*? Really? Give up a bright future with all the money and stability you could ever want, to go live with a guy who can't hold on to a job for more than six months?"

"Okay." Flo's eyes have lost some of their spark, but the determination is strong. "Someone told you. Guess it's not really important if it was Joss or Cédric, though I'm going to guess Cédric since I actually managed to convince him to follow you here." Joss had been by several times since she'd come out of the grave, and she'd talked to him about following her father, but to no effect.

"And now I even had to pay for *this*." Her dad kicks at the mausoleum, missing his daughter's ghost by mere millimeters.

"I'm sorry I'm always such a burden to you," Flo says. Her form flashes quickly to that of a much younger version of herself, then comes back to the version I know, anger flashing in her eyes. "At least you're rid of me now."

"At least I'm rid of you now," he echoes.

"Creepy," Clothilde whispers.

"Cédric came to me *crying*," the dad says, his own temper rising. "A grown man was crying in my lap because my daughter decided she didn't want him anymore. You take away everything we've worked for for *years*, and to top it all off, you break the one asset I could still use. What use is a man who starts *crying* over a *woman*?"

Clothilde takes off toward the back of the mausoleum. "I'm just going to check our little witness isn't going to do anything stupid until we have some definite proof."

"I can think of plenty of uses," Flo screams at him. "Cédric is a good man! He deserves a good life." She deflates a little and her voice lowers. "I couldn't give that to him. He might be sad right now, but I would have made him miserable in the long run."

"I was going to talk some sense into you," the dad says with a sneer. "Always standing on that bridge, wasting your time with God knows what. You'd just *sunk* my business, and there you were, *singing* and *shaking your ass* as if you were some ninny on TV who couldn't find anything more constructive to do with your time."

"I'm allowed to live my own life as I see fit!" Flo stands on her tiptoes, screaming into his face from no more than a centimeter away.

He flinches and takes a step back. He scans the cemetery, but doesn't seem to see any of us standing around him, least of all his daughter right in front of him.

"Jeez," he says. "I'm even seeing things. See what you've brought me to? I'm staying up all night to work on finding your replacement, on finding a new marketing strategy. On figuring out what to do with that lousy fiancé of yours. And all because you can't bloody swim!" His voice rose throughout his speech and at the end he's screaming so loud, I'm surprised the neighbors don't come running.

"I can't swim?" Flo has taken a leaf out of Clothilde's book and is standing on thin air to get right into her father's face. "I can't swim! You know bloody well I can swim, since you insisted I learn when I was five! But I can't swim if my head's bashed in, dad! I can't swim if I'm already dead! You did it, didn't you? You pushed me over the railing during one of your hissy fits, never thinking about the consequences of your actions!"

"Of course I did! You were just standing there, dancing, when everything was going to *shit*! You deserved to be thrown in! You deserved to pay the consequences! But you weren't supposed to die!"

Silence falls on the cemetery like a heavy brick.

"He just answered her question," Clothilde whispers as she pops her head around the mausoleum to meet my gaze.

"I know," I whisper back.

"Florence?" the dad asks, his voice shaky. He's looking right at her, not through her.

Flo's eyes are huge and her lips twitch as if she's about to start crying. "Daddy?"

The dad's eyes boggle, then roll to the back of his head. He falls to the ground as though someone pressed his "off" button.

Cédric comes scrambling out from his hiding place. He takes in the flowers, the man sprawled on the ground. He's searching for something else, but he can't see the three of us crowding around him. "What the hell just happened?"

***

WE STAND BY as the ambulance shows up and carts the father off on a gurney. While talking to the EMT, Cédric mentions what he'd overheard at Flo's grave and the police are called in. He shows them his recording.

"So it really wasn't a suicide, huh?" one of the officers says. "Good job on getting the evidence, kid."

After a while, even Joss shows up, and after a long discussion with Cédric where Flo listens in but I keep my distance, the two share a hug and leave together. There's not a dry eye in sight.

When there's only us ghosts left and the cemetery is back to its usual silence, Flo approaches. She's still here, but I can see straight through her as she's becoming more translucent.

"Ready to leave?" I ask her.

"You think I'm done?" she asks. "How do I know if it's enough?"

I smile at her and lean in for a hug while it's still possible. As I step back, I wave a hand to indicate her body. "You're already on your way," I tell her.

She looks down at herself, at the fact that she can see through her legs, her torso, as if she's only just a memory of herself.

"Oh," she says in wonder. "Thank you." Her eyes are on mine as she disappears altogether.

I walk over to Clothilde's grave, where she's sitting, her legs dangling with her worn Converse going straight through the stone on every swing.

"Nice job, detective," she says. She makes a show of looking me over. "Still not enough?"

I sigh as I sit down on my own grave—a slight hump on the ground next to Clothilde's, without so much as a temporary cross to mark it. "I'm not sure it will ever be enough."

Jerry Oltion is the most prolific writer of short stories in the history of Analog Magazine. *No one even comes close. And he still regularly publishes stories there.*

This really fun and original short, short story shows that Jerry not only has sold to many magazines, he has been around his share of slush piles. And cats. Great fun and more accurate than I care to think about.

Besides continuing his regular science fiction writing, Jerry is also a major amateur astronomer and does a regular column for Sky and Telescope.

Obsession

Jerry Oltion

BIG IS FAR away again. She sits here just before me, perched on her high-up sitting post, her forearms resting against the top of her put-things place, but she is not here. She stares at the flat whites, her gaze fixed on them even more intently than mine when I stalk a bird, and her eyes move like one who dreams.

I have stared at the flat whites myself, stared hard enough to bring out the shadow creatures that normally live only in the corners of rooms, but I never see what she sees. Her eyes track different movements than mine. She suddenly makes the happy noise for no reason, or gasps, startled, when nothing has happened. Like a mouse mesmerized by my steady gaze until it steps closer, completely unaware of its own motion, she turns one flat white over and stares at the next, searching, always searching for something she seldom finds.

It must be a very specific something, for most times she only looks at the first layer before pushing the entire bundle of them aside, obviously sure that what she seeks is not there. Other times she will turn all the flat whites in a stack, one after the other, moving through them faster and faster toward the end; then she will scream in frustration when there are no more and whatever she looks for has still not been revealed.

The strain shows. Her eyes grow red and her temper flares. When I or one of the others who live here tip something over or spit at one another, she comes back suddenly and shouts at us dammitcatyouscaredme and only if we apologize and rub her legs will she relax.

I sometimes jump to the top of the put-things place and lie on the flat whites so whatever horrible things she sees there will not be able to reach her, but she always removes me; most times gently, other times not so. If I prance and preen and make the good noise she sometimes lets me distract her longer, but she always puts me to the floor and returns to her hunt.

Once when she was truly asleep, resting with Even Bigger near the end of the long dark time, I found the clumsy one atop the put-things place, eating a flat white. I had always thought him slow until that moment, but I suddenly saw his genius. Yes, it was time for we who live here to act. We had to save her from this obsession. We had to destroy the flat whites, though it might take us all the rest of the dark and into the bright beyond to do it.

Less than half of a flat white later, the flaw in the plan became apparent. Flat whites taste terrible. Worse even than the dry food, and they are all edges. This one smelled bad as well, as if it were once near a fire. We bravely devoured what we could, but the clumsy one suddenly grew sick and coughed it back out. I fared little better. When we recovered we scratched and fanged as many as we could, hoping that would be enough to destroy their control over her, but even then we barely ruined a single pile of them before the bright came and Big awoke again.

Furious Big! Poor clumsy one, poor squeaky one, poor everyone. Much stomping of big flat paws. Things that should not fly did so poorly. Even Bigger came to investigate, stood amazed at the sight. Big threw a bundle of flat whites at him, too, and though they fluttered like leaves long before they even got close, he said whoashit and fled with the rest of us.

We were cute for many brights and darks before she calmed.

It did no good, of course. She still searches wearily for that which she seldom finds.

Seldom, but not never. Now, as I watch

from my own perch atop a stack of flat whites even taller than me, she turns over the last one in the latest bundle, leans back against the tall part of her sitting post, and sighs contentedly. Her eyes glitter with the thrill of a successful hunt. She stands, walks to the hole in the wall, and calls to Even Bigger. Inthekitchen he says from the food smells place, and she goes there to share her kill.

It is almost enough to make me pause in my own mission. The sight of Big so happy is nearly worth seeing her so weary. I consider the situation again, consulting the shadow creatures for inspiration. They say nothing, of course, but their presence focuses my attention while I think.

Big is happy. I do not want to change that. But something must be done or the flat whites will rob her happiness again, just as they have done so many times before.

My resolve hardens. I must do what I came here to do. I must give her a message she cannot misinterpret. No matter how great the pleasure she derives from the rare good one, these flat whites are bad for her.

But I need not destroy them all. In fact, I now realize, Big must find the strength to do that herself, or she will never be truly cured. I need only make a start.

Very well, then. I will only pee on one stack.

For Kristine Kathryn Rusch, who for six years bravely stalked manuscripts at the *Magazine of Fantasy & Science Fiction*.

~

J. Steven York is a master at the short-short powerful, nasty story with a bite. And this story is no exception.

Steve has been publishing novels and powerful short fiction for over thirty years now, and before that he worked in the gaming industry. Steve is also doing a really fun and off-the-wall Internet comic, one of which he has allowed me to put in each issue on the back page.

Flowers for Mother

J. Steven York

GRANDMOTHER DRUMMOND'S HEAD turned from side to side, occasionally stopping, as though she could somehow see through the thick leather blindfold. All was quiet except for the soft whir of the engine. The woman's grandson, David, shook his head in amusement and took another drink of champagne. She'd been that way since the drugs had started wearing off half an hour before.

David leaned back and the seat's leather upholstery creaked. He glanced to the driver's seat where Trenton, the butler, gripped the wheel in his frail but steady hands. Trenton glanced over his shoulder at David and nodded. Things were going well.

David leaned toward his dazed and confused grandmother. "I see you're awake, Grandmama. I'm so happy you could join me for a little Mother's Day jaunt."

She flinched at the sound of his voice, twisting so he saw a flash of the chrome-plated handcuffs binding her wrists. "David? Is that you? Something dreadful has happened. Set me loose at once!"

He nodded and ran his fingers though his thick, sandy hair. "Oh, yes, Grandmama.

Something dreadful has happened. But that was a long time ago. Today, we'll be together. Won't it be fun?"

Her blind eyes looked around even more urgently, taking in the environment with all her other senses, touching the leather seat cushion with her clawed fingers, feeling the soft carpeting under her feet, hearing the muffled sound of the motor, forehead bumping the cool glass of the window. "We're in a limousine, aren't we? Where are you taking me?"

David couldn't resist a smile as he savored the moment. Pregnant pause, and then: "It's Mother's Day evening. We're going to take some flowers to my mother."

Her thin parchment lips, lined with smeared lipstick the color of blood, fell open in surprise. "Your mother is gone, David. She was a bad woman. You know that. I sent her away myself."

David's smile faded with his amusement, displaced by an angry tightness in his chest. "I know nothing of the sort. I don't remember my mother. You took her away from me before I could even remember her face."

She licked her lips and struggled at the cuffs, causing a strand of slate-gray hair to fall across her face. "You couldn't know, David. She was a low-class slut. She tried to take your father, my baby, from me, you know. She let herself get pregnant just to trap him." She laughed softly. "But we showed her. She said she couldn't be bought, but there is a price for everything. She's far away, David, and you'll never find her."

David looked out the window. It was dark, and he could see very little. He glanced toward Trenton. "Are you sure we're going the right way?"

"Yes, Master Drummond. Your father visits her several times a year. I know the way well."

"You see, Grandmama. I know all your little secrets now, and I'll finally get to see my mother, and give her some flowers, and be the son she never had."

Grandmother Drummond paled, the skin on her cheeks becoming as white and translucent as waxed paper. "Trenton! You stop this car and set me loose at once. My husband will be furious when I tell him about this! I don't care how many decades you've worked for this family, you'll wish you were never born! Trenton! Let me go!"

The butler ignored her pleas. "Almost there, sir."

David nodded in acknowledgement. "Thank you, Trenton. Thank you for everything. I never would have known without you. The risk you're taking."

Trenton dismissed this with a small, dignified wave of his right hand. "Really, sir. The end is worth any risk."

David pressed his hands against the window, the better to see out into the darkness. Then he saw her, waiting for him, a thin figure in a flowing white dress, transfixed in the glare of the headlights. A single soft word escaped his lips. "Mother." The motor's sound faded as they slowed.

Grandmother Drummond struggled violently, almost slipping off the seat. "David! This is absurd. Let me go. You mother is dead, David. I had her killed myself. We can't see your mother because she's dead!"

David looked out at his mother, admiring the curve of her chin, the long blond hair that moved at the slightest current. She was as he had always imagined her, except for the many turns of heavy chain wrapped around her ankles.

"I know she's dead, grandmother. I know." He reached over and gently unbuckled the blindfold just as the little submarine settled into the silt at the bottom of Lake Michigan.

The old woman gasped as she looked out through the thick glass window and into the mummified face of her dead daughter-in-law, largely spared from age and decay by the cold, oxygen-poor lake water.

David climbed into the seat next to Trenton, where he could operate the submarine's robot arm. Gently he placed the bouquet of roses in his mother's bony, emaciated hand.

Grandmother turned away from the sight of the woman she'd killed so long ago. "Why have you brought me here, David. Why have you done this just to bring flowers to a dead woman?"

He looked at her intently, wondering if she would ever understand. "Because I am a good son, Grandmother. Now that I know, I'll visit Mother every year, and I'll bring her flowers.

"I'm a good grandson, too."

He opened the airlock's inner door and brought out the length of heavy chain. "Don't worry. "I'll bring you flowers every year.

"I promise."

KING
SAUCER
LATE NIGHT
BRITANNIA

I have been reading Jason A. Adams's stories for a few years now in various locations, knowing it was only a matter of time that I find one that fits in Pulphouse.

Of course, with this wonderful original story, it didn't hurt that Jason hit two of what Kris calls my editor reader cookies. He wrote a story about books and about collecting. Totally a home run for this editor.

For the Love of Books

Jason A. Adams

WICKFORD IS A lovely little village in North Kingstown, Rhode Island. The archaic Historic District is full of gallant white pre-colonial houses, narrow lanes of bumpy cobbles, fresh sea air from the nearby Narragansett Bay. Even in the middle of June, temperatures are comfortable. The air holds no hint of smog or the other olfactory sins of larger cities. Time has passed it by, save for the glow of electric lights and the occasional vehicle.

For nearly four hundred years, towns like this have kept the charm of the old Yankee world alive.

Peter Billingsworth strolled down Main Street past several historical buildings now housing tourist traps selling Chinese-made Americana, hand-knitted seaman's sweaters that cost more than a seaman made in a week, and bistro-ized versions of *Luso* seafood. It all struck him as tawdry, but in that comfortable New England way. Everyone knew the old fishing villages were now overpriced summer towns for well-to-do folk from New York and Boston, but everyone smiled, waved, and comfortably rooked the ignorant away folk.

Overhead, seagulls swooped and roiled in raucous clouds. More elegant birds—robins, chickadees, and such—chose to stay in the stately oaks and maples that lined the streets, impervious to the blight that had slain the old elm trees. Children and adults alike rode past on bicycles of various shapes and sizes. One tyke even had an antique metal pedal car that reminded Pete of his own, long vanished in the ancient mists of his boyhood. He chuckled softly at the melodramatic idea. His quarry must be influencing his thoughts. Which was fine. Hardy was allowed to do so.

Pete himself was an interloper, but was not here for crab cakes or "lobstah" stew. He had far bigger fish to fry, so to speak. He looked the part of bored summer visitor in his Harris Tweed jacket and shapeless linen trousers, hands in pockets as he glanced in the shop windows he passed.

He was not bored at all, however. Indeed, this could be his most important trip of the last decade. A trip dedicated to his collection, which up until now didn't hold the book he most wanted.

Not the world's most valuable book, nor the most rare. But one Pete was determined to make his own.

The true collector does it for love, not money.

A small body crashed into Pete's legs, and he nearly stumbled. Instead, he took the thin shoulders in hand and steadied both himself and a young tow-haired boy, not yet a teen by the look of him.

"Slow down, chum," Pete said, smiling. "What could your hurry be, on such a fine day?"

The boy squirmed and tried to break the grip on his arms, but Pete had seen a pretty young woman hurrying toward them, her sunny blouse and robin's-egg slacks combining with a golden ponytail to paint the perfect picture of a mother on a weekend jaunt. She held a maroon mass-market paperback in one hand, and as she yanked the boy toward her, she began waving it in his face.

"Where, Danny? *Where* did you get this??"

Pete saw that the book was a middle edition of Alfred Bester's classic, *The Stars My Destination*. The corners worn white, inner pages the color of aged honey.

"I just found it," Danny mumbled. "Can I have it back now?"

"No, you may *not!*" his mother said, anger and unwillingness to cause a scene reducing her voice to a low and furious hiss. "As soon as your father gets back from his boat ride, we're going straight home, and *you're* going straight to your room!"

She thrust the worn volume into Pete's hands.

"Thank you for stopping Danny," she said. Her cheeks flamed, whether with anger or embarrassment Pete couldn't say. "Please take this. I don't want anyone to see—I mean, I don't want Danny to have it."

Pete watched them walk down the lane, Danny with head and shoulders hanging low, she with wagging finger and stabbing tongue. Pete laughed a little, shaking his head and full of pity for young Master Dan.

But he tucked the paperback in his jacket and went on. He had an appointment to keep, after all.

***

AFTER TURNING LEFT on Church Street, he saw the tiny cottage he'd been looking for. He knew it by the large cherry tree in the yard, which had been described in detail, down to the century-old heart carved into the trunk. The cottage was white, naturally, but the front door was a dark woodland green that struck the eye forcefully in this town of staid whites and blacks. The quaint wooden signboard hanging from a polished black wrought-iron post depicted an open book, the pages curled and cracked at the edges. No establishment name, but that was for the best. Advertisement often covered for impurity.

Stopping on the brick sidewalk, Pete stared at the house, feeling his pulse rise. Inside was a man who claimed to have an original 1892 copy of Hardy's *Tess of the*

D'Ubervilles. Pete considered himself not an excitable man, but the chance to own his favorite author's masterwork in the first edition…

Well, it would be something indeed! Pete could picture the volume, red cloth binding embossed with the shamrocks denoting the Harper & Bros. publishing house, then a powerhouse of New York bookmakers. It would look fine sitting atop the lectern he'd acquired just in case the shopkeeper told the truth and would part with the work.

He could only hope the promise of a large payment, plus the fifty-year-old bottle of Glenlivet tucked under his arm, would persuade the bookseller, a Mr. Gorton, to part with the valuable tome. If not, Pete would have to think of something else. He couldn't help it. Books were his biggest weakness. Although his library was extensive and varied, with many rare and unique volumes, there was always room for one more.

A jaunty bell jangled as Pete pulled open the green door and entered the shop. Inside, heavy velvet drapes in royal blue kept the book-destroying sunlight at bay, but several brass lamps with green glass shades and Edison bulbs adorned low tables scattered among the display cases and shelves. Pete set the whisky on a fine example of Early Colonial woodwork and drank in the sensory feast. The sight of all those hoary volumes, a mix of masterworks and popular. Books of all genre and none. Tiny pocket books and massive folios. The scratchy cloth- and leather-bound cover boards that Pete longed to run his fingers over. Alas, he only had one pair of cloth gloves, and he was saving those for Hardy.

The sound of nothing, save the whistles and warbles from the town's high fliers outside.

And the smell. Ah, that aroma. Scents of ink and paper and glue and musty, musky, smoky volatiles blending together like fine Belgian chocolate, far finer than the Glenlivet.

And the mental perfume of all those lovely words. Words trapped within their bound prisons, waiting for days or years or centuries for someone to set them free and breathe them in. Someone like Peter Andrew Billingsworth.

Pete closed his eyes, leaned his head back, and breathed in until his belt left a mark.

Soft padding on the thick maroon carpeting alerted him. He opened his eyes and beheld the epitome of all bookshop owners approaching.

Samuel Gorton, vice-chair of the Association of Rhode Island Rare and Antique Book Dealers (ARIRABiD, a fine jest), was a rotund little fellow, barely five-five in stocking feet and of similar girth. A green eyeshade jutted from his bald pate, and a pair of wire-rimmed half-moon cheaters hung from a silver chain around his neck. A white Oxford shirt with mother-of-pearl buttons, unfettered by a necktie, tucked into tasteful charcoal slacks. Leather suspenders completed the image. Pete wasn't sure if Gorton reminded him more of a Las Vegas dealer or a steamboat captain.

On second thought, the lack of a derby—and the lack of shoes on his blue-stockinged feet—dashed both images. Bookshop owner it was, then.

And yet the red cheeks below the darting hazel eyes, the moisture in the neatly trimmed black moustache, and the stains spreading from his armpits belied the rest of his appearance.

"Mr. Billingsworth. Right on time, I see. I presume you're here to meet *Tess?*" The same tenor, reedy voice Pete had heard over several telephone conversations. With just a hint of quaver. DeMille would have looked no further, if he were casting a bibliophile.

Gorton took Pete's hand in his own sweaty, trembling grip and shook weakly.

"I am indeed," he replied. "If she's ready and you're willing, of course."

"Yes, yes. Certainly." Gorton retrieved his hand and then wrung both together, his plump fingers working over and through each other like so much bratwurst in a rock tumbler. "Well then. Right this way, please."

Gorton turned and Pete followed him to a second, smaller room. The light didn't try so hard to defeat the shadows in here. Subdued lighting shaded to protect the precious inhabitants from UV rays was tightly focused in small circles, enough to illuminate one book per station, and only if the book were exactly placed. To the usual pleasant odors of the bookshop were added the slightly acrid scents of disinfectant and desiccant, valiantly battling the ocean's humidity and all the life forms just waiting to feed on the Masters. No mass markets in *here*.

And there she was.

An archival clamshell, covered with buckram canvas dyed the Harper & Bros. signature scarlet, rested atop an elegant Victorian desk of African mahogany, unless Pete was very much mistaken. The soft glow of the desk lamp glinted off fine gilt lettering.

Pete's hands moved toward the box of their own accord, but he stilled them with a mighty force of will.

"May I?" he whispered.

A moment of silence, then, "Hm? Oh. Oh yes. Of course. Please be my guest."

Pete tugged the white cotton gloves from his pocket, pulled them over trembling fingers, and gently opened the case.

His breath caught. It was really there. And in very fine condition. Not perfect, no. But that was only to be expected after a century and more. But like a beautiful woman, the small marks of age only made her all the more handsome.

Pete carefully eased *Tess* open. Only an inch. Only enough to verify the pages within were in equally excellent condition. Then, not without a pang, he let the cover fall and closed the archive box over his treasure.

Stripping off his gloves, Pete turned to Gorton. The man stood, still worrying his hands, eyes unfocused. Perhaps he was ill?

"I am very pleased with the Hardy, Mr. Gorton. Shall we discuss a price?"

Gorton jumped a little. He seemed surprised Pete was still there.

"Price. Yes. Well, I'm afraid that, with the condition of the book, I'll have to ask nine hundred dollars."

Pete's mouth fell open. *"Nine??"*

"Plus tax, of course. I'm afraid I really can't budge, Mr. Billingsworth."

Pete had expected to pay six-fifty, maybe seven hundred. The 1892 was hardly a rare book for its age. And of course, it was actually the first edition of the third publishing. First was the serialized version in *The Graphic*, then the 1891 three-volume set. Still, book collecting was about love, not price. And this was a lovely copy.

With a sigh, Pete drew his wallet from within his jacket, pulled out his credit card.

Gorton had wandered back out to the front room and was staring through the drapes.

Pete followed, confused by the man's behavior.

"Ah. They're here. It's about time."

Gorton let the drapes fall and walked briskly to the door, which opened to reveal the same young mother and boy Pete had encountered earlier.

A man in the black uniform of the North Kingstown Police Department stood behind them, his laden equipment belt and bullet-proof vest a bit of overkill for the situation, in Pete's opinion. The officer's wry smile robbed the scene of any menace, however.

"This them, Mr. Gorton?"

Gorton smiled for the first time since Pete had met the man, the broad grin so out of place with the bookish demeanor that it changed him from shopkeeper to jolly old elf in an instant. St. Nick's accountant, perhaps.

"It is. It is indeed. Thank you, Bill."

The policemen, Bill presumably, gently but firmly guided Danny and his mother into the shop.

"You're sure?" he said, closing the door behind him. "They don't look much like hardened criminals to me."

"Yes, yes. Business has been quite slow today, and apart from Mr. Billingsworth here, these two were the only others in the shop."

"You are *grounded* until you turn eighteen," Danny's mother said, face burning with shame.

"Give the nice man his book back, son," the officer said, one hand resting on Danny's shoulder. "I'm sure we can all forget all this and go on our way."

Danny studied the floor, hands shoved deep in his jeans pockets.

"I don't have it anymore," he said, jerking his head toward Pete. "Mom gave it to *that* guy."

The three adults turned toward Pete. What in the world? He didn't—

But he did.

Pete laughed, and took from his pocket the battered old paperback the woman had thrust at him earlier.

"Is this what all the trouble is about?" He held up *The Stars My Destination*.

"Yes! There it is!" Gorton snatched the book away from Pete, his face aglow with delight, hands stroking the faded cover. "Thank you! Thank you, Mr. Billingsworth, and thank you Bill. Officer McTavish. You have no idea what this means to me!"

"I think you have something to say to Mr. Gorton, Danny." Bill gently squeezed Danny's shoulder.

"Sorry, sir," Danny whispered, kicking at the carpet. "It just looked really cool and Mom wouldn't get it for me. I think I've got a couple of bucks I can give you for it."

"No no, my boy," Gorton said. All traces of his earlier nervousness gone. "I can't let you have this one. But wait here just a moment."

He went to a bookcase filled with pulp paperbacks, studied the spines for a moment, then came back with a somewhat thicker volume, with starry black cover and bold white typography. He handed it to the boy.

"This is *Ringworld*, one of Larry Niven's finest. Enjoy it, my boy."

Danny held it in both hands, staring at the cover. Pete recognized that wonder on the young boy's face. The knowledge that an exciting journey awaits.

"Is two dollars enough, mister?" Danny said, freeing one hand to dig in his pocket.

Gorton smiled and held up a hand. "Consider it a reward for coming clean, young man. And Danny—" Gorton winked. "Might I suggest a library card or a summer job instead of thievery?"

Officer McTavish coughed down what sounded suspiciously like a chortle, then drew himself straight and put on a stern face.

"All right, you two. I don't believe Mr. Gorton will be pressing shoplifting charges, so I'll let you go with a warning. This time. Off you go, now."

"Thank you, Mr. Gorton. Officer," said the young lady. "Come on, Danny."

They left, she clutching the boy's arm, he clutching Niven to his chest. McTavish exchanged a few pleasantries with Gorton, then departed as well.

When it was just the two of them, Pete followed Gorton back to the room where *Tess* still sat, patiently waiting, and Gorton ran his credit card. *Tess* went into a thick canvas bag printed with *Samuel Gorton's Rare and Used Books*. Pete took up the bag, but didn't turn to leave.

He had to know.

"So tell me, Mr. Gorton," Pete said. "Why all the furor over the Bester? Surely that copy holds no value."

"Quite the contrary, Mr. Billingsworth." Gorton took the paperback up from where it sat beside *Tess*. He opened it to the flyleaf, carefully tucking back a few pages that tried to escape back into the cracked spine. He held it under the light and pointed to an inscription written in faded blue ballpoint.

"To Sam, from Dad. Happy birthday, Son!"

He closed the book and gently set it back on the desk, arranging it just so with practiced ease, fingers lingering on the cover.

"My pop bought this when he was in grade school, and gave it to me on my ninth birthday." Some of Gorton's culture had fallen from his voice. "It was my first grownup book. I've read I don't know how many since then, but I always go back to this one, and wouldn't give it up for all the tea in China."

He closed his eyes and smiled.

"Sam Gorton is my name, Rhode Island is my nation. Church Street is my dwelling place, the worlds my destination."

And Pete understood perfectly.

Collecting books isn't about value. It's about love.

Robert Jeschonek's stories just shout Pulphouse *in so many ways. I have been very lucky to have a story of his in every issue so far. Actually, readers have been lucky. And this wonderfully funny story is no exception.*

And seems to be a great bookend in this issue with Stephanie Writt's opening story.

Robert's stories have appeared in dozens of magazines and he has published dozens of novels as well. He has even worked for DC Comics and early in his career sold me a couple stories when I was editing for Star Trek *at Pocket Books. He seems to be able to do it all.*

The Spinach Can's Son

Robert Jeschonek

I AM THE CAN of spinach in a sailor man's hand. He squeezes, expecting me to burst open and launch a blob of green power into his gaping maw.

But I do not burst. He gets no mouthful of spinach, no surge of energy pumping up his arms to three times their size. That's not how it works on this side of the tracks, my friend.

You're not in the funny pages anymore.

Potpie the Sailor tries again with both hands, straining for all he's worth. "C'mon, ya rat-finsk!" He squints up at the threat looming before him, the whole reason he needs his spinach. "We've gotsk to drive this *she-hag* off me boat!"

What threat could be awful enough to strike fear in the sailor man's heart? Is it Bobo the comic-strip bully, back for another knock-down, drag-out?

Not even close.

The figure standing before Potpie and me isn't a drawing at all. There's nothing pen-and-ink about her. "Sir!" She's a three-dimensional woman in what looks like a spacesuit out of a 1950s movie—silver metallic tights and a bubble helmet. Her black hair is arranged in tight waves beneath the glass. "Please, calm down! I just want to ask you some questions." She pulls a photo out of a pouch on the belt slung diagonally over her hips. "Have you seen this man?"

"Never seen 'im before in me lifesk!" Potpie squeezes me harder than ever. I try my best to help, pushing from within, for one simple reason.

I recognize the man in the picture, with his dark brown hair and square-jawed features. I know him like I know my own self, in fact.

Because he *is* myself. Myself in another life.

And I know her, too. Her name is Molly. She's my wife.

And I know why she's after me.

"Take another look, please," she says. "It's urgent that I find him."

Potpie shifts the corncob pipe from one side of his mouth to the other without ever touching it. "I ain't seen him, she-hag!" He shakes a fist at her. "Now putsk 'em up!"

Molly takes a step toward him. "You're sure you haven't seen him?"

Potpie scrambles backward, knocking over a stack of spinach crates. Crying out, he puts me to the only use he can think of—hurling me right at her.

Molly ducks, and I go sailing over her head. It's not a clean getaway, though; the bracelet on her wrist starts beeping as I pass.

Here in the Underfunnies, I'm an anomaly, a deformity in the panel geography—the panelography—and her equipment has detected me.

Good thing a true Panelnaut like me can swim the currents here like a dolphin through water. Focusing my energies, I dive deep into the sea of words and images, hunting a good place to resurface.

Found it. I cross the borders in full flight and land with a shock that takes my breath away.

This time, I am the brick in the hand of a mouse.

I bounce lightly in his grip as he jounces along through a strange landscape, surrounded by abstract objects straight out of a surrealist painting. He gives off a thick smell of stinky cheese and whistles a jaunty tune from his pointy gray snout.

I know him well—Ixnay the Mouse. Once again, I've gravitated toward my favorite stomping grounds, the panelography of the early twentieth century. In this case, the *Hazy Kat* strip.

Or should I say, the *Underfunnies* version of that strip. The reverse of it, the flip side where things don't work the way they should. The negative space that accrues in the collective unconscious of the readership around these tiny, panel-bound stories. The land of things unsaid and hopes unrealized.

For each time Potpie the sailor pops open a can, gobbles the spinach, and beats up the bully, we know in our hearts there must be times when the can doesn't open. That's just the way life works. And our expectations create this flip-side place that until recently no one knew about.

I am a Panelnaut, an explorer of this place. Though "fugitive" might be a better word for what I've become.

"Boy," says Ixnay. "Have I got one cooked up for that idiot cat this time." He hops up on what looks like a warped sundial and calls out into the hot wind. "Oh, Haaazyyy!"

Without delay, the creature known as Hazy Kat comes bounding over the horizon. She's wearing a polka-dot scarf and matching tutu. "Comink, mine treasur-ed pession flour!"

"Make it snappy, willya?" hollers Ixnay. "Yer burnin' daylight here!"

Hazy flops to a stop in front of us and gapes with a love-struck goofy grin. "Dost Rumeo have a heart-wiltin' sonnet plucked out to make his Joliet swoon'st?"

"Ohh, yeah." Ixnay turns me over in his grip. "Ya ever hear of *iambrick pentameter*?"

Hazy claps her paws together and giggles. "Butter 'course, o' bard o' the mousehole! Hit me with that iambrick pentagrammer to yer li'l ol' heart's continent!"

"You asked for it." Ixnay hauls me back, ready to throw. "Be sure to notice the rhythmic counterpoint of strike and release. Or should I say the *opposite*?"

At that exact moment, Molly flashes to life between us and Hazy. The second she materializes, her bracelet starts beeping.

She points her wrist in my direction and nods. "I know you're here, Everett. You've figured out how to assume local forms, haven't you?" Watching the bracelet, she walks toward us. "You're inside the mouse, aren't you?"

Before Ixnay can say a word, Molly suddenly snaps backward. As she drops to the dusty ground, I see Hazy has her paws on her.

"You stays awake from my lettle Ixnay mouses!" Hazy flaps her paws like pancakes at Molly's helmet. "He is my preshiss poet and certifiable booblekins! Don't try steelin' his heart, you hussy!"

"Everett!" Molly shoves the cat away and scrambles to her feet. "I've come to talk to you! You sent me a message through the comic strips—our prearranged emergency signal! Don't pretend you didn't!"

She's right, I can't, because I sent it. But the signal wasn't a cry for help—it was bait. All part of the secret I've been keeping.

"I'm serious, Everett." Molly takes another step toward us. "I'll do what it takes to get through to you."

Ixnay just watches, juggling me from hand to hand. "Whoever this dame is, I gotta admit, I like her style."

Hazy, never much good in a fight, weakly bats at Molly's calves. "'Ev'ritt,' you say? Is that some other word for 'mouses?'"

"Shut up, cat!" says Molly. "Everett, listen…"

Ixnay's little mouse heart thumps like a big bass drum. It pushes out his chest in the shape of a cartoon heart as it throbs. "I think I'm in love!"

Naturally, this makes him raise me into throwing position again.

Molly sees the danger but doesn't stop talking. "It's time to come home, Everett. You can't keep running away." She spreads her arms wide. "We both miss him, Everett. But you can't make things right on your own."

I want to tell her how wrong she is, but I don't get the chance. Ixnay whips me at her glass-helmeted head before I can get the words out.

"Sech fe'rce percision!" says Hazy Kat. "His peshion must be deeper than I yimagined!"

As I blast toward her helmet, I focus my strength on changing course. Ixnay's throw is off, which helps; in the Underfunnies, things don't work the way they normally do, including his brick-pitching aim.

So I fly wide and hurtle on past, soaring through the ochre skies…casting my mind toward another refuge. I've gotten so good, I find one instantly, and I set my sights.

But I wait another moment to dive. Because the truth is, I'm not trying to lose her at all.

Her bracelet has alerted her to my presence in the brick, and she charges after me, calling my name. Calling another name, too.

"Henry's gone, Everett!" That's what she says just before I dive. "I miss him, too! But we need to move on without him!"

She's wrong. Dead wrong. And I'm going to prove it.

When I'm sure she's got a lock on me, I throw myself into the panelography. I ride the swirling currents of the Underfunnies, swooping away from the bizarre realm of Hazy Kat.

As I travel, I think of Henry. I think of our son. I remember how miraculous he was, how full of life and personality from the day he was born. I remember his bright blue eyes fixing on me with pure love and expectation. The way his lips moved as he repeated the things I said, as if he were memorizing each and every word.

He was the greatest thing to ever happen to me, to us. A dream come true—a dream I'd never known I had until he arrived.

A dream that ended the day he died.

I remember the sound of screeching tires, the screams of Molly as she ran. But never a sound from Henry. Not even a last gasp of breath when I got to his side in the street. Only silence from him.

And only blame between Molly and me. Blame become hatred, hatred become rage. I threw myself into my work, pioneering the exploration of the richest vein of the Underfunnies, born of the comic strips of the early twentieth century. Anything to lose myself in the black and white of simple line work, the discoveries of Subtextual Space. Anything to forget Henry and stay away from Molly.

And then, one day, I got The Idea. And I knew it would work. It *will* work, if only I can get her to where she needs to be.

Suddenly, the flow of my thoughts is interrupted as I pop free into a fresh setting. I feel the tingle of something sparking on my body—the crackle of a tiny flame burning at one end of me.

This time, I am a lit stick of dynamite in the hand of a child.

"Zo!" says the little boy, a chubby creature with thick hair as black as his old-fashioned waistcoat. "Vhat do you say, Fritzie? Vill der Admiral like zis special *bratwurst* ve have for his dinner?" He holds me up and grins.

"Oh, ja," says his brother, also chubby but with blond hair and white coat. "I zink maybe he von't haff zo many *chores* for us tomorrow, Helmut!"

We're in a kitchen, surrounded by the smell of cooking sauerkraut. The boys' auntie toils away on the other side of the room, stirring a bubbling pot. Her work is never done, taking care of the mischievous and ungrateful Schnitzeljammer Brats.

"Time to serve der first course!" Blond Fritz grabs a plate and holds it out.

Helmut drops me on the plate with a devilish smile. "Vhat a lovely presentation! Der Admiral ist sure to ask for *seconds*!"

"Ja!" Fritz laughs. "*Thirty* seconds till she *blows*!"

With that, they march me out through the swinging door to the dining room. The Admiral awaits them, sitting at the table in his seaman's cap and scrub-brush mustache.

"Dinner iss served!" Fritz plunks the plate in front of him.

"*Bomb Appétit!*" says Helmut, and then he catches himself. "I mean *Bon Appétit*!"

The Admiral doesn't seem to notice there's dynamite on his plate instead of bratwurst. He raises his fork and knife, ready to dig in…

But before his utensils make contact, his cap leaps off his head and flops down over me. Cut off from the air, my fuse fizzles and stops burning with just an inch to go.

Then, I hear her voice—Molly's voice, speaking from the substance of the cap. "You're not the *only* one who knows how to manipulate the supertexture of the Underfunnies!"

I'm surprised. Following me into the panelography is one thing; possessing resident iconography is quite another.

Apparently, my wife did her homework before she got here.

"Now *listen* to me," she says. "I want you to come *home* with me, Everett. You've been in here too *long*."

For the first time since she found me, I answer her. "You don't know what you're talking about."

"Oh yes, I do," she says. "Don't you think I tried to hide from the world, too? Don't you think I wanted to run away and never come back—never remember what happened to Henry? Don't you think I loved him, too?"

Her words settle around me like comic strip snow. Should I remind her, again, that I was trimming hedges in the backyard when it happened, and she was the one who was supposed to be watching him when he wandered into traffic? That she was the one who turned her back to talk to a neighbor when she should have had her eyes glued to Henry at all times?

Only if rubbing salt in the wound is my goal. "Leave me alone," I tell her. "Go back to reality."

"I'm not leaving without you. That's final." Just as she says it, she's lifted away, leaving me uncovered on the plate.

Fritz makes a grab, but I dive out of the realm of the Schnitzeljammer Brats before his pudgy hand can touch me. I've got to keep moving, keep running, keep drawing her along in my wake.

Until it's too late to stop what I've got planned.

It wouldn't be enough to tell her the story straight up, to tell her The Idea I've set in motion. I can't take the chance she won't believe it's possible, that she won't cooperate.

Not to mention that it breaks every tenet of the Panelnaut protocols. Protocols that I helped create.

Diving through the foamy black-and-white tides toward my next destination, I remember the early days of exploration. I wasn't the first to discover the Underfunnies, but I found the first doorway and made the first trip inside.

It was so thrilling back then, such a novelty—plying the byways of this vast psychic substrata. Jumping into manifestations of comic strips from various eras, existing side-by-side with beloved characters as well as obscure ones. Before long, I discovered I hadn't accessed the primary reality of those strips, but a flip-side echo where nothing works the way it should—a negative space where expectations can't be trusted. The place where Potpie's spinach can won't burst on cue, where Ixnay the mouse can't toss a brick on target, where the Schnitzeljammer Brats' dynamite sticks won't stay lit.

Did I understand the full implications back then? Hell, no. The best I thought we Panelnauts could do was influence the collective unconscious—plant messages that guide humanity toward a state of peace and harmony. We wrote protocols forbidding extreme intervention, anything that disrupted the essential integrity of the panelography.

And now I'm throwing them all away. The ultimate disruption is in motion; every moment brings it closer to final fruition.

And I'm the one who engineered it. I'm the one who knows how close we are to the grand finale.

Very close, now. It's time to pick up the pace.

I need to move her along quickly, not give her time to think or catch her breath. I need to flash like a skipping stone from world to world to world until we reach the last one.

The one I've prepared.

So I fling myself out of the current and surface in another place. This time, I'm a cigar in the mouth of Moo Mullet, rascally gambler and ne'er-do-well. Seconds later, I hear Molly's voice coming from the black derby hat on Moo's little brother, Kozy.

"Please, Everett," says the derby hat. "No more running."

"Say! What gives?" Moo snatches the hat from Kozy's head and gives it a smack with the back of his hand. "Now I gotta take *lip* from a *lid*?"

"We can get through this together," says Molly, "if you'll just come home."

"That topper's positively *brimmin'* with yap, ain't it?" says Kozy.

"Leave me alone!" I shout, just as I dive out of the scene.

"Now my *cigar's* runnin' at the mouth?" I hear Moo say as I leave. "What's next? My *racin' form* tellin' me which *horse* to bet?"

Once again, the currents bear me onward. I'm closer still to our final destination and the consummation of all my efforts.

Leaping from the flow, I become a club in the hands of Allie Hoop the caveman. Molly becomes the collar around the neck of his pet dinosaur, Finny.

"Please give me a chance!" The sound of her voice makes Finny grunt and run into a tree.

"What the heck?" says Allie. "How come you sound like a *girl* all of a sudden, Finny?"

I leap away without a word, and she follows.

Next, I become the fireman's hat on Smokin' Stovepipe, and Molly's the bell on his kooky one-man fire truck. I linger there for less time than it takes Smokin' to utter his catchphrase, "Fwoooo."

We're closer now, almost there. I speed up even more.

At our next stop, I'm the clodhopper boots on Li'l Asner the hillbilly. Molly's the pipe in his old Maw's mouth.

Then, I'm the giant sandwich in Ragwood Rumstead's hands, and she's the polka-dotted bow tie at his throat.

Another hop, and I'm the TV wristwatch on Rick Tracer's arm. She's his lemon yellow trench coat.

Then, I'm the bald head on Daddy Bigbucks, and she's Orphan Agnes's curly orange hair.

"Please stop!" says Molly, giving Agnes quite a start. "Just stop running!"

"Bleepin' blizzards!" yelps Orphan Agnes.

In spite of Molly's pleas, I leap again just the same. Because finally, we've reached the end. My whole purpose in leading her on this chase through the Underfunnies.

I swoop through the currents and burst free at our last stop. This time, I appear as myself, not disguised as some comic strip prop. She does the same, returning to her familiar form in the silver spacesuit and bubble helmet.

Finally. Here we are. In a child's darkened bedroom.

"What is this?" She stares at the black-haired boy on the bed between us. "Who is this?"

"His name is Little Nino," I tell her. "And he's a dreamer."

Even as I say it, Little Nino stirs and sits up in bed. He rubs his eyes, and then he looks at me, and smiles.

"Oh!" he says. "You are here!"

Grinning, I tousle his hair. "Just like we talked about, Nino. Are you ready?"

He smiles and nods.

"What's happening here?" Molly scowls. "What are you talking about, Everett?"

"Little Nino's been having a crazy dream," I tell her. "Haven't you, Nino?"

"Why yes, I have." Little Nino crawls down off the bed and pads across the room in his fuzzy white footie pajamas. "I have been dreaming about the music in my closet."

As we watch, he opens the door of his closet. Beams of rainbow light stream out around him.

At the same time, a sweet piping song skirls forth—the sound of flutes and chimes and strings weaving in delicate harmony.

Little Nino smiles back at us. "Do you hear it?"

"Yes, we do," I tell him. "Let's have a closer listen, shall we?"

"That will be fine." Without hesitation, Little Nino shuffles through the closet doorway, disappearing into the rainbow light.

"Come on." I take Molly's elbow. "I want to show you something."

She frowns at me. "That song. I know it, don't I?"

I just shrug and pull her toward the closet.

As soon as we cross the threshold, the doorway disappears behind us. Suddenly, we're standing on a beach at night, facing a bonfire that burns in rainbow colors.

At first, we're alone there with Little Nino. "I remember what comes next," he says. "Would you like to see the rest of the dream?"

"Yes, we would." I let go of Molly's elbow and take her hand. "We would like that very much."

Little Nino waves his arms, and figures descend from above, floating down one at a time from the starry sky. They are comic strip women, all of them, descending like wingless angels to land lightly on the wet sand around the rainbow bonfire.

There's Potpie's girlfriend, Olives… Ragwood's wife, Blonder…Li'l Asner's gal, Dandelion Meg…Rick Tracer's true love, Bess Bluehart…Allie Hoop's cavegirl, Moolah…and so many more. Every woman you can think of from the funny pages, every one of them from the sublimely beautiful to the utterly ridiculous. Dozens of them, hundreds of them.

This is it. This is what I've been working for; this is why I summoned Molly.

Because this is where the impossible can happen. Here in a child's dream in a flip-side place where things don't happen the way they should.

Only here could I do what had to be done.

Hand in hand, Molly and I walk to the fire. We stand before the women, their faces and forms flickering in the dancing rainbow light.

"Oh!" Suddenly, Little Nino runs forward and gazes into the flames. "There is something inside!" Without hesitation, he plunges his arms into the fire.

When he pulls them back out again, unburned, there's a bundle in his hands. Something wrapped in a comic strip blanket, all black ink and wooly cross-hatched texture.

Grinning, Little Nino turns and offers the bundle to Molly. "Please take this," he says. "It is for you."

"From all of us," says Olives in her nasally voice. "Every last one of us."

That's exactly what it took—the combined power of several hundred female icons projected together. Merged with my own hopes and memories in one supreme act of will.

Not sex, but creation nonetheless. The ultimate surrogate motherhood.

Molly peels back the blanket, and a tiny face looks out at her. The face of a comic strip baby boy, eyes big and dark and shining.

This, then, is my secret son, a child conceived in the panelography. A child of pure hope and imagination—an homage to the son we lost.

And perhaps much more than that.

"Think of Henry," I tell her. "Remember everything you can about him. Every detail."

She looks at me with tears rolling down her face. "But that won't…this isn't…"

"Trust me." I lift the helmet from her head and kiss her wet cheek. "Think of Henry."

She casts her eyes up at me with a look of anguished disbelief. I brush the dark hair back behind her ears and shake my head.

"I can't do it myself," I say. "I need you. Your half of the memories. Your half of who he is." I kiss her cheek again. "Please try."

I watch as she cradles the squirming bundle in her arms. As she closes her eyes and frowns, reaching deep to dredge up those memories.

The comic strip women huddle close, caught up in the moment. I can practically see the pen-and-ink waves of hope ripple out from their exaggerated forms.

Maybe it's the force of their collective willpower. Maybe it's the power of the dream we're in, a dream within a dreamlike realm where human disbelief is suspended. Where comic-strip life works in reverse, so harsh human reality can change direction, too.

Or maybe it's just her memories and love for him. *Our* memories and love pouring into a vessel of India ink. Pulling him back from the vanishing point—pulling all three of us back.

Whatever the reason, a new strip debuts tonight, a full-color single-panel above the fold in the Sunday pull-out section. Here's how we kick off the run:

A mob of famous comic strip women stands around a rainbow bonfire. At panel center, classic child character Little Nino stands on tiptoe, gazing at a swaddled babe in the arms of a woman in a skintight silver spacesuit.

Little Nino says, "Oh my! Look at his eyes! They're not black anymore!"

The woman in the spacesuit weeps with joy. The square-jawed man beside her bends down to kiss the infant's forehead.

We can see, in the firelight, that the baby's eyes are the brightest blue that the four-color printing process will allow.

The caption at the bottom of the panel reads as follows: "Welcome back, Henry!"

Minions at Work - "Bar None"

J. Steven York

Printed in Great Britain
by Amazon

61705000R00097